EVERYONE IS TALKING ABOUT
THE RIDERS OF THE APOCALYPSE SERIES

Praise for *Hunger:*

★ "Realistic and compassionate. . . . The writing is never preachy, and it allows an interesting exploration of both intensely personal food issues and global ones."
—*SLJ,* starred review

"Jackie Morse Kessler does a fine job of taking a critical issue that has been explored in writing no small number of times, and putting a new and thought-provoking spin on it. . . . Sheer genius."—*New York Journal of Books*

"Powerful, fast-paced, hilarious, heart-wrenching. . . . This story will grab the reader and never let go."—*RT* magazine

"*Hunger* is not just a good book. It is a great book. It is funny and sad, brilliant and tragic, and most of all, it speaks truth. . . . I adore it."—Rachel Caine, author of the Morganville Vampires series

"A fantastic and gripping read that never shies from its difficult subject matter. . . . This book is a knockout."
—A. S. King, author of *Everybody Sees the Ants*

BREATH

BREATH

JACKIE MORSE KESSLER

Houghton Mifflin Harcourt

Boston New York 2013

Graphia and the Graphia logo are registered trademarks of
Houghton Mifflin Harcourt Publishing Company.

www.hmhbooks.com

Text set in Adobe Garamond.

Library of Congress Cataloging-in-Publication Data
Kessler, Jackie Morse.
Breath / Jackie Morse Kessler.
p.cm — (Riders of the Apocalypse; 4)
Summary: "In the fourth and final volume of the Riders of Apocalypse series, high school
senior Xander Atwood has a secret. Death, the Pale Rider, has lost his way. What happens
when the two meet will change the fate of the world" — Provided by publisher.
ISBN 978-0-547-97043-1
[1. Four Horsemen of the Apocalypse—Fiction.]
I. Title.
PZ7.K4835Br 2013
[Fic] — dc23
2012023509

Manufactured in the United States of America
DOC 10 9 8 7 6 5 4 3 2 1
4500402219

If you've ever had your trust broken so badly
You asked yourself, "What's the point?"
Then this book is for you.

ACKNOWLEDGMENTS

So many people made this book possible, in so many different ways, and I'm grateful to all of them.

To Julie Tibbott and the entire Houghton Mifflin Harcourt team: Thank you for your vision and your support.

To Sammy Yuen: Your work never ceases to amaze me—thank you for the wonderful covers.

To Miriam Kriss: Best literary agent ever! Thank you for your ongoing enthusiasm, advice, and encouragement. (And, you know, for selling my stuff!)

To Shalaena, the grand-prize winner of the *Loss* contest: I hope you like how I used the name you chose.

To Kevin Hearne: Thanks for being so awesome and letting me write Perry's final scene. Nothing like a little bit of meta to kick things off!

To Matt Krain: Years ago, you gave me permission to use one of the best lines I'd ever heard. I finally found the right place for that line. Thank you so much!

To the awesome people at my dojang: You're all fantastic! Here's to Team Not Dead Yet (and Team Not Yet Not Dead Yet). And a special hat-tip to Kimber and Chuck Coler, who gave me permission to use a terrific line. Thank you!

To Ty Drago: For more reasons than I could ever name, thank you, thank you, thank you.

To Renee Barr: For Girls' Day Out and so much more, you're the best. Thank you — twenty-five years of thank you! (My God!)

To Ryan and Mason: You're the most phenomenal Tax Deductions in the world!

To Brett: Always, forever. It's all good, love — and that's because of you. (Cue sappy music!)

And to all of the readers who have written and shared so much: Thank you for everything. You're amazing, each and every one of you. Now go thee out unto the world — rock on!

Xander Atwood hated heights. Always had. Ever since he was a kid and chickened out of jumping off the high diving board at the community pool — much to the irritation of the kids behind him, who had to make way as he climbed down the ladder, shamefaced — Xander staunchly preferred for the ground to be within easy reach. Going to the top floor of buildings was fine, as long as it wasn't in one of those funky glass-walled elevators. Driving over bridges gave him fits. Airplanes were right out. Let others soar with the eagles; Xander was perfectly content with an ant's-eye view.

So the fact that he was leaning over the balcony railing of his parents' apartment building, thirty floors above the street, was a very big deal.

"So," he said. "Want to talk about it?"

"Not really," replied Death.

BREATH

PART ONE

THE MÖBIUS STRIP

Möbius strip: a one-sided surface that is constructed from a rectangle by holding one end fixed, rotating the opposite end through 180 degrees, and joining it to the first end.

— *Merriam-Webster's Dictionary*

A sound, like the screech of tires—or maybe the boom of a door slamming shut. Impact, then echoes of contact, then nothing.

And then, a beep.

And another.

And again, until the beeping became an insistent shrill.

And then . . .

XANDER

Xander Atwood woke with a start. He inhaled quickly, as if he'd forgotten that he'd been holding his breath, and he swatted his alarm clock until he hit the Off button. The shrilling beep stopped midshriek. An echo lingered, weighing the air with frantic urgency, but it quickly faded until all Xander heard was the soft, electric hum of the clock. He exhaled slowly, then grinned. Today was the big day.

He was finally going to ask Riley out.

Xander hopped out of bed and ducked into the shower. As he shampooed, he went over the plan: During fifth period, when they were both in the library for study hall, he'd casually mention that he was going to grab some pizza after school, and maybe Riley would like to join him. Okay, so maybe it wasn't exactly a date, but it was a start.

All Xander had to do was not vomit all over his sneakers, then he'd be set.

No problem. He'd be fine. Calm. Cool. Not at all freaked out from the thought of talking to Riley Jones.

His belly flipped.

Maybe he shouldn't eat breakfast, just in case.

Five minutes later, he was grabbing his clothing. Definitely the royal blue T-shirt, the one that made the blue in his eyes pop. He'd heard Riley mention in passing that there's nothing better than gorgeous eyes, so Xander wanted to play that up. His friend Ted would bust a gut if he knew that Xander was obsessing over what to wear, but hey, Ted wasn't the one who was going to be asking Riley out for pizza.

Which Xander would absolutely not be too nervous to eat.

He got dressed, then looked in the mirror and frowned at the fresh crop of pimples on his brow. Thank God for long hair. Xander busted out the gel and spent ten minutes working on his hair until he got it to that perfect style, the one that looked like he spent no time on his hair and also managed to hide the zits.

He could practically hear Ted's guffaws as he told Xander that he was being such a girl. Of course Ted would say that; he never worried about anything. Ted was strictly a play-it-by-ear sort of guy, whereas Xander liked to plan his spontaneity. Could he help it if he had a thing for details?

Xander glanced at the clock. He had about five minutes before he had to leave, twenty if he didn't want to stop at Dawson's for coffee before school. More than enough time for him to practice his smile.

Yikes—way too much tooth.

He tried again. Now he looked like he was constipated.

Third time was the charm. Smiling his winning smile, he launched into his Asking-Riley-Out-But-Not-Really question. After a few tries, he thought he nailed the inflection, making it sound like he was interested but not too interested. He figured Riley would answer in one of four ways.

Scenario 1: All Goes Well

> XANDER: Hey, Riley, I'm gonna grab some pizza af-
> ter school. Want to come?
>
> RILEY: Sure! Hey—are you wearing contacts, or
> are your eyes really that blue?

Scenario 2: Delayed Gratification

> XANDER: Hey, Riley, I'm gonna grab some pizza af-
> ter school. Want to come?
>
> RILEY: Thanks, wish I could, but I can't today. I've
> got track.
>
> XANDER: Maybe another time.
>
> RILEY: That would be great. Hey—are you wear-
> ing contacts, or are your eyes really that blue?

Scenario 3: Could Be Worse Somehow

> XANDER: Hey, Riley, I'm gonna grab some pizza af-
> ter school. Want to come?
>
> RILEY: No.

Scenario 4: Kill Me Now

> XANDER: Hey, Riley, I'm gonna grab some pizza af-
> ter school. Want to come?
>
> RILEY: . . . Sorry, do I know you?

He thought those possibilities covered the bases. Even though
part of him was terrified that Riley would opt for either scenario 3 or 4—thus the potential for puking—the rest of him

focused on having a 50 percent chance of either scenario 1 or 2 coming to pass. Fifty-fifty: That was a flip of a coin.

He spotted his pile of change on his nightstand, and he plucked a bright penny from the top of the heap.

"Heads," he said, then tossed the coin high. He caught it, slapped it onto the back of his hand, and took a look.

Heads.

He flipped it again. Heads.

Once more for good luck—and again, it was heads.

Grinning like a fool, Xander pocketed the coin. Yeah, today was the day. His lucky day. He felt it.

He stuffed his backpack for the day's classload: his evil math textbook, massive enough to be a doorstopper; his equally massive but less evil philosophy textbook; his sketchbook, along with his set of pencils and two erasers; his overstuffed, overworked looseleaf binder. Finally, he plucked a novel off his nightstand—Gaiman and Pratchett's *Good Omens,* which he was rereading for the gazillionth time—and jammed it into his backpack. He grabbed his wallet and his phone, made sure he had his keys, and then he quietly headed down the hall. Xander took pains to walk softly, because he didn't want to wake his mom; she hadn't been sleeping well since her very pregnant belly had started entering a room before the rest of her. He didn't worry about waking his dad; that man slept like the dead. Then Xander was out the door and on his way.

The entire time he walked to Dawson's Pizza, he played and replayed the possible scenarios of him (kinda sorta not really) asking Riley out. By the time he got to the pizzeria—open for breakfast starting at the crack of dawn—he was feeling thoroughly nauseated. What if Riley laughed at him? Or worse: What if Riley pitied him?

What if the answer wasn't just No, but Hell No?

He squeezed the penny in his pocket and told himself to stop worrying. Today was his lucky day.

He walked into Dawson's and waved to a handful of guys clumped around tables, but the group he was looking for was off in the corner by the window, basking in the morning spotlight. There was Ted, darkly casual, all lean good looks and radiating mischief, smiling wickedly as he tried to steal a homefry. Across from him, petite Suzie slapped his hand away and stuck out her tongue. Next to her, Izzy laughed and shook her head, her sloppy ponytail swinging across her shoulders.

Xander grinned. The table changed daily, but the group was always the same: the four of them, kicking off the school day at the pizzeria. Life was good. He bought a large coffee and a breakfast special, then headed over to join them.

"Hey," he said as he slid onto the bench next to Ted.

"Hey," said Ted and Izzy.

"Morning, Zan," Suzie said around a yawn.

"Boring you already?"

"Sorry. Up all night studying. Got a constitutional law test, and then debate team after school."

Xander grinned. "I'm sure you're gonna do great when you fall asleep in the middle of proving your point. Ow." That last was after Suzie kicked him.

"That's why I don't study," said Izzy. "I need my rest."

"You girls and your beauty sleep," Ted said, grinning big enough to blind.

Izzy smiled sweetly. "Don't make me kick your ass before breakfast."

"You soccer girls are all so scary."

"I wanna be scary," Suzie said with a pout.

"Your GPA terrifies me," said Xander, sipping coffee. "Hey!"

Ted flashed him that blinding grin, then took a bite from half of Xander's breakfast-special sandwich.

"He's practicing to be a starving actor," Suzie said, glaring at Ted.

"Not so starving." Xander took a bite of his remaining sandwich. "I licked the bagel on that side, by the way."

"Knew it tasted off this morning," Ted said around a mouthful of special. "Here I thought it was because they don't use real eggs in the egg sandwiches."

Izzy snorted. "That's what you get for ordering eggs in a pizzeria."

"Someone should tell management they need to do pizza for breakfast."

"Egg pizza?"

Suzie made a face. "Ew. Hey, nice shirt, Zan. Makes your eyes real blue."

"Thanks," Xander said happily.

"Okay," Ted said. "You look like you're about to burst into song. What's up?"

Xander grinned hugely. "Today's the day," he said, feeling like he could fly. "I'm gonna ask Riley out."

Ted, Izzy, and Suzie exchanged a look, then the three of them cracked up.

"What?" Xander said, perturbed. "I am. Really."

"Even if I believed you, which, for the record, I don't," said Suzie, "your timing is terrible."

"Why?"

Izzy laughed. "You really don't know? Riley's got mono."

Xander's heart sank to his toes. "Aw, man."

"You're such a bad stalker," Izzy said, wagging a finger at him. "It was all over Facebook this morning."

"That explains why he didn't know," said Suzie. "Love you, Zan, but you're social-networkly inept."

Ted was still chuckling. "Kissing disease. Good thing you haven't asked Riley out yet, or you'd be down for the count too. Oh, wait, no you wouldn't—you'd never kiss the Amazingly Perfect Riley Jones."

"He'd be too busy worshiping the very ground the Amazingly Perfect Riley Jones walks on," Suzie agreed.

"Too amazingly perfect for him to ever ask out," said Ted.

"Ah, it's just the universe's way of telling me to wait," said Xander, sighing.

Ted snorted. "Spoken like the deluded lovestruck fool that you are!"

"The universe doesn't need to tell you anything," said Suzie, nibbling a homefry. "You've waited for . . . how many years now? Two? Three? You've got the waiting thing down pat."

"Seriously," said Izzy. "Just ask Riley out already. You know, once the whole mono thing is history."

Ted nodded. "What they said."

"I will." Xander took the penny out of his pocket and flipped it. It came up heads. "I swear it on my lucky penny."

Ted declared, "All hail the lucky penny!"

They all said, "All hail!"

Xander grinned and took another bite of breakfast. "So to-day's not the day," he said, tucking the penny into his pocket. "That's okay. I've got time."

"But I need more time! There's so much I still have to do!"

Like he'd never heard that one before. "Sorry, Perry," he said. "This is what you get. But hey, you've done a lot with your life in the time that you've had."

Perry—or, more accurately, the essence that most recently had been Perry Thomas—stared at him for a moment, then shook his head and sighed. "I guess. If you say so."

"I do," he said cheerfully.

"Aw, man." Perry looked down at his body, which was sprawled on the ground just outside the bookshop where h worked. "At least it happened before the store opened. The c tomers would've totally freaked, what with me having a h attack right there in front of them. That's what it was, My heart?"

"In the end," he said, "it always comes down to hea one way or another."

"Yeah, I can see that. Man, Kevin is gonna lo sighed again. "He'll find me dead on the ground solutely lose it."

"Kevin is a strong guy. He'll be fine."

Perry darted a look at him. "You know hi

"I know everyone."

"Oh." Perry looked back at his corpse. "Wish I could've done more with my life."

"There's much for you to be proud of. Your life impacted many others. The stories you've told to your customers, and sold to your customers, left impressions that became inspirations. And the homemade herbal teas you sold to them have comforted many."

Perry's nose twitched. "I didn't get a chance to mix the tea."

He sensed the regret, so he waited.

"Kevin was finally gonna teach me how to make some of his teas, you know? The special ones that've been in his family forever. For the longest time, I just couldn't mix the herbs the right way, so he'd mix everything and put 'em into their sachets and tell me to add water. And that was fine. I mean, I'd been working here in the store for two years, and I was cool about not being able to make the homemade teas. We all have things we can't do, right?"

He nodded.

"But then last week, I woke up and I said to myself, I'm done with not knowing how to make the tea. I'm gonna learn how to mix those herbs, and Kevin is gonna be proud." Perry laughed quietly and shook his head. "I don't know why learning to do it suddenly became so important. It's just tea. But it's like I had a new goal. And Kevin *was* proud that I wanted to learn how to do it right. He was. He's real picky about those teas."

"All artists are picky about their work."

"It sounds silly, hearing me say it out loud, but I was looking forward to him showing me how to do it."

"That doesn't sound silly at all."

"It's just tea."

"But it mattered to you."

Perry sighed. "Yeah. It really did." He dug into his pocket and pulled out a coin. He squeezed it for a moment, then looked up at him. "I've got this to give to you. But could I make you a cup of tea first? Just to see if I could have done it?"

He smiled, delighted. "Homemade tea would hit the spot."

And so, in the early hours of the morning, the police milled around a body found outside a bookshop while Death and a dead man sat inside the store and shared a pot of tea. They were both pleased to discover that it was not at all bitter.

Lynn Tyler was bitter. "But I'm only twenty-six! This can't be it!"

"Define 'it,'" he said.

"It. Over. Finished. Done. The end." She kicked her body, or would have, had her foot not ghosted through the flesh. "Dead!"

"I'm afraid that this is it, then. You're dead."

She stared at her corpse, at the splayed limbs by the foot of the stairs. "All because I didn't want to wait for that stupid elevator. I was running late, so I ran down the stairs."

"Exercise is healthy," he said. "Well. Usually."

"It was that loose heel again, wasn't it? I thought I heard it snap, right before I fell. I was going to fix it. I was," she insisted, turning to face him. "Let me fix it, and I promise I'll be more careful! I'll slow down!"

"You wouldn't have fixed it," he said patiently. "And you never would have slowed down. Between work and school and socializing, you barely had time for sleep. You squeezed more into each day than many do in a month."

"Yeah, and for what? I didn't even get to take the bar." She kicked through the corpse again. "All that work, and all I got out of it was bills and exhaustion. I'm pathetic."

"Of course you're not. You lived your life. You pursued a dream. You wanted to be a prosecutor, someone who helped make those who hurt others pay for their crimes. It was a noble calling."

"But I didn't get the chance to do it!" She looked at him again, pleading. "A second chance. You can do that, can't you?"

"I could," he agreed.

"Please. *Please.* I'll do anything." She fell to her knees. "Anything you want. Just give me more time."

"This life is done, Lynn."

"But you could give it back!" she screamed, tearing her hair. "You said you could!"

"I can. But I won't. Rules," he said, shrugging.

"There has to be a loophole. There are *always* loopholes!"

He didn't bother replying. There were loopholes, of course; he was the one who had put the rules in place. But either people knew the loopholes or they didn't. He wasn't about to teach them. So he shrugged again, and gave her another minute— roughly speaking; time was relative for him—to rage over the unfairness of it all. And when her anger finally played itself out, he said gently, "Come, Lynn. It's time."

Lynn was crying now, her sobs filling the narrow stairwell. "It's so unfair."

"If you say so."

Sniffling, she took one more look at herself—the splayed limbs, the snapped neck. Her corporate-chic skirt had bunched up when she'd landed, and she tried to nudge the hem back into place. Her hands passed through the clothing, through her body, and she sobbed harder.

He reached over and tugged the hem until the skirt protected her modesty.

She tried to say "Thank you," but the words stuck in her throat. Even so, he knew her intent—he always knew their intent—and he said, "You're welcome."

With a trembling hand, she offered him a coin. He accepted it somberly and tucked it into a pocket. "Ready for what's next?"

Sniffling, she nodded.

He took her hand, and then Lynn Tyler moved on.

He inhaled souls; he exhaled lives.

He breathed, and the world turned.

Another breath; another death. Every ending was personal; every encounter, unique. He knew them all, better than they knew themselves.

And they all knew him.

Ruben Morris (76, third and final heart attack) was devastated that he was going to miss his grandson's wedding in three months' time. With a sigh, he kissed his wife—who was so busy shrieking at the paramedics to keep trying to resuscitate him that she didn't feel the chill upon her cheek—and then fished a coin out of his pocket. "It is what it is," he said to his wife, who couldn't hear him, and then he offered the coin to Death, the Pale Rider.

Mohammed Hassan (68, kidney failure) was surrounded by family and friends as he whispered, "I bear witness that there is no god but Allah," and after he died he gave thanks for a gentle death, even as he gave Death a coin.

Huang Mei (102, old age) was pleased to have died a five-blossoms death—she had been married, had a son, was respected in her community, had a loving grandson, and died in her sleep after a long life. She dropped to her knees and bowed, knocking her head to the floor nine times before she presented him with a coin.

Ramesh Ravi (56, lung cancer), with his wife and two sons by his side, died with the mantra *Aum Namah Shivaya* in his ear and the taste of milk on his lips. His heart full, he touched Death's feet and gave him a coin.

Frances Caprio (66, Alzheimer's) was worried that she had died before giving her last confession, but he assured her that last rites had been performed. Grateful, she smiled as she presented him with a coin.

José Martinez (82, influenza) had a last request: *"Como yo te amo"* had just come on the radio, and he asked if they could wait until the song was over. Less than three minutes later, he smiled as he presented his coin and thanked him profusely.

"You're such a sap," the pale steed said after José moved on.

"I'm patient," Death corrected.

"You say tomato . . ."

He smiled. "It is what it is."

Not all of them moved on right away. Not all of them were ready.

Some were angry. Shelley Silber (23) wanted to haunt the drunk driver who had slammed into her car; Lincoln Archer (18) wanted to wreak havoc after learning he'd been cut down by a stray bullet. He tended to let the angry ones work out their issues before they moved on — and not because he was a sap, no matter what his steed said. Human essences remembered pain, clung to it as they moved on. It made things messy in the long run. Dying was messy enough; why bring that baggage with them?

Many were scared. Franco Coppola (82, liver failure) had been a thief for most of his life, and now he didn't know if that was going to make him burn for eternity. Golda Siegel (63, stroke) had poisoned her philandering husband years ago, and now she was certain he was waiting for her. Timmy Jones (8, leukemia) didn't want to move on without his parents to keep him safe. Li Feng (one month, sudden infant death syndrome) was terrified of being alone forever.

Some were tired. The ones who'd lived their lives and had made their peace with dying were usually pleasant, even friendly. The ones who'd died after a debilitating illness tended to welcome him. There were the ones who had been used and abused by the world, and he sympathized with them even as he accepted their coins.

And then there were those who had lost hope somewhere along the way, the ones who, after a long and dark desperation, had finally given up—the ones who had stopped living long before they stopped breathing.

All of them had stories to tell before they moved on.

And so he listened, and he gave them all what they needed.

He listened to the oak tree's song of its life, a chorus for every ring. It was a nameless song, for names are as meaningless to trees as legs are to worms, and it was a slow, winding tune, full of rustles and sighs, at turns mournful and joyous. It was a song of quiet triumphs over hurricanes and floods; it was a song of remembrance for its offspring, lost to the Great Burning.

Eventually, the tree fell silent, and it listened to him sing the tree's song of death, how its body would continue to provide shelter and nourishment to countless living things.

When he, too, fell silent, the oak rustled one last time in a final farewell, and it moved on.

He gently scooped up the kitten, which had been too young to open its eyes, and nuzzled it until it blinked up at him. It purred him a question, and he answered. The kitten stretched, kneaded his arm—careful not to stick him with its claws—and then moved on.

In the cardboard box behind the garbage can, its littermates slept on, as did its mother, who twitched once as Death passed by.

The livestock after slaughter. The prey after the hunt. Flies after a swatter.

He was there for them all — them, and for all living things. He spoke to them all, and they all spoke to him in the ways of their own kind.

And then they moved on.

It had been a long day, even as one such as he considered time. He felt the age in his bones. That, and something more.

Something colder.

It was coming. It wasn't here yet, but it was coming: winter's frost creeping in amid the autumn branches.

Soon.

Next to him, the pale steed nickered, "You okay? You seem . . ." The horse stumbled for a word. "I don't know. Sad."

"I'm fine," he replied. "Just tired."

"Want to stop?"

Of course he did. He knew what was to come.

But he would do what he had always done when that knowledge became unbearable: He would step into the Slate and find that one thing that he needed to see him through. If he were alive, it would have been the one thing he lived for.

Yes, soon he would have to retreat to the Slate, retreat and replenish. But soon was not now. Until then, he had things to do, dead people to see.

"A couple more," he murmured, "then a brief respite."

The horse nodded, in the way that horses do. "Respite is good. Maybe call the others, play a game of cards?"

"Maybe."

"Just be careful with War. She cheats."

That made him smile. "None can cheat me. They only think they can."

"You're too trusting." A pause as the steed snorted. "Would that be a fatal flaw?"

He groaned. "Oy."

"Sorry, has that been done to death?"

"You're trying to cheer me up, aren't you?"

"Is it working?"

He chuckled. "It is. My thanks." He patted the steed's neck. "All right. A couple hundred more for today, then a break."

XANDER

The late bell rang. Actually, it beeped — which, Xander thought as he peeled down the school hallway, was exceedingly strange. Bells didn't beep; they rang. Or, in the case of the late bell, it shrilled like a fire alarm. But not today. Today, the late bell beeped exactly once, then gave up the ghost.

He raced inside his philosophy and film studies class ten seconds later. "Sorry, sorry, sorry . . ."

"The late Mr. Atwood," said Ms. Lewis, shaking her head. "At this rate, you'll be late for your own funeral."

He grinned as he slid into the seat to Ted's right. "Wouldn't you want to be?"

Ms. Lewis sighed loudly, then turned her back to finish writing on the board.

"You're only half as clever as you think you are," Ted whispered.

"Which is still twice as clever as you."

"Ouch. You practice that comeback as much as you practice smiling in front of a mirror?"

Xander should have known it was a mistake to share that tidbit with Ted. "Riley has no complaints."

"Yeah, yeah." Ted snorted. "Can five minutes go by without you mentioning Riley? Never mind five — can *one* minute go by?"

Xander grinned. "Nope."

"And you've only been dating for what, two months? God help me if you make it through the end of senior year. You'll be insufferable."

"It's good to have goals."

Riley was the reason Xander had been late for class, again —they'd been hanging out by the lockers, just talking and touching and making plans for after school, and then the late bell had rung. Well, beeped. Xander knew that Ms. Lewis was marking down every time he bolted into class after the bell, but he couldn't help it; he loved spending as much time as possible with his significant other. Was it because of Riley's amazing smile? The black hair styled in those elaborate braids? Those dark chocolate eyes that he could drown in? The infectious laugh? Those were all part of it and yet didn't begin to scrape the surface of why he was obsessed with Riley Jones. He knew he was a little crazy, but it was a good sort of crazy, the kind of feeling that made him believe anything was possible.

He thought he might be falling in love.

Ms. Lewis turned to face the class. On the blackboard, she had written a quote.

I think; therefore, I am.
　　　　—*Descartes*

"Before we get started," said Ms. Lewis, "a quick reminder that if you're going to get involved with the school musical, today's the last day to sign up. I promise not to be an evil faculty advisor and micromanage everything. My job is to make sure no one does anything illegal or dangerous. That's it. Everything else is up to you."

Ted shot Xander a look: *You signing up?*

Xander nodded. Of course he was; he did so every year as part of the musical's Art Squad. He didn't crave the spotlight like Ted—the leading man for two years running—but Xander absolutely loved making something from nothing. When he looked at a blank canvas, he didn't see emptiness; he saw potential. In his creative writing elective, they talked about world building. He thought that concept applied to art as well, especially as part of the Art Squad: He helped build the world of the school musical with every stroke of a brush. It was like playing God. Total head rush.

"Now that my public service announcement is done," said Ms. Lewis, "I have your existentialism essays to hand back. Overall, very well done. I'm glad most of you enjoyed *Rosencrantz and Guildenstern Are Dead.*"

When Xander got his paper back, he noted the big A at the top—unsurprising, since Ms. Lewis gave everyone an A as long as the work was handed in on time and answered the assignment questions completely—and then he scanned the rest of her comments.

Good job showing how the main characters struggle to define themselves and their confusing world, and how they eventually come to the conclusion that their destiny is their own fault.

Xander grinned. Was that what he'd done? He thought he'd just been using meaningful quotes at opportunistic times. He liked the "film" part of the elective, but the "philosophy" part was weird. Whatever—it was still an easy-A class.

After she returned all the essays, Ms. Lewis said, "Time for our next segment. Let's talk about solipsism." She pointed to the quote on the board. "The idea of solipsism is that we can be sure that our own minds exist, but that's it. Everyone else's minds, even the world itself, might not exist at all."

Ted raised his hand. "That's stupid," he said when Ms. Lewis called on him. "The world's right here. I see you."

"But what you're seeing might not be real. I might not be real."

"Of course you're real. I'm looking right at you."

"What if I'm an illusion?"

"Like in *The Matrix*?" Xander asked, belatedly raising his hand. "Everyone thought they were in the real world, but that was just the machines fooling them so they could feed off of them."

"Good example," said Ms. Lewis. "If you want to get technical, *The Matrix* falls under Cartesian skepticism." She pointed again to the quote on the board. "If you doubt everything, then the only thing you can know for sure is that we exist as thinking beings. I think; therefore, I am." She smiled. "Descartes went on to say that there's no way for us to know whether the world we're experiencing isn't really just an illusion created by a 'malevolent demon.'"

An appreciative murmur rippled through the class.

"Cool," said Xander.

"That sort of explains my math grade," said Ted.

"Or, you know, your lack of studying."

Ms. Lewis continued: "Descartes's notion leads to the idea of solipsism. Keep in mind that what one person perceives to be true may not be true for another person. It's subjective reality. Which brings us to this week's film." She nodded at Xander. "It's similar to *The Matrix* in that the main character lives in a false reality. But the main difference is that the main character is the only one fooled by what's false. And now, the first part of *The Truman Show*."

As Ms. Lewis got the DVD set up, Xander settled back in his seat. He was all about getting graded for watching movies — especially movies he'd already seen. The lights went off, and he propped an elbow on his desk and his head in his hand.

Naptime.

His eyes closed as the movie began. He heard an announcer's breathless voice setting the scene as background music began to swell, rising, building until the sound carried like a scream—

—there's a sound like a scream he's screaming in pain there's so much pain and he can't move can't think can't get away he has to get away because something's coming for him so he screams again screams until the roof of the world is ripped away and there's noise and glaring lights and a dark shadow reaching for him—

"Xander? Seriously, dude, wake up."

Xander sat up with a start, his breath caught in a scream, his heart lodged in his throat. He blinked at Ted, then looked

around. He was in a waiting area of some sort, complete with
pseudo-art-deco chairs and low tables wedged between them,
bookended by magazine racks overstuffed with reading mate-
rial. Large windows would have let in daylight, if only it were
daytime.

"Um," Xander said. "Hey. Weren't we in class?"

Ted grinned, shaking his head ruefully. "That explains the
screaming. You must've been dreaming about school. Waste of
a good dream, if you ask me."

"Dreaming . . . ?"

"Nightmaring, based on how you were yelling." Ted chuckled. "At least you grabbed a little sleep. You've been here what,
six hours, yeah?"

Xander blinked again. "I have no idea."

"Bumped into Riley. Said you guys came here right after
school."

They did? He didn't remember anything like that. He didn't
even remember being with Riley. He mopped his hair away
from his face and looked around. "Riley's here?"

"Riley was on the way out when I got here. Had to get
home, make an appearance for the parents, do homework. You
know. The usual. I got here to see you snoozing. Or, more accurately, thrashing. Hey, want me to grab you some food?"

"Food," Xander repeated. He felt like his brain had been
turned into tapioca pudding—his thoughts felt too thick, almost soupy, and he had a nagging feeling that something was
wrong. He just couldn't figure out what it was. He dug a hand
into his jeans pocket and found his lucky penny, squeezed.

The cold flat metal was reassuring. Solid.

Real.

"Food," Ted agreed. "Or, in the case of hospital fare, over-priced food-like substances. I bet the coffee's decent. If Suzie was here, she'd be all mother hen and insist you eat something. Riley mentioned you were too anxious to eat. Said it was, and I quote, 'adorable.' Hear that, dude?" He clapped Xander's shoulder. "You're adorable!"

Xander frowned. Hospital. They were in the waiting area of a hospital. Why . . . ?

Before he could ask, a door opened. Xander turned, and for one moment, one crystalline moment in which time itself froze, he saw a shape filled with shadows, saw a man who was not a man standing in the doorway, standing and looking right at him.

The shadows beckoned to him, whispered his name.

Xander's throat tightened and his stomach clenched. He gripped his penny tightly.

The crystal shattered and time resumed: The shadows gave way to Xander's father, pink-faced and grinning like a lunatic, wearing ill-fitting hospital scrubs and calling his name.

"Xander! Xander, it's a boy! You officially have a little brother! A healthy, six-pound-six-ounce baby boy! Mom's great, your brother's great, life is great!"

Xander's head spun. He felt his mouth pull into a grin, felt himself stand and then sit back down again, felt Ted clapping him on the back in a volley of congratulatory thumps. He was giddy with relief, and somewhere in the back of his mind, he thought that was wrong—he should be giddy with excitement, with joy over having a baby brother. But he couldn't quite convince himself that he was feeling anything other than a palpable sense of relief, like something dark and terrible had passed over him and left him unscathed.

He let out a laugh, even as he gave his lucky penny a final squeeze. Of course he was relieved; his mom wasn't exactly young, so there had been some risk with the pregnancy and the birth. But his dad just said that she was fine — and so was his brother.

He had a little brother.

His dad said he'd let Xander know when he could visit Mom and meet his brother, and then he retreated. The door shut behind him, swallowing him whole.

"So cool," said Ted. "Hope you enjoyed being an only child for so long, because now everything changes."

Xander grinned. Change was good. Change meant life.

When you stop changing, you die.

"Spare some change?"

"Actually, Kate," he said, "I believe you have something for me."

Kate Bromley, 53 — toothless, homeless, and (she thought) penniless — dug a gloved hand into her oversized pocket. Her entire face lit up when she pulled out a shiny coin. "Hey! When did I get that?"

"You've had it since the beginning," he replied. "It's my covenant with you."

"I know every cent I have, mister. And I tell you, I never had this penny before now."

"It's not a penny."

She dropped the coin into his outstretched hand. "Of *course* it's a penny. It's . . . hey. *Hey.* You're *him.*"

"Yes."

"So I'm dead." She turned and saw her body, half covered by a pile of garbage bags that had done little to keep her warm. "Too proud to go to the shelter, that's me. What was it — the cold?"

"That, and malnutrition, and a host of other maladies. But exposure is what officially killed you last night."

"So you didn't get here until what, half a day later? What're you, lazy?"

He shrugged and smiled as he stuffed his hands into his pockets. "I've been accused of being a slacker in my time."

"So do I get any last requests?"

Ah, one of *those*. Some people believe in an afterlife; others believe in a do-over. He asked, "What do you have in mind?"

"Something with a steady income would be nice."

"You make your own destiny, Kate Bromley. I don't play the soothsayer."

"Humph. Lazy."

He chuckled.

She tapped her chin as she pondered. "How about a redhead this time? Natural, not bottled. Can't stand the bottled stuff —always looks so fake. And maybe tall. Yeah, I'd like to be more than armpit-level to the world this time around."

"Done."

She eyeballed him. "Just like that?"

"Just like that." Whether it would happen remained to be seen.

"Well. Okay." She looked at her shopping cart, which was overflowing with bags, and the piles of garbage on the floor— the sum of her existence, shoved into plastic. She sighed once, remembering things she would rather have forgotten, then lifted her chin and met his gaze unflinchingly. "Yeah, okay. Let's go."

Kate Bromley moved on.

The mud snails crawled along the bottom of the Hudson River, scraping up algae and debris as they moved. Josh Hume watched the mollusks as they scavenged, and he envied their simplicity.

"Only humans make it complicated."

"I didn't mean to," Josh said. "I just . . ." He closed his eyes and sobbed. "It hurt. It hurt so much. I *trusted* him, and he —" His voice hitched, failed.

"Is that why you jumped?" he asked. "Because he betrayed you?"

Josh cried quietly for a minute before he replied. "There was no place that was safe anymore. Everyone laughed. Everyone knew. And . . . everything was dark and bleak and thick, like here on the bottom of the sea, and all I could think about was having to live every day for the rest of my life feeling like my heart was being crushed, like I was moving under water while everyone else was doing laps in the daylight. And I knew, just knew, that no matter what I did, that feeling would never go away. Never." He looked up to face Death. "I jumped because I finally had hope, and it got ripped away."

Between them, the mud snails slowly trekked along the river floor.

"You lived," he said, not unkindly, "and possibilities spread before you too numerous to count. You jumped, and became nothing more than a statistic."

"I know. I'm sorry. It just hurt too much." Josh's hand trembled as he offered his coin. "Next time," he whispered, "can I be a snail? Please?"

As if he could control what happened next. But instead of saying so, he replied, "Done."

Josh smiled sadly, and if Death had a heart, it might have broken, or at least cracked. But Death was heartless, and always had been.

He felt Josh Hume move on, and he contemplated the notion of hope, and of hopelessness, and how the one could so easily lead to the other.

He left the river, shedding icicles as he passed by.

Michael Tucker stared at the pool of red beneath his body. His mom was going to have a stroke trying to get the stains out of the carpet.

"You really think that's the thing that's going to upset her?" Death asked. "The bloodstains on the carpet?"

Michael shrugged. "You don't know her."

"I know everyone."

"So you know she's all about appearances. I woulda blown my face off if I had Dad's gun."

"I know you did this to hurt your parents. You threw away your life in a temper tantrum."

"Whatever."

A pause, and then Death repeated, "*'Whatever'?*"

"You heard me. My life sucked. Thanks for nothing." Michael pulled a coin out of his pocket and waved it. "Here."

A far longer pause, one that stretched and pulled taut. When Death finally spoke again, his words frosted the air. "Keep thy trinket, Michael Tucker."

Michael blinked. "But . . . but you get a coin. You have to. That's, like, the rule."

Death smiled an empty smile. "It is the rule for those who move on."

The meaning behind his words hit Michael, and he stammered, "But *why?*"

"You insulted me."

Michael had no idea how he'd done such a thing. It was yet another item to add to his shit list, to his personal vendetta against the world. If there was one lesson he had learned in his sixteen years, it was that life is grossly unfair.

"So . . ." His voice cracked. "So what happens to me?"

"Nothing."

Relief washed over Michael, and he let out a laugh. "Man, you got me good. I was actually scared for a moment there."

"You misunderstand me, Michael Tucker. Nothing is what happens to you." Death's smile sharpened. "You are nothing."

Michael reached out, perhaps to beg, but then he felt an insistent tug at his feet. He looked down and watched, horrified, as he began to unravel. The pain didn't kick in until his legs were gone below the knees. He screamed, and screamed, and screamed again as he was slowly erased from existence. He screamed until his voice was taken away, and even then his eyes screamed silently until they, too, were gone.

His coin winked once, as if holding on to the memory of light, and then it blackened and turned to ash.

Nothing remained of Michael Tucker.

On the bedroom floor, a discarded corpse began to rot.

"Cold," the pale steed commented.

"He insulted me."

"Oh, I didn't mean what you did. Agreed, he was a piece of work, and should've known better than to mouth off to you. I meant the temperature. It's cold."

He allowed himself to feel the chill of the wind, and he had to admit that his steed was correct: The temperature had plummeted. His fault; he had allowed himself to get distracted. "Sorry."

"I don't mind. I was just pointing it out." A pause, and then the horse snorted, "You know what helps the cold? Heat."

"Indeed."

"So? You going to see her?" When he didn't reply, the horse said, "Or maybe escape to Club Med. I hear the vacation packages are to die for."

Despite himself, he smiled. "Fine. I'll see her."

He walked among the rubble, pausing every time he came across another victim. Most were soldiers, and they gave him their coins and, more often than not, a salute before moving on. Others were bystanders who had been in the wrong place at the wrong time, according to the media. The time and place meant little to him; everyone came to him at one point, whether sooner or later, whether violently or peacefully.

He breathed in; he breathed out.

They moved on.

Overhead, War circled on her red steed. He smiled up at her, but he didn't make his presence known. He liked to watch her work. She was passionate, of course—all of the Red Riders were passionate. That was a prerequisite for the job. She was also compassionate, which was rare. Bloodshed for this particular War was secondary to catharsis. She was angry over the bombing; he felt that deeply. He could feel *all* mortals when he wished, but the Horsemen were connected to him on a much more personal level; in a very strict sense, they were part of him.

Or had been, at one point. Now? They were something else. Something different.

A frown played on his face. They had changed since their conception, hadn't they? War's need for control had turned inward. Famine's quest for balance had turned outward. Pestilence quietly inspired people to stand and be strong. Battles and starvation and sickness still took millions of lives, and yet the Riders who oversaw those functions had become much more than caretakers of mortality.

They had changed.

Not he. He was the same as he'd always been. He continued to watch life evolve while he himself remained aloof, apart. Disconnected.

Cold.

He closed his eyes. It was coming. He knew the signs far too well. It was coming, and soon.

A sound, like a door slamming shut.

Chasing after the sound, a memory, fleeting and imprecise, of contentment. Of completion.

He reached behind him for the guitar slung across his back —the guitar that until just now had been in the Slate. Eyes still closed, he touched the piece of him that had, at one point, been a songwriter and a singer. That wasn't exactly correct; he himself had never sung a song or played the guitar. Before he had been Death, the concept of music had been unknown to him. But just as pieces of himself were in all life, all life touched him. Part of him housed the essence that had been a musician, and it was that musician's likeness he had taken for this current cycle.

There had been something in the way that one had lived, the words and songs he had created, that had resonated deeply.

As people lay dying and dead, crushed by debris or blown to pieces by a bomber out for vengeance, his fingers strummed guitar strings. Amid the cries of humanity, he began to sing about touching feelings he didn't understand and losing a soul he didn't have.

"Oh, come on," Suzie said grumpily. "Brown is brown."

"Well," Xander replied, "yes. Brown is brown. But there's also burnt umber, raw umber, auburn, chestnut, coffee, and chocolate. To name a few."

"Chocolate! You're singing my song, Zan . . ."

Always one to take a hint, he nudged the bag of M&M's closer to her. "You see what I'm saying? You can't paint the tree just brown. It's too plain."

"That's stupid," she said, popping a handful of chocolate into her mouth. "Tree trunks are brown. Even trunks that are part of magic wish-granting trees."

He pretended she didn't just insult something that he took seriously. She was about as book smart as a person could be, but when it came to the creative end of things, Suzie was as hopeless as a mathlete in an MMA tournament.

"Magic wish-granting trees would definitely have hints of gold, like burnt sienna." Xander dumped the tube of acrylic into Suzie's hand. "The tree has to appear three-dimensional."

"It *is* three-dimensional. Marcie's going to be inside, playing Cinderella's Mother." Suzie frowned. "And that's another thing. Why doesn't the mom have a name? She's just 'Cinderella's Mother.'"

"You understand that she's a minor character, right? *Into the Woods* isn't about Cinderella's mom."

"That's not the point."

"There's a point?"

She threw an M&M at him.

"Look," he said, grabbing a brush. "Light adds depth to colors, changes them, sometimes subtly, sometimes drastically." He squeezed raw umber onto his palette and added a few streaks over Suzie's patches of brown. "See?"

"Yeah, sure. But this is silly. You want light? The spotlight will be on Marcie when she has her lines. Why bother being so finicky about the colors on the tree?"

"Because it's important. Details matter. Especially the small ones. Look." He led her around to his section of the prop tree, and he showed her where he'd painted a few objects into the bark: Prince Charming's sword, gleaming brightly, with hints of ruby by the pommel; Cinderella's silver crown; a set of bronze scales the Baker used to weigh his ingredients before baking bread; knotholes that were actually pennies, winking copper.

"Okay, admittedly, that's cool," Suzie said, tracing the outline of the sword. "But what's the point? No one's going to see the hidden drawings."

"Maybe not. But I know they're there."

She took another handful of M&M's. "Seems like a waste of time. Like you always bringing chocolate to Art Squad when you don't eat chocolate."

"I do," he said, but that wasn't true. He hadn't had a bite of chocolate since he was a kid. "And chocolate inspires creativity."

"It inspires my waistline," Suzie said around a mouthful of M&M's.

"You don't really care about any of this stuff, do you?" He motioned to the prop tree, to the scenery, to the backdrop waiting to be painted.

"Not really."

"So why'd you join the Art Squad?"

"For the intense social scene," she said innocently, batting her eyes.

Xander chuckled. There were, officially, ten students on the Art Squad, but on any given afternoon, four showed up: Xander, who loved it; Deb, the art director; and any random two students whose names were on the squad roster, like Suzie. "Had to pad your college applications, huh?"

"You know it. I've got the academic activities nailed," Suzie said. "But nothing on the more artistic end of things. Mom and Dad had a fit when they went over my applications. It was either this or learn how to play the clarinet."

"It's not like Harvard's gonna turn you down because you didn't work on the school musical. You're a straight-A student."

She sniffed. "Colleges don't care about grades."

"Okay," Xander said. "It's official, Suzanne. You're insane."

"I mean, they don't look just at grades. If it comes down to me and some other Jewish girl with straight-As, they're going to compare our school activities. All I have is the debate team and mock trial and student government and the chess team."

"That's all, huh?"

"I need something creative to round it out."

"I don't know. I think your ability to rationalize anything is pretty creative . . ."

She threw another M&M at him, and he grinned.

"Come on," he said. "I'll tell Deb that you want to paint part of the wall. No extra colors required."

As he got Suzie set up with a roller, she asked, "Hear anything from Carnegie Mellon yet?"

He shrugged. "You know how it goes. I'm doing the hurry-up-and-wait thing."

"Thought you applied early admission."

He had. He'd even received the acceptance letter, but he hadn't said anything about it to anyone—not to his parents, not to his friends, and definitely not to Riley.

And he certainly hadn't told anyone what he'd done after he'd gotten the letter.

He was just waiting on one thing, and then he wouldn't have to keep his secret any longer.

He could hardly wait to tell Riley.

Just as he was going to say that he was positive good news was coming, his phone let out a harsh beep.

"Earth to Zan."

A hand waved in front of his face, and he blinked at Suzie, who was holding a dripping roller. She'd finished painting her section of backdrop—all one color, and relatively smooth strokes. She was looking at him oddly, like he had drool leaking out of the corner of his mouth.

He said, "Sorry, what?"

"I *said*, are you and Riley going to Marcie's thing on Saturday, but maybe you should stay home and catch up on your sleep, based on how you just zoned out on me."

"Yeah, we're going to the party," he said absently as he pulled out his phone. There was a new text message. Odd — he could have sworn he had it set to Vibrate, the way he always did at school. He must have accidentally hit the switch that put it back on Sound.

"Xander? You're acting all weird . . ."

"Hang on, Riley texted me."

"You get reception in school?" Suzie humphed. "I get no signal until I'm outside."

"Just lucky, I guess." He read Riley's one-word message, and then he sprouted a grin.

STANFORD!!!

Riley must have gotten the acceptance letter today. Xander's grin broadened. That meant he had to wait only a little bit longer.

And maybe, just maybe, at the party on Saturday, he'd be able to share his great news with Riley and the others.

"Someone looks happy."

"Oh yeah," he said, texting back a quick congratulations to Riley. "It's all good." He hit Send, then pulled out his lucky penny and flipped it. "Heads!"

And it was heads.

"All hail the lucky penny," said Suzie.

"All hail," Xander agreed, flipping it once more.

Heads.

Still grinning, Xander put his phone into his back pocket. Yes, it was all good. With luck, everything would be even better soon, real soon. And he had luck. He squeezed his penny and tucked it into his front pocket, and for the rest of Art Squad that afternoon, he pretended to listen to Suzie babble about her college plans as he daydreamed about telling Riley his secret.

He had to wait a little longer, that was all.

No worries. As he'd said to himself again and again before he'd had the courage to ask Riley out six months ago, he had time.

He was out of time. Literally. He was in the Slate between time and space, standing on the edge of all things and no things as history and potential sparked like fireflies at midnight. It was breathtaking. Or it would have been, if he had actually been breathing.

In the Slate, he never breathed.

He ignored the definitive yesterdays and focused on the probable tomorrows. Normally, he reviewed the past with the same playful curiosity with which he observed the possible, and there were times when he came between that he watched the befores and afters simultaneously. Those were the times when he visited the Slate out of whimsy.

But not now; now he was far too pensive to be playful. Work was getting to him again.

That happened more and more lately. In the last thousand years, humanity had exploded all over the world; in the past ten years alone, another billion people crawled along the planet.

So many people. So many lives.

They took so much out of him.

It was enough to make him lose his sense of humor.

Before entering the Slate, he had taken two humans, Holly Owens (27) and George Greene (29). They had been lovers, and they'd done the clichéd leap off a seaside cliff in Cape Cod, momentarily obscuring the scenic view with their desperate attempt to make a statement about life in general and their love in particular.

"We'll be together forever," George had promised Holly. "This world has nothing for us. Come on—you and me, in the next world. Let's do this!"

They did it. And they quickly discovered that promises made while living mean exactly zilch once dead.

He had been waiting as they picked themselves up from the bottom of the cliff, and he told them about the future they had just aborted. George would have gone on to become a defense attorney who got an innocent man off death row, and Holly would have opened a women's shelter, affecting countless lives. When they realized what they had just thrown away, George wept bitterly over the unfairness of it all, and Holly begged for a second chance.

Suicides always thought it was about *them*.

So he'd taken George and Holly, and after they had moved on, he'd found himself in a funk. Or, more accurately, he'd found the dead dolphins as he and his steed walked along the Cape Cod beach and he realized he was in a funk. Eighty-one of the mammals, dying or already dead, littered the shore.

Whoops.

His steed scolded him as he took the dolphins, and then the dolphins scolded him before they moved on. He'd put up with it—the dolphins were understandably annoyed, and his steed had never been one to let silence reign—and he'd decided that he'd had enough. More than a hundred thousand people died every day, as humans told time; he deserved a break.

And so, he had finally retreated to the Slate. It was his place, where he could slip his skin and be himself, where he could remember and reflect, where he could ponder and plan. It wasn't home—no, never that, never again—but it was a place of hope.

Especially now, when it was coming soon. Coming fast.

Because his time was approaching quickly, he had retreated to the Slate to seek a glimpse of a specific possibility, the one that would be enough to clear his head and return his focus to the big picture. A gleam of promise, a hint of *maybe*—that would do.

For as long as he could remember, that one particular glimpse had always been enough to keep him going.

Now, in the Slate, futures beckoned and he followed. The most likely paths were first, as always, followed by the ones slightly less probable. And so on. And so on, again, and again, until he was traveling down paths so unlikely they were constructed from little more than fancy.

And for the first time ever, the hint of *maybe* that he needed wasn't there.

He frowned, and he began again.

This time, he didn't simply follow the paths but searched them instead, seeking the one thing that had kept him going for countless millennia. As he searched, he rationalized, in the way of humans: He had simply missed that one possibility, that was all. This particular tomorrow had always been faint, and he had been so distracted lately—of course he had overlooked it.

Even one such as he could make mistakes. Just ask the dolphins.

When this second search turned up nothing, he searched a third time. And then a fourth.

Still nothing.

Perhaps he hadn't made a mistake at all.

Now he was experiencing something else in the way of humans: a growing sense of emptiness, as if he were slowly being hollowed out. It was the subtle shift from optimism to pessimism, the turn of the glass from half-full to half-empty.

It was the birth of despair.

He stepped out of the Slate and back into time and space.

"He returns," his steed nickered fondly. "Good holiday?"

"It was fine."

The steed snorted. "I can tell by how tan and relaxed you are."

"I said it was fine." He patted the steed's neck. "Come. There's work to be done."

"War's doing a flyby over the Middle East. Want to join her?"

"Maybe later."

He reached down for the saddlebag that just appeared—along with the saddle—and opened it. From within, he removed a fiery red plume. It had belonged to the previous incarnation of War: Joan, the Maid of Orléans. He held the feather for a moment, remembering her passion, remembering the ferocity that had shone in her eyes. From the moment that he'd offered her the mantle of the Red Rider, she had fervently believed that her purpose was to be his handmaiden. She belonged by his side, she had proclaimed, when he would eventually lead the Horsemen to the Last Battle.

She would be his sword arm when he finally destroyed the world.

He had been fascinated by her conviction. Her belief had made her strong—first in life, and then after.

Even so, now she was dead.

He, too, had a belief, one that had both grounded him and buoyed him. Now that belief was as dead as Joan's War, yet here he remained—for the first time ever without hope.

Even hope died, but that didn't make hope his to take.

Distracted, distraught, he climbed atop his steed and went out unto the world.

Behind him, a cold wind began to blow.

XANDER

Everyone had shown up for the party. No surprise there; Marcie's shindigs were famous for being parent-free and alcohol-heavy. As Riley had said on the way, Marcie's parents were either incredibly cool or incredibly oblivious.

Xander, who was on his fifth beer, voted for incredibly cool.

The party blared around him, with music blasting from hidden speakers and people resorting to screams to be heard. As a result, the volume was just under migraine-inducing. Xander barely noticed. He'd begun drinking to toast Riley's acceptance to Stanford, then kept right on drinking.

He still hadn't told Riley what he'd done—he hadn't told anyone yet—but he knew he would have to, and soon. But soon wasn't now. Thus, the drinking. That and, hey, free beer! Whoever said you can't get something for nothing had never been to a Marcie party. He took another pull from his beer and stared up at a nude blue woman.

He and Riley and Ted had arrived at Marcie's some time ago —it had taken them a little while longer to get there, because it had been crazy windy outside, which had made driving quite the challenge—and had done the initial circuit of the house together, after a pit stop in the kitchen to grab a couple of drinks. Ted quickly peeled off to join a larger group. Riley soon found the track team, and Xander hung out with them for a

few minutes before his inner social butterfly needed to take
wing. He made his way through the house again, alone this
time as he sought his friends.

There was Deb and other fellow art geeks, which soon
morphed into the thespian crowd, where Ted was well on his
way to getting smashed. They had invented a drinking game
that had something to do with show tunes—Ted warbled that
he was the model of a modern high school twelfth grader—so
Xander stayed until the chorus, then excused himself and
found Suzie. She was with a handful of others who dominated
the high end of the GPA spectrum, and they were talking pas-
sionately about their local U.S. senators. When Xander found
himself nodding along without understanding a thing, he
grinned, shook his head, and moved on.

Izzy was entrenched with the varsity soccer girls and guys, so
Xander joined the conversation about who was going to make
it to the World Cup. Not like he really cared—he could never
bring himself to tell Izzy that he didn't really like soccer, even if
it was called "football" in some places—but he could fake his
enthusiasm with the best of them. Soon Xander's beer was
empty, so he wandered into the kitchen to toss the old bottle
and get a new one.

Fresh drink in hand, he meandered his way around the
house again, slower, fascinated by the sheer size of the huge
split-level home that clearly belonged on the set of some popular television show (complete with about a hundred people acting as extras; Marcie's parties were always a hit). He took in the
furniture tastefully arranged just so, the sculptures and vases
proudly displayed on shelves, and he decided, as he drank, that
homes were really nothing more than backdrops to people's

lives—they set the scene, gave a hint of what to expect, but nothing more. Nothing revealing.

And then he found the blue nudes.

There was plenty of art decorating the walls, mostly original works by artists he didn't recognize. But what had arrested his attention were two pictures framed side by side in a small room. He probably shouldn't have opened the closed door, but the drinking had made him bold, and he wanted to find a little quiet. The room was probably a home office, based on the furniture: a large desk with a massive computer monitor, a high-backed chair with wheels, overstuffed bookcases, grim curtains shrouding the windows.

And on the wall opposite the bookcases were two prints of famous paintings, one by Matisse and one by Picasso. Xander had studied them in his art elective junior year, and as he stared up at the pictures, he found himself dumbstruck.

Matisse's blue nude showed a clearly female shape sitting on the floor with one hand clasped behind her head, one leg wrapped around the other. There was no face, no details, just the outline of a woman, and yet that lack of detail was what made the pose so mesmerizing—she was on the cusp of springing, of raging, of doing *something,* but what that action was didn't matter, because she would never do it. Faceless, featureless, she was forever caught in the moment before, coiled. Trapped.

Next to the Matisse, Picasso's blue nude showed a woman from behind, closed in on herself and hugging one of her knees. Everything about her, from the set of her shoulders to the curve of her back, gave voice to her grief; that the painting was entirely in shades of blue made the effect more profound. Xander didn't have to see her face to know, to feel, that she was sad. Tension radiated from the Matisse print, but Picasso's nude emanated waves of sorrow.

He stared at those paintings, captivated by faces he couldn't see, until he was jostled out of the moment and back into the party when someone opened the door and slurred something about trying to find a bathroom. He pointed her in the right direction and went back to his friends.

Over the next hour, every time he passed by the home office, he went inside and looked at the framed prints. They made him think of ghosts: devoid of detail, nothing but swirls of emotion. The women in those paintings were long dead— ghosts in truth as well as art.

Dead and gone, their memories forever encased in canvas and gilded frames.

Frozen in a moment, in the confines of that moment, forever.

Smirking, Xander shook his head. He should stop drinking, he told himself, because clearly, the alcohol was making him feel melancholy—especially as he looked at Picasso's grieving blue nude.

Instead, he had another beer and walked out to the back deck to get some air.

It was a beautiful night, crisp without being cold, the sky full of stars and promise. The wind had died, leaving the trees to stand quietly with their leaves unbothered. Xander found a spot that wasn't too crowded. He leaned against the rail, quietly taking it all in as he nursed his beer. Around him, people laughed and smoked and drank, some faking it, some reveling in it, all putting on a show for him, here with this glamorous house as a backdrop. Some of the teens were quieter in their roles than others, keeping mostly to themselves as they smiled and tried to fit in; others, like Ted, were bombastic and screamed for the spotlight, chugging to chants and proclaiming their lines to the back row. And there were those in the middle, not quite one or the other, content to be slightly social in the play that was Marcie's party—social-lites instead of socialites. Those were the Suzies, the Izzys, the Debs and Marcies.

And then there was him, Xander Atwood, standing outside of time in some in-between state, watching the performance while he himself remained aloof, apart. Disconnected.

He was like the blue nudes, he realized—frozen in a moment.

He took another sip.

He had to break free. He had to stop waiting for the right time, had to go to Riley right now and say what he'd done—

A beep, like a fire alarm on the fritz.

Xander frowned at his empty beer bottle. How long had he been outside, staring off into space? That's it, he was cutting himself off.

After one more beer.

He threaded his way back inside, waving at Suzie as he headed to the kitchen. It was packed sardine-tight with partiers, everyone hovering around the booze like they were ready to body slam anyone who dared to take the last one. Xander managed to snag a can of the cheap stuff—the only kind left —and then retreated to the small room again, finding himself in front of the Picasso.

Maybe she wasn't just sad, Xander thought. Maybe she was

aching, suffering from a pain that was far beyond physical. Maybe she'd lost someone.

Maybe she'd learned something that had broken her.

The more he looked at her, the more he thought that was accurate: Picasso's blue nude had learned a devastating truth, and all she could do was hug herself and hide her agony from the world.

A sound, like the screech of tires.

Xander whirled, startled, and saw two people stagger into the room, close enough to get drunk off each other's breath.

"Zan!" Ted announced. "Here you are! Been looking for you!"

Riley grinned, swaying a little, saying nothing.

"Couldn't hear myself think," Xander said, shrugging.

"Who comes to a party to think! Come on, join us!" Ted grabbed one arm and Riley took the other, pulling him out of the room, away from the blue nudes.

For the rest of the party, Xander grinned and laughed and pantomimed having fun, like the others acting in the play of Marcie's party.

And he absolutely didn't think about what he thought he'd seen when he was in the small room.

There had been a moment, just a moment, when out of the corner of his eye he thought he'd seen someone come into the room, someone not quite real—the shape of a man, but without the details. A ghost, like the blue nudes.

A dead man, made of shadow.

No question about it: He'd had too much to drink.

Well, he'd go home—eventually—and sleep it off. And tomorrow, he'd finally tell Riley what he'd been keeping secret for weeks. Part of him wanted to do it now, in front of Ted and Suzie and the others, too, but the rest of him insisted that it be just him and Riley first. The *what* behind what he'd done was less important than the *why*, and he wanted that *why* to be shared in private.

He dug into his pocket for his lucky penny, and he tossed it high, calling heads. He missed it on the way down — the five beers had messed with his timing — and the coin bounced on the carpet and landed next to his foot.

Heads.

"All hail the lucky penny!" Ted hooted, and they all lifted their bottles in salute.

Grinning, Xander scooped up his penny and managed to get it back into his pocket without dropping it. Tomorrow. Yes, tomorrow would be the big day. He could feel it in his bones.

Tomorrow.

Tomorrow would never come.

He knew that now. He understood it, accepted it as truth: The only future that mattered, the only possibility that had kept him content eon after eon, would never become actuality.

When he had returned to the Slate, he had felt the weight of probabilities pressing down, crushing him in various degrees of potential as he'd searched again and again for the one future that held his salvation.

For that's what it had been, he realized now as he rode atop his steed and wandered along the dying world: That possibility had been his deliverance, his very purpose.

And now that purpose was gone.

That particular tomorrow, always slight, would never come to pass. The still, small voice would be silent forevermore.

He had not made a mistake before; something had changed, something irrevocable. He could search through the yesterdays to determine what it had been, but why bother? Understanding why his *maybe* had ceased to exist wouldn't change anything.

If he had no hope of salvation, did that leave him damned?

Humans fretted over such things, he knew — hell, the Chinvat Bridge, Gehenna, Tartarus. So many names for punishment, but none of them touched the truth. Damnation wasn't eternal fire, wasn't a world of devils sent to torment and tease. It wasn't a lack of heaven or nirvana.

Damnation was being abandoned and forgotten.

Aimless, he drifted.

There was a polite nicker from the steed, and then it commented, "You're blighting the ground."

He did not reply.

"Maybe you're doing it on purpose," the steed said diplomatically. "Nothing like a good blight every now and then to remind the earth of its place. But in the event that you're just distracted, which, by the way, you have been ever since you returned from the place you go when you go away, I wanted to let you know that you're leaving a trail of scorched soil."

A long pause before he replied: "So?"

The horse's ears quivered, and the steed said nothing more.

In silence, a man who was not a man and a horse that was not a horse walked the patch of land, leaving a desert in their wake.

Eventually, he spoke. "The time has come."

The steed, already uneasy, hazarded a question. "Will you let the others know?" When Death did not reply, the pale steed continued, "None of them have seen your cycle come to completion. Well. Not directly. The Riders have, of course, but not these Riders. If you take my meaning. They might not understand."

A stretch of time in which there was silence. And then, finally, he murmured, "You're right. I will visit them."

The horse blew out a satisfied breath, thinking—incorrectly—that the Pale Rider meant he would explain to the others what was to happen, now that the cyclical change was upon him.

And Death, still without purpose, was momentarily at peace. There would be a tomorrow after all, a tomorrow that mattered. A tomorrow for farewells.

Tomorrow would be the day the world ended.

PART TWO

THE BEGINNING OF THE END

Then I heard one of the four living creatures say in a voice like thunder, "Come and see!"

—Revelation 6:1

DEATH

The day that Death decided to destroy the world began almost like any other day. People woke up or were woken up or didn't wake up at all; they got ready for school or for work or for nothing of any importance; they were ambitious and they were aimless; they prepared for celebration and they prepared for mourning.

They lived.

But there was one difference: All the babies cried. In every dwelling in every corner of the world, all of the babies woke screaming. They didn't cry because they were hungry or soiled or in pain. They cried because words eluded them.

They knew what was coming.

So the babies cried, and their parents tended to them with false promises and temporary comfort as Death prepared for the end of everything.

XANDER

Lex was crying again.

Xander pried open one eyelid and stared at the digital clock on his nightstand, then he burrowed under the blanket and tried to go back to sleep. No good; Lex wouldn't shut up. The kid had quite a set of lungs.

With a sigh, Xander yanked the blanket back down. He heard his mom go through the calm-the-baby motions — the soft, off-key singing about rainbows; the creak of the old rocker-glider, back and forth, back and forth; the rustle of plastic as a diaper was checked for deposits. He heard it all, just as he had every morning since his little brother had taken his first breath three months ago. He loved the baby, really he did, but right now at oh-my-god o'clock in the morning, he would have happily sold Lex to the first bidder on eBay. Had there really been a time when he'd been woken by an alarm clock instead of his brother's piercing screams?

Speaking of which, the baby was still crying.

Xander groaned, peered at the clock once more, then groaned again. There really should be a law about getting up before sunrise on a weekend.

Recognizing a lost cause, he stumbled out of bed and headed toward the nursery. Lex was still wailing loud enough to wake the neighbors—just not loud enough to wake their father. Nothing short of a nuclear annihilation would be enough to wake Dad. And really, who wouldn't want to sleep through the end of the world?

(today)

Xander blinked as the thought triggered a memory—no, a dream from last night. It was little more than a vague feeling of dread, an impression of pending doom: shadows swirling through the nighttime sky, staining the midnight blue with tendrils of ink.

Something was going to happen today. Something bad.

Uh-huh. It was probably just another nightmare about running late for a math test. Naked. Xander shuddered. Doom, indeed.

He opened the nursery door and stuck his head inside. His mom, looking more wrecked than Xander felt, was standing over the changing table on the dresser, trying to coax a pacifier into the baby's mouth. No luck; Lex just spat it out and screamed louder.

"Want me to try?" Xander asked sleepily.

His mom's head hung low and her shoulders slumped. "God, yes. Please."

Xander walked into Lex's shoebox of a room and squeezed between the crib and the rocker-glider, careful not to bang his elbow against the dresser. Lex would need a real bedroom next year, but by then Xander would be living in a college dorm, so Lex would get his room. When Xander would come visit, he'd stay at Ted's house. A room for the baby; no broken sleep for Xander. Win-win.

His mom stepped aside. "Nothing's working," she said dully.

"He's not hungry, doesn't care about a new diaper, won't take the binky."

Probably because the baby had too much class to call a pacifier a binky. "Tried duct tape yet?"

His mother half smiled, half grimaced. "Don't tempt me."

Lex shrieked.

"It was a joke, kid. A joke. Get a sense of humor." Xander bundled his brother into a baby blanket and scooped him up. Lex squirmed and fussed, so Xander brushed his fingertips across the baby's cheek to quiet him, just a soft touch to let him know that his big brother was there and all was right with the world.

The moment his fingers skimmed his brother's face—

(the Pale Rider comes)

—a dark window creaked open: Xander remembered shadows gathering into a shape filled with wonders and horrors, remembered it stretching and standing tall as death spread across the land like butterflies with wings of poison.

"The Pale Rider comes," he murmured.

His mom said, "What? I didn't catch what you said."

In his mind, the window slammed closed.

Xander blinked at his now silent baby brother, then shrugged. "Had this weird dream. Just remembered part of it."

"Anything good?"

He frowned, trying to make the images return, but he was met with static. "Don't remember. That's crazy, I just had it a second ago."

"Dreams are like that," his mom said. She reached over to stroke Lex's hair, but she pulled her hand back with a jerk before her fingers made contact. "He must be in a big brother sort of mood."

"Lucky me."

"Lucky *me*. You mind if I crawl back to bed?" She punctuated her question with a haunted, hopeful look.

"Go ahead," Xander said, sighing. "I've got this."

She squeezed his shoulder in thanks. "You're a saint, Son. A saint."

He smiled faintly. "A saint who could use a new car . . ."

"Couldn't we all." With a yawn, his mom staggered out of the nursery and aimed for her bedroom.

Xander closed the door behind her and rocked Lex in his arms. Illuminated by the small night-light in the wall, his brother took on an almost ethereal glow.

"Now you listen to me, kid," he said. "The game's on at one. You have to have this crying thing all sorted out by then, because Ted's picking me up and we're off to Izzy's to watch, and you'll be alone with Mom. Dad, too, but let's face it: He's useless until you're more than furniture with an appetite."

The baby said nothing, which Xander took as complete agreement.

"Oh, he's a good dad and all. He's just helpless around babies. Play your cards right, he'll be wrapped around your finger before you're two. Like me with Riley." He grinned as he imagined Riley's full lips pulling into a lush smile. Oh, that smile. "So. Wanna hear just how much I've fallen in love with the amazing Riley Jones?"

The baby yawned. That had to be Baby for "Of course I want to hear, tell me everything, I'm a great listener."

He told the baby his secret—and then the clock on the dresser let out a harsh beep.

Xander blinked at the baby, who was on his lap, tucked neatly into a blanket, as Xander rocked on the chair. Frowning, he stared at the clock, which showed that he'd been in the nursery for twenty minutes. He could have sworn that he'd just walked into Lex's room maybe a minute ago.

"Huh," he said aloud. "I think I'm sleep deprived."

Lex's tiny face scrunched up, as if he were mulling over his brother's words. Then he passed gas and settled down, closing his eyes.

Xander chuckled. "Nice. You'll be stinking up the bathroom in no time."

He rocked Lex gently as he hummed an old *Sesame Street* tune. He stroked Lex's hair and looked at the crib, ready and waiting for its precious cargo; looked at the changing table atop the banged-up dresser; looked at the desk lamp and book on the nightstand next to the rocker-glider. It was a novel by an author named Ibáñez. The title read *The Four Horsemen of the Apocalypse*. Curious, he flipped the book over and scanned the back cover. He'd thought it would have been something along the lines of *Good Omens* or some other romp about the end of the world, but no; this book was historical fiction about a family just before and during the First World War. Much more his mother's taste than his.

When he thought his brother was really sleeping, he kissed Lex's head, ready to place the baby into the crib. As his lips brushed the peach fuzz of Lex's hair—

(kiss them all goodbye)

—an image caught fire in Xander's brain: something dark and incomplete, like a silhouette given life.

A dead man made of shadow.

Xander shook his head and chuckled again. *Definitely* sleep deprived.

He carefully placed the baby into the crib. Lex didn't stir as Xander silently backed away, channeling his inner ninja as he aimed for stealth. He waited until a count of fifty before he slipped out of the nursery and gently closed the door. With luck, Lex would stay asleep for at least two hours. By then, it would be a proper sort of Sunday morning, one that included actual daylight.

Back in his room once more, Xander threw himself into bed and waited for sleep to come.

It didn't.

Instead, he saw a dark vision rise behind his closed eyelids —humanlike, filled with horrors and yet hollow, empty. A black hole sucking in all light, all life.

The end of everything.

Xander shoved his pillow over his head and made himself remember holding Lex—his fragile baby brother, with the soft spot on his head that still hadn't closed.

He'd kissed the baby and had seen something dark and full of dread.

A kiss before the end.

A kiss goodbye.

His eyes snapped open. A kiss goodbye, because it was the end of everything. The end was here . . . no, the end was coming, heralded by empty space in human form.

The Pale Rider was coming—coming soon.

That was it: the finale in four letters, a coda leading to full stop.

The urgency of *soon*.

Xander turned on the table lamp that rested on his night-stand and grabbed the spiral sketchbook and drawing pencil that waited there. It wasn't his main sketch diary, and it wasn't the sketchbook that he used as part of his portfolio when he'd applied to Carnegie Mellon and other art-heavy colleges; this was a small book, almost a notepad, meant for him to quickly touch on ideas and thoughts. Capture the notion, tease it out with the immediacy, the intimacy, of paper and pencil and return to it later to better refine it.

Get it down; get it out. Turn the page and move on.

He set the point to the paper's surface and began to draw. He played with shapes, toyed with impressions, quickly filling the page with half-formed images. Art breathed; if you over-powered it with meaning right away, it suffocated. He sketched four horses trampling the world, a world riddled with coins. Each horse had a color, a purpose: bold, thick strokes turned one horse solid black, like charred food; flames outlined an-other horse, suggesting the fiery red that was its coat, and he dotted droplets around the horse's mouth to represent blood —that horse was a biter; the third horse he left stark white, with dust beneath its hooves that hinted at filth; as for the last, he smudged the outline until it only suggested a horse, leaving it pale, ghostlike.

A horse that was not a horse, for a man who was not a man.

He wrote a few words, too, when the pictures in his head didn't translate properly onto paper as a form. One word, *kiss,* he knew he'd remember in the sense of a kiss good night, a kiss goodbye—something intimate, something final. Sealed with a kiss. A promise, irrevocable.

Another word: *end,* as in the End, game over, hit the lights on your way out. The end of everything.

And a final phrase, one that made his chest tighten and his heartbeat quicken.

The Pale Rider comes.

Yes.

He didn't understand what he had drawn, and it wasn't exactly what was banging around in his head, but it was close enough for now. It touched on the inevitability, the sense of finality. Of farewell, forever.

A kiss good night. A kiss goodbye.

He let out a shaky laugh. Must have been one hell of a dream.

Xander tossed the sketchbook and pencil onto his nightstand, where they landed with an indifferent thud, and he stared at his lead-darkened fingertips and debated washing his hands. No point, he decided; he was just going to get them dirty again later in the morning, when he would do his next round of sketches. Then he settled into his bed and pulled his covers high.

When he was a kid, his mom used to tell him that after he had a nightmare, the rule was he had to have a good dream next. "It's only fair," his mom would say as she mopped his sweaty hair from his face and soothed him. "After the bad comes the good. Time for a good dream, Xander."

So Xander said aloud, "Time for a good dream." Ideally, one about Riley. And him. And maybe a new car.

And doing things in the new car that didn't involve driving.

Xander grinned and reached for his lamp, but then he paused. His fingertips, stained from the pencil, had left dark streaks along his pillowcase. He frowned at the white fabric marred by black, then flipped his pillow.

Good enough, he decided as he shut off his lamp. It didn't matter that he knew the black was there.

He was good at hiding the truth.

The bride wore white, of course. She looked radiant in the way that most brides do — something about the pledge of eternal love and devotion heats them from within and sets their cheeks aglow. This bride, in particular, wore her silk gown splendidly; the beading over the bodice emphasized curves and softened angles, helping turn the woman in white into a delicate work of art.

The groom was equally brilliant as he gazed adoringly at the one who'd stolen his heart. His tuxedo was the same as those worn by the other men in the wedding party; from behind, they all could have been waiters at a particularly upscale restaurant where you have to pay a hundred dollars for a dollop of food set upon the plate *just so.* But the groom could have been dressed in jeans and a ratty T-shirt, and he still would have been majestically handsome because of the light in his eyes, the joy in his smile.

It was enough to make Famine want to puke.

The Black Rider of the Apocalypse stood in the back of the room, clad in ink and shadow, frowning at the loving couple. They didn't notice her, of course, just as no one in the room noticed her. The Horsemen were visible to mortals only when they wished it, and right now Famine didn't want to be seen.

What she wanted was to be happy for the bride and groom, but they were just so pathetic — two meat sacks decked out in Vera Wang and Ralph Lauren. Sure, they were sated for the moment on love, but let them go a week with no food, then see how blissful their looks would be.

A touch of frost skimmed the back of her neck.

"You couldn't stay away, either?" she asked, not turning around.

Death slouched up next to her. "Of course I could stay away. As could you. Yet here we are." A pause. "There's something about weddings that gives people a new appreciation of life, don't you think?"

Famine declined to answer.

In the back rows, the guests began to shiver. An old woman loudly wondered if the air conditioning was set too high, and she was shushed by the people around her.

"Do you miss her?"

Famine scowled. "She made her choice long ago."

"Not to be the Black Rider? Or not to be your friend?"

She turned to glare at Death, but then she paused in her indignation. "Why are you wearing pajamas?"

"Too lazy to put on a tux." His blond hair was a tangled mess that crashed over his ears, and his blue eyes gleamed with winter's secrets. He smiled as he offered her a bouquet of pink and white flowers, bundled together in a wide satin bow. "For thee, Black Rider. They don't really go with my outfit."

Startled, she took the flowers. As soon as they touched her gloved hands, they began to wither, starved.

"They were already dead," Death said cheerfully. "Cut in the prime of their beauty, all for impact and style. Absolute murder on the bride's mother's allergies, but it's merely one of her many sacrifices for her daughter. Or so she'd tell you. Frequently."

Famine smiled thinly, a sliver of lips and teeth. "She hasn't changed."

"People rarely do."

She saw the truth in that.

They watched the bride and groom gaze at each other lovingly by the altar as the officiator recited the words that would bind them with love and affection for all eternity, or at least until divorce court.

The Black Rider frowned at the bride. Could the woman dressed in white sense Famine's presence? It was possible; even though the bride was no longer anorexic, she had once wielded the Scales of office. Did she miss flying through the skies on horseback, feeling and fueling the appetite of the world? Or did she pretend that part of her life had never happened?

A phrase from the clergyman nudged Famine from her bleak thoughts, and she sneered from the presumptuousness of the words.

Love is stronger than death.

Ridiculous. A previous incarnation of the Black Rider had died of heartbreak. Nothing was stronger than death.

"Such flattery," Death murmured. "One would think you want something."

"Not this time."

He smiled. "Liar. You just don't know what it is you want. But you want something. All living things do."

"I'm not like them," she said. "Not anymore."

"You think just because you've turned your back on your

humanity that you're no longer human?" He chuckled. "You're adorable. And you didn't answer my question. Do you miss her?"

The Black Rider said nothing. In her arms, the dried flowers flaked to ash.

"Of course you do," Death answered for her. "Despite your protest, you're only human. And so you miss her like a starving man misses food."

She lifted her chin. "You're wrong."

"I'm many things, but I'm not wrong. She was your best friend—past tense, verging on the pluperfect—and yet here you are, present tense, at her wedding. You miss her."

"You're *wrong*," Famine insisted.

"Am I now?" He gazed upon her, gazed through her with his empty blue eyes. "Since you know so much, do you want to know what you were to her?" His smile turned sly. "Nothing."

A lump formed in the Black Rider's throat, and she choked it down.

"In the scheme of things, you were just a distraction to her. That's all." Death stood in his ill-fitting green and white striped pajamas, and he stared blankly at the bride and groom, even as that sly smile played on his face. "She cut you out of her life so that she might live. As for him, he never cared for you in the first place. You didn't matter then. And neither of them thinks about you now."

Stung, Famine cringed.

"It doesn't matter that you emulated her. It doesn't matter that you followed in her footsteps. Lisabeth Lewis left you stranded in a field of dust."

The Black Rider whispered, "Why are you being so cruel?"

"If truth is cruelty, then I am a sadist." He turned to face the Black Rider, and this time she flinched as his empty gaze fixed upon her. "You look so hurt. Don't be. Embracing the truth can be cathartic. Rather like purging, wouldn't you say?"

She bit her lip until she tasted blood.

"Here's more truth for you: People make choices, and each choice brings with it repercussions." He laughed softly, the sound like a graveyard wind. "A butterfly flaps its wings and the earth trembles. Lisabeth chose to walk away from you, and as a consequence you chose to become Famine. In doing so, you chose to walk away from your humanity. What do you think the consequence of that action will be?"

"Nothing," the Black Rider said tersely. "I may as well have never existed before I took the Scales from you. I'm Famine, now and forever."

"Nothing is forever, Tammy."

The room filled with thunderous applause.

Her lip sore and already swelling, Famine glanced at the altar. The groom was kissing the bride. And kissing. And kissing. It looked like he was eating her face. When they finally paused for air, Lisa giggled and her groom, James, kissed her again, to the hearty approval of their guests.

Famine dropped the dead bouquet to the floor, where it landed in a pile of black stems and ash. The satin bow fluttered to the ground, a discarded memory of something bright and festive. The Black Rider sighed. She wanted to be happy for her former friend, but she just couldn't manage it. She was too raw inside. Empty, like Death's bouquet.

Just as well, she decided. Famine didn't go hand in hand with happily ever afters.

Nothing is forever, Death whispered in her mind. *Especially happiness.*

She turned to argue the point, but he was already gone.

Even though she wasn't cold, she couldn't stop herself from shivering.

XANDER

Xander glanced at the thermostat as he headed toward the apartment's front door. The needle was set at seventy degrees, which did nothing to explain his sudden chill. Whatever—he was probably coming down with something. The weather had been nuts lately; instead of the balmy temperatures that had been predicted, it had been unseasonably cold, almost frigid. Between the freaky weather and his adventures in broken sleep, he was a candidate for the flu of the week.

Or maybe he was absolutely fine and the thermostat was on the blink.

He opened the door just as the bell chimed—actually, beeped; that was weird—a second time. Ted stood in the doorway, grinning his trademark grin, the one that made parents frown and teachers reach for their detention slips. He waved and said, "Hey."

"Hey," Xander said. "Tip for you: Ringing the bell a lot doesn't make me get to the door any faster."

For a moment, Ted didn't reply. Something lit behind his eyes, something that Xander couldn't read, and then Ted's grin softened into a tired smile. "Tips are for *mohels*. And it works for elevators."

Xander stepped aside, and Ted walked into the apartment, sipping from a Styrofoam cup.

"Uh-huh," Xander said. "You probably press the Walk button when you want to cross the street."

"Nah. I just jaywalk."

"Such a rebel."

"Got to get my jollies where I can. You ready to go? We've got to make a pit stop at the package store before we get to Izzy's."

Xander winced. "Say it a little louder. My parents might not have heard you."

"Please, they're over forty. As if they hear anything if we don't shout."

"It's selective hearing. It's like a superpower." Xander frowned at his friend. The grin on Ted's face couldn't disguise how exhausted he looked: skin too pale, circles under his eyes dark enough to be bruises, hair that would have given a brush a case of the nerves. "You okay? You look like you met the business end of a baseball bat."

Ted slid him a look, as if he was weighing Xander's words. Finally, he said, "Just tired. Nothing a little coffee won't cure." He took another sip as if to prove the point.

"Late night?"

Now Ted was staring at him. "Dude. Marcie's. Last night." He paused. "Remember?"

"Right." Of course Xander remembered. Well, sort of. His memory was spotty, like he couldn't quite focus on any one thing from the party. He grinned to cover his embarrassment. "Late night."

Ted was looking at him oddly. "How much did you drink, anyway?"

"Dunno," he admitted. "It's sort of a blur. Head's a little weird today."

Ted saluted him with his cup. "That's why God invented coffee. And aspirin. Are we going, or what?"

"Wallet's in my room, give me a second."

He raced to his bedroom and snagged his wallet, keys, and phone, pausing for a moment to glance at the framed Escher print hanging over his dresser. It showed a figure eight that had been twisted into a Möbius strip, flipping the figure 180 degrees, with ants crawling along both sides. Because of the extra twist, the ants would never meet, and they would crawl along the perpetual surface of the figure eight for all eternity.

Xander frowned. He was definitely having a moment, because for the life of him, he couldn't remember when he'd gotten the poster, let alone framed it and put it on his bedroom wall.

Whatever. It was yet another side effect of having a baby brother double as an alarm clock.

Tucking his phone into his shirt pocket, Xander ducked into the nursery to tell his mom that he was headed out. He thought maybe she was changing Lex's diaper, but no, she was sitting in the rocker—nursing the baby.

Xander blushed and turned his head so he couldn't see anything he shouldn't be seeing. "Mom! Hang a sign up or something!"

"I've got a nursing cloth covering me," she said reasonably. "Nothing's exposed, I promise. Besides, breast feeding is perfectly natural."

Maybe so, but the thought of accidentally seeing his mother's

naked boob was enough to give him the heebie-jeebies. Bad
enough that his parents obviously had had sex. Still not looking
at her, he said, "I'm going with Ted to Izzy's house to watch the
game."

"You'll be home before six, right?"

He sighed. "I promise for the zillionth time I'll be home to
babysit."

"My son the saint," she said happily.

Not so saintly; he was hoping to build up enough good
karma that his parents would reward him with a car. Xander
was a believer in the power of positive thinking. Besides, he was
going to ask Riley to come by tonight. He didn't mention that
part to his mom, who had definite ideas on when it was appropriate to leave two horny teenagers alone—also known as
"never."

Next he ducked into the kitchen, where his dad was playing
yet another round of online poker. "Off to Izzy's for the game,"
Xander announced.

His dad didn't look away from the screen. "You guys could
watch here."

"Izzy's got surround sound." And beer, but Xander didn't
mention that part.

"Damn it, should've held! Would've had four of a kind!" His
dad let out a frustrated snort. "Guess no one sees something
like that coming."

(the Pale Rider is coming)

For no reason he could name, Xander thought of his frag-
mented dream, the one that had led him to sketch four horses
breaking the world. Suddenly uneasy, he forced a grin onto his
face. Dreams were stupid and meant to be forgotten.

"Heading out. And yes," he said before his dad could mention it, "I'll be back by six."

His dad grunted, "Good man." Then he cursed at the virtual players at the online poker table.

Xander said, "At least it's not for real money. Which is good, because I'm guessing we'd be bankrupt by this point."

"I swear," his father muttered, "I don't know why I bother. It always ends the same way, with me wanting to win even more."

"So stop playing."

His dad glanced at him, an odd twinkle in his eye. "But playing's so much fun. Go, enjoy the game. Home by six."

Xander agreed, collected Ted, and left the apartment. An elevator ride later, they were outside the building and walking to Ted's car, which was parked across the street. It was a gorgeous day, with the sky so blue that the white of the clouds looked almost sharp. A cawing sound heralded a slice of black that suddenly cut through the blue—a flock of birds, taking flight.

No, not just birds, but crows. A murder of crows, marring the summer sky.

On impulse, Xander took out his cell phone and snapped a picture of the crows. Their cries hung in the air, echoing after the flock passed on to another patch of sky.

Soon, the birds warned. *Soon, soon.*

"Come on," Ted said, unlocking his door. "Places to be, beer to drink."

"Yeah, okay," Xander replied absently, staring at the place where the crows had been. The last of the caws faded, leaving only an impression of doom.

He shook his head and finally got into the passenger seat of Ted's secondhand beast of an automobile, which Xander thought of as the Death Car. The shocks were nonexistent; the brakes were questionable; the seat belts were an afterthought. How the thing always passed inspection was anyone's guess. Ted had gotten it for his seventeenth birthday last year, and he swore he'd drive it until it fell apart. Which, based on the odometer, could be any second now.

Once Xander shut the door, Ted gunned it out of the parking spot. The Death Car lurched down the street, belching exhaust. Ten seconds later, Xander was clinging to the grip over his door.

"I think you missed a pothole back there," he said through gritted teeth.

Ted grinned at him. "Nope. Got 'em all. I'm talented like that."

Maybe it was because he was behind the wheel of his beloved evil car, but Ted looked worlds better than he had at Xander's house: the paleness of his skin softened from sickly to merely sun-starved, and the shadows under his eyes gave him an air of mystery, even danger. He could have been on his way to a casting call for beautiful vampires, except vampires didn't sip from old Styrofoam cups and grimace every time they swallowed.

Xander asked, "Want to grab some fresh coffee before we hit the package store?"

"Zan, the man with the plan."

"You know you said that with your out-loud voice, right?"

"I blame the bad coffee."

Ted pulled into a fast-food drive-through, although the

word "fast" was a horrible tease, considering the line of vehicles ahead of them. Once the Death Car stopped moving, the air became oppressive — the car didn't have luxuries like air conditioning — so Xander and Ted both opened their windows.

"Love the smell of garbage and hot oil in the morning," Xander said, breathing deeply.

"That's because you're disturbed. Damn it!" Ted swatted at a mosquito, which avoided his hand either by luck or insectile agility. "Stupid bugs. What's the point of mosquitos?"

"Food for fish."

"Can't they just eat a pizza?"

"Maybe if they had teeth."

"They bite, don't they?"

The mosquito whined by Xander's arm. He waited until it touched down, just below his elbow, and then he smashed it to a smear. Bug guts and Ted's blood combined in a deathly streak that marred Xander's skin.

"Zan the skeeter killer," Ted said.

"Still using your out-loud voice."

"Look at that. That's my blood on you. Freaking bugs. Hate them. Wish they'd all just disappear."

"Seriously?" Xander said. "You'd waste a wish on mosquito genocide?"

"Hell yes."

"You're crazy. If I had one wish, I wouldn't use it to kill bugs."

Xander's phone vibrated, and he checked it quickly to read the new text. He'd expected it to be from Riley, but instead it was a message from Suzie.

U OK?

He chuckled.

"What's up?" Ted asked.

"Suzie's being all mother hen. Wants to know if I'm okay. I must have really drank a lot last night, huh?"

Ted shrugged, said nothing as he inched the Death Car forward.

Xander texted back that he was fine, that he and Ted were on the way to Izzy's to watch the game. He asked if she'd be there, even though he already knew the answer: Suzie did many things, but watching televised sports wasn't one of them. Thirty seconds after he hit Send, he got a new text.

?????????

"Huh."

"What?"

"Nothing, Suzie's just being weird." He put his phone away.

"That's our Suzie," Ted said, moving the car forward again.

"Yeah." For a second, he thought he remembered Suzie yelling at him—no, yelling something at him, trying to tell him something, something important, but he couldn't make out the words.

He thought he heard the screeching of tires, but it was just the Death Car coming to a jerking halt.

A chill whispered over Xander, leaving goosebumps on his flesh like secret kisses. He glanced out the window. Even though the crows he'd seen before were long gone, he thought he could hear their warning lingering in the air.

Soon.

PESTILENCE

The volunteer patiently taught a group of village women about the importance of using mosquito netting in their homes. The bed nets were treated with a chemical that would help prevent malaria. A child died from the disease every thirty seconds, the volunteer said somberly, then she went on to explain that malaria was spread by mosquitos, which bit people mostly at night. Sleeping under the treated nets would help keep their families safe in two ways: It would act as a barrier, and the chemicals on the nets would kill the mosquitos.

But the women were afraid. They would suffocate, one declared. The chemicals would harm their children, another insisted. A third proclaimed that white was the color of death, and all the village women nodded knowingly.

Unnoticed by the women, Pestilence snorted. White, the color of death? Ridiculous. Death didn't wear white.

Actually, Death wore whatever the hell he wanted to wear, and no one said boo about it.

Pestilence, the White Rider of the Apocalypse, stood beneath a large acacia tree, his snowy uniform a stark contrast to the sunbaked browns and greens around him. Creepers of dust clung to the edges of his coat sleeves, marring the pristine whiteness with hints of decay. A silver band rested on his forehead, winking beneath thick strands of white-streaked hair. His face was clear of acne and blackheads—a slight vanity, but he figured he was allowed the occasional perk. Next to him, a thin white horse nibbled contentedly on the parched grass. It didn't need to eat, but it found the action comforting; Pestilence knew this, because there was a connection between a steed and its Rider, one that surpassed the need for words. Besides, who didn't like a little comfort food?

Well. Other than Famine, who didn't like a little comfort food?

Absently patting the horse's back, Pestilence focused on his work. While the volunteer attempted to fight superstition with fact, Pestilence battled disease. Coaxed, really; there was no need for him to fight it. He controlled disease. If he wished, he could eradicate the malaria with a thought, banish it like small-pox, rather than slowly absorb parts of it into his system and leave the rest to feast upon mosquitos and plague humanity. But Pestilence had learned the hard way that completely elimi-nating a disease only made things worse—another sickness would take its place, one that was far crueler. Far more deadly.

Pestilence frowned as he continued to rein in the parasites that spread malaria. Was it he who had learned what happened when sickness was thrown out of balance? Or had it been a previous White Rider? He didn't know. Lately, it was becoming more difficult to separate his thoughts from those of his prede-cessors. If he didn't know better, he'd be worried. Figments whispering to you, telling you things you otherwise didn't know? That could be a sign of anything from fatigue to schizo-phrenia.

But the difference was that the voices in his head were real.

Gently, gently, the Elder said. *If you are too heavy-handed, they'll fight you.*

I know.

Pestilence had come to recognize the voices of the previous White Riders, from the soft-spoken Slave, who had been a helot in Sparta, to the commanding tones of the King, ruler of the land of Phrygia. He knew the King best and liked him least. Pestilence's favorite voice was that of the Elder, who had been the magic man of his tribe. The Elder had taken the Crown after the sky had fallen and the land had turned to ice.

He'd seen the end of the world, and it had begun on a sheet of white.

Pestilence shook that thought away. That was the King whispering to him, attempting to cloud his perception. The King didn't like the cold.

Happily, he didn't have to worry about the cold, not in this part of the world. As Pestilence continued to nudge the malaria into something less widespread, he ignored heat that otherwise would have left him drowning in sweat. That was just one of the side effects he had as the White Rider: temperature control. Other benefits of being a Horseman of the Apocalypse included uniforms, company cars, and picking up new skill sets—as long as you didn't mind single colors, cars that were really flying horses, and wielding phenomenal power that sometimes had a mind of its own.

Focus, the Elder scolded.

I'm focusing, Pestilence sighed.

Now the village woman were debating whether the netting

would be put to better use if it were sewn into fishing nets, much to the chagrin of the volunteer. Their words sparked a memory in Pestilence's mind: he saw himself as a boy of ten, trapping fish in nets of flax, remembered the joy he'd taken as he'd pulled his catch ashore.

No. That hadn't been him. That had been the Fisher, who'd taken the Crown after a plague had decimated his village.

Pestilence laughed softly. It was a pleasant memory, even if it wasn't truly his own.

A murder of crows fell upon the acacia tree, and the birds jabbered and cawed as the White Rider fished for malaria. Just as the volunteer convinced the villagers to take the mosquito nets, the opening chords of "Mad About You" filled the air. The birds squawked disapproval, but none of the women reacted. Everything about the White Rider went unnoticed by them, or maybe they just weren't Sting fans.

He gave his steed a final pat, then took his cell phone from his pocket and glanced at the number. Smiling, he took the call. "Hey."

"Hey! What're you doing?"

"Working."

"I'll keep it quick. Free for dinner?"

"Sure," he said, glancing at his wrist, which was covered by a white glove and therefore a completely pointless gesture, but some habits were hard to break. "When?"

"An hour from now? You bring the pizza, I'll take care of dessert?"

"Is that a euphemism?"

A smoky laugh, and then: "One way to find out."

His smile transformed into an infectious grin that spread warmth through his body. "It's a date."

"You, me, and a deluxe pizza." A happy sigh, punctuated with a giggle. "This is love!"

Still grinning, he murmured, "Is that what this is?"

"It is if you order the pizza with extra olives."

"For you? I'd order extra anchovies. I wouldn't eat them, but I'd order them."

"What a guy. See you in an hour. Love you."

"Love you too," he said warmly, then put his phone back in his pocket.

"In sickness and in health," said an amused voice from behind him. "Which, in your case, pretty much covers all the bases."

The white horse lowered its head and backed away, blowing nervous puffs of air.

Pestilence frowned over his shoulder. "You're scaring my steed."

Death was leaning against the acacia's trunk, wearing the form of a dead rock legend in green and white pajamas. His mop of dirty blond hair shrouded his face, casting his eyes in a sky of empty night. He nodded at the white horse.

"My sincerest apologies, noble steed," Death said in perfect Horse, which Pestilence understood. Pestilence understood all languages. Another side effect of being a Horseman of the Apocalypse. You haven't lived until you've been cursed out by a pigeon while speeding over the Hudson River on a flying horse.

The white steed shivered, but it accepted Death's apology. It was a nervous horse, not a stupid one.

The village women suddenly dispersed, as if they were flee-
ing to escape a squall. The volunteer hastily packed her things
and drove away from the clearing like there was no tomorrow.

Two Riders of the Apocalypse stood beneath the shade of an
acacia tree, with a trembling horse and a murder of crows bear-
ing witness.

"I like your pajamas," said Pestilence.

"They're not mine. I just borrowed them. It's all I can do. I
borrow. I rummage." He smiled. "I steal. I'm not a Rider. I'm a
pirate."

"Maybe you should trade your steed for a parrot." Pestilence
paused. "Say. Where's your steed?"

"Not here."

Pestilence's mouth suddenly, inexplicably, went dry. "Why
not?"

"I need a steed that leaves me to my own affairs, without the
benefit of commentary." Death's voice, never warm, now was
laced with frostbite. "Good help is so hard to find. But not as
hard as finding true love. That's what you think you have with
her, don't you? True love."

Pestilence felt his stomach cramp and twist.

Stomach pain. Gastroenteritis, said the Elder. *Lactose intoler-
ance. Anxiety.*

Fear.

"What happened to your steed?"

If Death heard the question, he ignored it. "You and your
girl sound so cute on the phone. Love as conveyed through
pizza. War would be sickened by the notion, but Famine, I'm
sure, would be amused. Or maybe bitter. She's not exactly sta-

ble when it comes to affairs of the heart. But she'd appreciate the food, even if she doesn't tend to eat it herself."

"I do love her," Pestilence said quietly.

"Who, Famine? Well. You and the Black Rider do have quite the history . . ."

"Not Famine. Marianne. My girl, as you called her. The one who sounds so cute on the phone. I love her," said Pestilence. "I have for a long, long time."

"You have no idea what a long, long time truly is, William."

Cold, the King wailed. *So cold.*

Pestilence stared at the Pale Rider, and he saw how Death's eyes gleamed with winter frost even as sunlight spun his hair to summer gold. "Something's wrong."

Death's shoulders bobbed from silent laughter. "Wrong? Everything is in balance. The Four go out unto the world, and all manner of living things bleed and sicken and starve and die. What could possibly be wrong?"

A lump formed in Pestilence's throat.

A lump. Globus hystericus, said the Elder. *Reactive adenitis. Mononucleosis. Cysts. Cancer.*

"I hear it in your voice," the White Rider said. "I see it on your face."

"So perceptive, and yet so limited. A human failing, that. Limited perception." Death motioned to the sky. "You see the sun and assume it rises and falls at the earth's pleasure. You see the horizon and insist the world is flat. Then you get science as religion. Hallelujah! Suddenly there's an entire solar system and gravitational pulls and orbits, and you think you've unlocked the secrets of the universe. You discover quantum physics and assume you understand your place in the scheme of creation. Such conceit." Death chuckled, the sound like broken glass. "The philosophers would weep from such rampant arrogance, but they're all dead and dying."

"Please," Pestilence said. "Tell me."

"Dead and dying," Death said again. "That's because philosophy is a lost art. You people are so busy finding new answers, you've forgotten that you've stopped asking questions. You people used to have an embarrassment of questions. Now it's all scripted reality television and a soundtrack."

"Tell me," Pestilence implored. "You've come to me before, when you needed my help. You've come to me now. Tell me what's wrong."

A pause, filled with tension and something more, something foreign. Something *other*.

"And so he presumes to command one such as me. Oh, humanity. There's nothing wrong, little Pestilence. Nothing at all."

How did one call Death a liar? Pestilence held his tongue.

The Pale Rider stepped forward lazily. Where he'd leaned against the tree, bark flaked like dandruff. "But it's kind of you to be concerned. For thee, White Rider. A gift."

Something dark rushed forward, pressed against Pestilence and moved through him, past him. He gasped as he felt parasites disintegrate. Where there had been malaria, now there was nothing but potential disease.

"Go back to your girl, William," said Death. "Your work here is done."

The white horse sneezed in despair.

Pestilence stammered, "But—"

In his head, the King screamed. *A SHEET OF WHITE! THE END OF THE WORLD! THE PALE RIDER COMES!*

The White Rider flinched. He squeezed his eyes closed and commanded the King to be silent. When he opened his eyes again, Death had disappeared.

A black rock fell from the tree, landing by Pestilence's feet.

No, not a rock. A bird.

A dead crow, frozen solid.

Another bird fell, and then another. Soon all the crows were tumbling to the grass, all black ice and petrified meat.

Pestilence didn't realize he'd fallen to his knees until his horse nudged his shoulder. The White Rider stared up at his steed, stunned, his gloved hands splayed by his sides.

"I don't understand," he whispered.

Go back, the Elder said sadly. *Go back, and kiss your girl goodbye.*

"And kiss that lead goodbye!" Ted whooped for joy, pumping his fist in the air.

On the sofa, Izzy muttered something physically improbable.

"It's not even halftime," Xander said. "Anything could happen."

"Don't remind me."

Xander shrugged and cracked open another can of beer. He wasn't hanging out at Izzy's because he was an avid football fan (he tended to root for whoever was winning) or because she had the best surround-sound entertainment system known to mankind (her parents inhaled sports and insisted on the best-quality viewing experience possible); he just liked hanging with his friends. Granted, the beer was a bonus. Feigning interest, Xander settled back and kept watching the game, making sure to "ooh" and "ahhh" at the appropriate times. When the first half came to an end, Izzy's team was down by ten.

"Don't worry," Ted said smugly. "I'm sure they'll give away even more points before the game's over."

Izzy glared at him. "You're such an ass."

"Don't be mad at me. Not my fault your boys suck."

"Shut up."

"Aw, someone needs a hug."

Izzy muttered, "Touch me and die." She stared murder at the television.

Ted grinned, stood up from the sofa, stretched. "Gotta see a man about a horse."

"Really?" Izzy said, rolling her eyes. "You have to announce when you're gonna take a piss? I swear, you're worse than a girl."

"And you'd know that how?"

"Swear to God, Edward, I'm gonna kick that scrawny ass of yours."

"She totally could," Xander said.

"Totally couldn't. You're a goalie, Isabella, not a center. You're all hands." Ted's grin spread to shit-eating proportions. "Wanna get grabby with me?"

"Not even if you were the last man on earth."

"Hey," Xander said to Ted, "weren't you gonna go pee?"

Izzy said, "And put the leftover pizza in the nuker, yeah?"

"What am I, your mother?"

"You're the guy eating my pizza."

"Says the gal drinking my beer."

"Whose beer?" Xander asked, arching an eyebrow.

"So possessive!" Ted blew him a kiss, then swaggered out of the den.

"You're right," Xander said, chuckling. "He *is* an ass."

"So," Izzy said. "How're you doing, anyway?"

"Buzzed."

"Not what I mean."

Xander frowned at her. "Not following."

Izzy glanced in the direction Ted had gone. "Sort of stunned you're actually talking to him."

"Who—Ted?"

Izzy said nothing, but her look was cutting.

"What the hell? First Suzie's all weird, now you're acting weirder." Xander set his beer can on the coffee table, a little harder than he'd planned. "What's going on, Iz?"

Izzy was leaning forward, elbows on her knees, long ponytail draped over her shoulder, as she stared intently at Xander. "Last night. Marcie's." She paused. "Don't you remember?"

Mouth dry, Xander shook his head.

"Nothing? About what happened with you and . . . ?"

Voice tight, Xander said, "Me and who?"

Izzy looked down at her feet, then back up at Xander. "So here's the thing. I was in the house with everyone, so I didn't catch the beginning. But when I heard the yelling, and I saw what was happening, I went out back, onto the deck. When I got there, I saw you and—"

Xander's head, already fuzzy from the beer, suddenly began to pound. Wincing, he pressed a hand to his temple, but that didn't stop the pressure. He screwed his eyes shut and tried to ride out the pain. Izzy was still talking, babbling on and on and *on,* but he couldn't hear the words because there was a loud beep from the kitchen—the microwave, signaling that the pizza was ready—and now there was something else.

A voice.

"Come on, Zan," the voice said. "Come on, open your eyes."

He opened his eyes.

Ted, behind the wheel of the Death Car, was crowing about his team winning the game. "Man, you'd think Izzy would smarten up and root for my boys, but no, she's got this thing for the underdog." He sang the *Underdog* theme song in a piercing baritone.

Xander, disoriented, rubbed his head. "Stop. Just stop."

"Such a critic."

"Uh. So." Xander blinked, looked at the houses streaking away as they passed by. "Game's over."

"Yeah, and has been for twenty minutes." A pause. "Dude, you've been out of it all day. You feeling okay?"

"Yeah. No." Xander pressed his hand against his forehead. It wasn't hurting, exactly, but there was an echo of pressure, like a memory of pain. "Head's hurting."

"Want some aspirin?"

"No."

"Good, I don't have any." Ted laughed, but it sounded off, like a guitar slightly out of tune.

Xander leaned his head back against the seat and closed his eyes and remembered pain—

—so much pain and he can't move can't think can't get away he has to get away because something's coming for him so he screams until the roof of the world is ripped away and there's noise and glaring lights and a dark shadow reaching for him and there's a face in the shadow a face made of shadow and he screams even louder because now there's a voice telling him that it's time—

"Time to wake up, Zan," Ted said. "You're home."

Xander sat forward with a start, his body pulling the shoulder harness taut. His head was a mess, and his heart was screaming in his chest, and he kept thinking that a man made of shadow was looking for him.

But no; as Ted had said, they were in front of Xander's apartment building. Xander blew out a shuddering breath and mopped his hair away from his face.

"Hell of a dream," Ted commented.

"Not sleeping well."

"No shit, Sherlock. You were whimpering."

Xander took another shuddering breath and told his heart to calm down. "Stupid question. When did we leave Izzy's?"

A long pause before Ted said, "About thirty minutes after the game ended. You had to get back because you promised your folks you'd babysit for the rugrat. You don't remember?"

"I was watching the game," Xander said dully, "and then it was halftime. You went to put the pizza in the microwave. And then I was in your car, on the way home." He turned to face Ted. "I don't remember any of the second half. It's like I jumped from Izzy's house to your car."

"It's a . . . what do you call it, a blackout. You're losing time." Ted paused, darting a glance at Xander. "Maybe you should stop drinking for a bit."

"Not like I'm a boozer," he said, perturbed. "Just, you know, at parties and stuff."

"Still. Blackouts aren't good."

Xander sighed, closed his eyes. "Think I just need a good night's sleep. I'll tell Riley not to come over tonight."

Ted's knuckles whitened on the steering wheel. He didn't

say a thing, but Xander could feel the tension of the unspoken words clogging the air.

He snapped, "What?"

Ted said nothing, but his eyes were troubled. Guarded.

Angry for a reason he couldn't name, Xander threw his door open — then slammed it shut as he heard a screech of tires, like a car was about to plow into them. Panicked, he looked for the oncoming car, but the street was empty.

"Zan," Ted said quietly, "are you okay?"

Still hearing the prelude to a collision that didn't happen, Xander didn't know how to reply. He closed his eyes and wondered if he was losing his mind.

War, the Red Rider of the Apocalypse, smiled as she opened her eyes. She'd had a magnificent dream, one of passion and perfection, one that made her blush as she remembered the things she'd done. The blush wasn't from embarrassment; one such as she didn't get embarrassed. Instead, her cheeks flushed because the memory heated her. And she did so enjoy the feeling of heat along her skin. It was a good way to wake.

She felt like today, anything could happen.

Still smiling, she stretched languidly, arching her back to feel the pull in her shoulders. Her blanket slid down her body, revealing naked skin. War enjoyed sleeping naked. There was so much to *feel,* so much sensation waiting to be experienced, that it was a shame to swaddle her skin in clothing when it wasn't necessary. She didn't have to feel fluctuations in temperature—she could plunge into the heart of a volcano and not pop a sweat—but she preferred to experience heat and chill and everything in between.

War was a creature of feeling; without it, she was dead inside.

She rolled onto her hip and glanced at the clock on her nightstand. It was early, as far as mortal time went. And for the moment, she was in her mortal skin. Along with being a Horseman, she was a human teenager—well, technically, she was in the limbo of twenty, neither a teenager nor a full-fledged adult, but in her heart she was still sixteen and would be forever.

That had been the year she had accepted the Sword of office, when her life had changed completely.

Yes, it was early. Later that day, she would be attending her sister's high school recital—family first, as her parents liked to say; how things could change in four short years—but she didn't have to start getting ready until eight o'clock. She had hours to go. More than enough time for her to do a little work. Wreak a little havoc. Shed a little blood.

Her exposed skin suddenly bumped with chill.

"Lounging in bed," said a bemused voice, "yet thinking of work. I don't know if that makes you a workaholic or a slacker."

Neither Death's sudden appearance in her bedroom nor his easy ability to read her mind bothered her. Nothing about him bothered her. He'd been the one who'd saved her when she hadn't known she'd needed saving. He hadn't just given her the Sword of office years ago—he'd given her the world.

And she'd given him her heart.

"Contrary to popular belief," she said with a grin, "the wicked do rest. We just don't get a lot of sleep."

"*Wicked?* Isn't that a musical?"

"And a state of mind." She rolled over, unselfconscious about her nudity, to face Death. And then the grin slid off her face.

She saw him perfectly, there in the dark of her tiny bedroom, saw his long golden hair and the scruff of a goatee framing his face, saw the twin maelstroms of his eyes, their color so blue and deep it was like drowning in the Mediterranean. She saw those things, blinked at his green and white pajamas—

some things about him, she'd never understand — then looked back at his face, into those bottomless eyes, and she knew with perfect clarity that something was wrong.

She asked, "What is it?"

His mouth quirked into a smile. "A pronoun, usually. Unless you had something more specific in mind."

War sat up, her gazed fixed upon the Pale Rider. She had learned to trust her gut, even when her brain attempted to muffle emotion with rationalization, and her gut was insisting that the figure standing before her was in pain.

"Something's hurting you," she insisted.

He laughed softly, and though she heard the humor in that laughter, there was also an unspeakable sadness. "Nothing can hurt me."

"Bullshit."

"Such eloquence."

"That was extremely eloquent. You should have heard what I was thinking."

"I did."

Yes, he probably had. "Then instead of listening to me curse up a blue streak, talk to me."

"I'm talking to you now."

"Tell me what's wrong. You're hurting, love," War said softly. "I feel it like it's my own pain."

Death leaned against the wall of her bedroom, wearing the form of a pajama-clad dead rock legend and keeping his secrets close.

"'Love,'" he repeated. "A noun, a verb, a term of endearment. Is that what you think of me? Am I dear to you?"

"You know you are."

"Well then, Red Rider. A gift for thee."

He was suddenly next to her, smothering her with his close-ness, leaning down and sealing his lips on hers.

Kissing her deeply.

She felt herself falling into him, into a cold so complete it threatened to leave her numb. For a moment, she almost strug-gled — she was War, and she was defined by struggle and con-flict. But he was Death and she was his handmaiden. She trusted him. So she opened herself up to him, allowed herself to sink into his kiss.

It was a moment trapped in time, ongoing and echoing, one she would replay again and again: the memory of Death kissing her, lulling her.

Stealing her heat and her breath.

When the Pale Rider finally pulled away, War's hand flitted by her mouth. If her lips were swollen from his kiss, she couldn't feel it.

She couldn't feel *him*.

"What . . . ?" Her voice trailed off as she stared at him in horror. Nothing. That was all she felt from him: nothing. It was like hitting an iceberg, all slick and perilous and so very cold. Desperate, she reached out with her senses and almost sobbed with relief as the emotions of her neighbors licked at her like fire.

She could still feel. She just couldn't feel *him*.

Through gritted teeth, she hissed, "What did you do?"

"I gave you a gift." He smiled at her, but it was empty, de-void of meaning. "My feelings, such as they are, are not meant for you. So I took away your ability to feel them."

"You . . . !" Words failed her, so she punched him in the face, right in the center of that vacant smile. He didn't even have the decency to bleed.

"So violent." His eyes, so fathomless just moments ago, were now as empty as his smile. "But then, you've always defaulted to violence."

Seething, War clenched her fists and forced herself not to hit him a second time. "Why did you come here?"

He paused, as if considering his words. "I wanted to see you. To speak to you."

"Well, you have," she said bitterly, "and you even stole a kiss in the bargain. Now get out."

"I'm a thief, Melissa. I always have been." Death smiled at her again—so empty, so hollow—and he tilted his head in a bow. "Enjoy your sister's recital."

She squeezed her eyes shut. "GET OUT!"

A tickle of frost on her brow, and then nothing.

She waited for a count of sixty, and then she opened her eyes and fumed. That sorry excuse of a Horseman! She had half a mind to summon her Sword and chase after him and slice him head to toe, and then toe to head, maybe even julienne him like fries and serve him to Famine. How dare he just shut her out like that? Did he really think he could turn off her feelings for him by literally turning off her feelings *of* him?

That stupid, sorry, *miserable* Horseman!

A ripping sound made her look down. She blinked, nonplussed, when she saw that she'd shredded her blanket.

But soon her fury cooled and settled into something thicker, something more troubling.

Unease, peppered with fear.

That hadn't been a kiss goodbye.

Tears stung her eyes, and she clutched her blanket to her chest as she cried. Less than five minutes ago, she'd felt like anything could happen. And something had—something overwhelming and horrifying.

Death hadn't just kissed her goodbye.

He'd kissed her farewell.

He had finished his task. He had said his goodbyes, in his own way. Now he was free to end it all. The cycle was coming to a close; there was no way to deny that. The only heat left to him now was the memory of War's passion.

He absently rubbed his mouth, where she'd struck him with her fist. He was far too cold to feel either the impact or the echo of that blow, but he held on to the memory.

She'd been so angry with him. She hadn't understood that he had spared her as best he could. Now she was as numb to him as he was to all living things. She couldn't feel him. And that was how it should be; what he was to do, he had to do alone.

In the end, everything dies alone.

He was ready. Soon had finally stretched into now, and it was his time. The cycle was hovering by its endpoint. But this time, for the first time, there would be no renewal.

This time, done was done.

So why, instead of welcoming the end, was he wandering this particular city street? Was he stalling, or had he been drawn here by some unfinished business? Around him, life flowed— people going and coming, all of them absorbed in their momentary distractions—and as he walked down the block, mortals made way for him without knowing why they side-stepped. He noted them, took tally of their names and lives, and wondered again why he was walking among the humans instead of bringing about the end of the world.

If his steed had been with him, perhaps it would have had an answer.

Vexed, he opened up the woven purse dangling from a cord slung over his hips, a purse that previously had been a saddle-bag. He rummaged through it, ignoring the countless coins, the various feathers in their clashing shades of red, the iPod. His fingers closed on an item, and he pulled it out.

A chocolate bar.

Ah.

He glanced up at a building, up toward one of the higher floors. Yes, there he was, puttering from room to room, doing human things in his human way.

The boy with the chocolate.

Death smiled. He had unfinished business after all.

XANDER

Xander's mom kissed him goodbye, and his dad clapped him on the shoulder, and then the two of them fled the apartment, ready to let their hair down and do whatever it was that grown-ups do when they don't have to think about being parents. Xander waved to them and told them to have a good time. He shut the door behind them and turned the lock.

"Well," he said. "Just you and me, kid."

In his bouncy seat, Lex gurgled agreement.

For the next hour, Xander took care of his baby brother. He fed him a jar of mashed peas — or, more accurately, attempted to get more peas into the baby's mouth than onto the baby, and was only moderately successful. He gave Lex a bath to get rid of the remnants of dinner. He diapered the baby, pajamaed the baby, repajamaed the baby after the Horrible Spit-up Incident, disposed of the baby's diaper after the Stinky Poop Bomb, gave the baby a second bath after forgetting that there should always be a blocking cloth involved when changing a baby boy's diaper, rediapered and repajamaed the baby again, and, all in all, discovered a new respect for his parents for doing this crap every night.

"Swear to God," he said, exhausted, "I wasn't this much trouble with Mom and Dad."

Lex agreed as he passed gas.

"Nice." Xander popped the pacifier into the baby's mouth, then selected a picture book from Lex's bookshelf. "Tonight's reading selection will focus on trucks. Big trucks, little trucks, all sorts of trucks. Sound good?"

Lex sucked on his pacifier.

"I'll take your thoughtful silence as complete consent."

Xander settled into the rocker-glider, made sure Lex was propped up on his lap, and then opened the book and began reading to his brother.

"Big rig. Cement mixer. Pickup truck," he said, pointing to the picture. "Remember, for a pickup truck, you need a pickup line. Repeat after me: 'Hey, baby, come here often?'"

Lex dropped the pacifier and said, "Bbbbbbpbt."

"Very good," said Xander, scooping up the pacifier. He frowned at it, decided that being on the carpet for two seconds wasn't enough time for deadly bacteria to infest it, then popped it back into the baby's mouth.

Lex spat it out again.

"Come on, kid. Give me a break." He put the pacifier into Lex's mouth, and Lex spat it right back out.

The brothers stared at each other.

"You know you're a pain, right?"

Lex began to cry.

"Aw, come on, I didn't mean it. What, you want a bottle, maybe? Is that what this is about?"

Lex cried harder.

"I'll take that to mean, 'Yes, you idiot big brother, I'm hungry because I wore most of my mashed peas instead of eating them, feed me now.' Come on," Xander said, and sighed, picking up the squirming, squalling mass that was his brother. "Let's get a bottle ready."

He brought Lex into the kitchen and plopped him into the highchair, strapping him in and settling the tray into place. The baby began to play with the toys affixed to the tray.

"Let's hear it for a short attention span," Xander muttered. He began to prepare the bottle. "So what do you think: Should I ask Riley to come by tonight?"

In his highchair, Lex kicked his feet.

"Yeah, I know," said Xander, mixing in the formula. "I'm wrecked, and my head's been all weird. Seriously weird. Like, losing time weird. Blacking out, Ted says. Thinks I'm drinking too much. I think he's stupid. And he smells. Even so," Xander said, screwing the bottle top into place, "maybe I should take it easy tonight. Maybe text Riley instead of make face-to-face plans. Go to bed early. What do you think?"

Lex banged on the highchair tray.

"Yeah, it's hard for me to think on an empty stomach too."

He gave Lex the bottle. Xander watched his brother drink, and he smiled, thinking about how sweet it must be to live in the now, to want only the basic comforts—food when hungry, warmth when chilly, a place to sleep—and not have to worry about friends hurting him and . . .

He blinked. Where had *that* come from?

Xander dug at the thought. Why would he think that one of his friends was hurting him? He remembered Suzie's odd text, remembered Izzy's conversation with him—well, no, he remembered part of it, something about how Izzy had heard shouting at the party—but that was it.

Wasn't it?

Ted at his front door, looking exhausted and wane.

Xander frowned. Was there something about Ted . . . ?

Lex pushed away the bottle. "Bbbbbpbtt."

"Yeah. I hear you." Distracted, he burped his brother, and then cursed when the kid spat up all over his pajamas and Xander's shirt. One of these days, he'd remember to get a bib on the baby.

After the third pajama change for the night, he got Lex settled into his crib. "Bedtime, kid," said Xander. "When you're a little older, we'll talk about how to wheedle Mom and Dad into letting you stay up later. Love you. Sweet dreams."

The baby blinked up at him. Xander couldn't be sure because of the pacifier, but he thought Lex was smiling at him.

He turned on the baby monitor, then quietly walked out of the nursery and shut the door. He tiptoed his way to his bedroom and threw himself down onto the bed. He was exhausted. Taking care of a baby was hard! No wonder his parents went to bed practically at nine o'clock. And here he'd thought it was just because they were old.

He glanced at the clock—not even eight p.m.—and then he grabbed his cell phone. It was completely dead. With a sigh, he plugged it in. He really had to be out of it to forget to charge his phone.

There were seven texts waiting for him. Most were from Suzie, who wanted to know if he was all right. And one was from Izzy, wanting to know the same thing.

Xander stared at the texts, and he wondered what exactly had happened last night at Marcie's party that had everyone so concerned about him.

Maybe he'd had more to drink last night than he'd thought. He hoped he didn't do something completely stupid. As tempted as he was to ask Suzie or Izzy or Ted for details, he realized that he didn't want to know.

Some things were better left forgotten.

He laughed uneasily. Talk about melodramatic. Ted would have been impressed. Smiling, shaking his head, he texted Riley.

Whatcha doing?

He hit Send and fired up a computer game while waiting for a response.

Three lives later, Riley still hadn't texted back.

Xander checked on Lex, found the baby dead asleep, and then went back to his room. He thought about eating, but he had no appetite.

Riley still hadn't gotten back to him.

Something dark and cold wormed its way into his brain, and he wondered yet again what had happened at the party last night. Did it have something to do with Riley?

A sound like a screech of tires.

He flinched, waiting to hear the telltale crash, but there was no impact. A near miss, maybe.

He blew out a breath. He was being ridiculous. So what that he hadn't heard from Riley yet? Not everyone was glued to a cell phone. Maybe Riley was in a place with spotty reception. Maybe Riley's phone was off, or the battery had run out, like Xander's had.

Maybe, maybe, maybe. Tons of maybes. A world of maybes.

Sometimes, a hint of *maybe* was all that mattered.

His head began to throb, so he grabbed a bottle of aspirin from the bathroom medicine cabinet, then went into the kitchen and poured himself a glass of water. He'd have a quiet night tonight, he told himself as he downed the aspirin, would go to bed early. He'd been stressed out and sleeping poorly, even before Lex's morning wakeup howls had begun in earnest a month ago.

Xander was sure the stress was due to his decision to drop Carnegie Mellon. When he had turned the school down, that had been ugly. Colleges, as it turned out, didn't like it when you reneged on early admission.

And he'd had to keep it quiet for so long. He hadn't said a word to his parents, let alone to Riley or his friends.

It had all been worth it — the lying, the silence, the stress. The sleepless nights.

He was going to Stanford to be with Riley.

It wasn't the best art school, not like Carnegie Mellon or Yale or any of those, and it was insanely expensive; he didn't have any scholarships, and the thought of how he was going to foot the bill was enough to give him a minor heart attack. But he'd figure it out. Stanford was where he was supposed to be — because Riley would be there.

He just had to figure out when to share the news, and how to do it. His folks were going to be mad, but eventually, they'd come around. The two of them had fallen in love in high school, even though they dated other people in college and didn't get married until their midtwenties. Xander knew all this because he'd heard their love story plenty of times. His parents would understand that when it was love, you had to listen to your heart and not be tied up by your brain. All the planning, all the hopes for the future—none of that mattered, not when it came to love.

Love didn't conquer all; love *was* all. Love was everything that mattered.

He'd do anything for Riley Jones.

Absently rubbing his head, he drank the rest of the water. Between the stress over his secret college plans and his choppy sleep, he was a bit of a mess. No wonder he was having so-called blackouts, and never mind the drinking. All he needed was some quality sleep, then everything would be fine.

Sleep, and figuring out when to tell Riley he was also going to Stanford, that they didn't have to worry about a long-distance relationship.

They were going to have a happily ever after—starting right now, he decided, setting down his water glass. He'd tell Riley everything. No more waiting for the right time, waiting to come up with the right way to say it. He'd just blurt it out.

He marched back to his room and checked his phone.

Still no text from Riley.

No matter; he wanted to say it, not text it. He punched in Riley's number, then hung up when he got voicemail. This wasn't voicemail news.

Nuts. Looked like he had to wait after all.

Sighing, Xander went to the window and glanced out. He liked looking at the cityscape at dusk, just as the sun was beginning its slow descent from today to tonight. Granted, he didn't care for being thirty stories up, but he was behind glass, safe. So he watched the colors play across the sky—the blues darkening and bleeding into purples streaked with pink like the air had gone punk. Clouds stretched lazily as they striped the sun. Xander looked, amazed by how easily something so radiant could be muted, subdued. Molten gold marred by cotton white, framed by twilight skies whispering promises of starlight and first wishes.

Xander made a wish, made it with all his heart.

The sun, still bright behind its barrier of clouds, stung his eyes. He blinked and turned to the right, catching a partial view of the balcony off the living room.

And he blinked again.

A man was sitting on the balcony ledge.

(the Pale Rider)

Xander's eyes watered, and he frantically wiped away his tears.

There was no one on the balcony.

Of course there wasn't, he told himself, and so what that his heart was screaming and his head was throbbing and it felt like he couldn't breathe? There was no one on his balcony. The very thought of it—

(the Pale Rider comes)

—was ridiculous.

Panicked, and feeling stupid for his panic, he grabbed the baby monitor and ran into the living room, over to the glass door that opened to the balcony.

And there he saw a man in green and white striped pajamas sitting on the rail. The man was facing away from Xander, his long blond hair catching the wind and whipping around his shoulders.

In Xander's mind, a dead man made of shadow whispered his name.

He squeezed his eyes shut—

—but he sees the glaring lights and a dark shadow reaching for him and there's a face in the shadow a face made of shadow and he screams because there's a voice whispering his name and telling him to kiss them all goodbye because today's the day the world ends and—

"The Pale Rider comes," Xander whispered.

He opened his eyes.

He saw a man perched on his balcony railing, ready to jump off the high board and plunge thirty stories into the cold. And he saw beyond that, saw that the man was not a man at all. He saw a ghost, like the blue nudes—trapped in a moment, frozen in rage and grief.

His heart thudding in his ears, Xander approached the glass door of the balcony. He unlatched it and slid it open.

"Hey," he said, his voice sounding tinny and far away. "What're you doing?"

The man's head and shoulders bobbed, as if he was silently laughing. "Contemplating." His voice was cold and deep, and Xander felt it echo in his bones.

"Okay," Xander said, feeling very small. "Contemplating what?"

"The end of everything."

"Yeah, I sort of got that, given that you're sitting on the balcony rail. If people want to admire the view, they tend to do that from a window."

"I'm not a person," said the blond man.

"Yeah, I got that, too."

And he did. Xander recognized him for who, for what, he truly was. He wasn't sure how he knew, but he didn't question it. It felt right.

Just as the blond man sitting right there on the railing felt wrong—tragically, horrifically wrong.

Something was going to happen. Something bad.

Without knowing why he was doing it, Xander stepped forward. This close, there was no way to mistake the blond figure for a person; there was a presence about him, something alien that spotlighted his humanity as a mask, a disguise. Part of Xander wanted to retreat—actually, his brain was screaming at him to get the hell away and not look back—but he kept walking until he was next to the figure. He carefully placed the baby monitor on the floor, and then he leaned over to rest his elbows on the railing. He was terrified of being so close to the edge —it would be so easy to just lean down and let gravity take him.

But this wasn't about him at all.

Xander looked over his shoulder at the man who wasn't a man. He was thin with scruffy hair and beard stubble, and if he was nervous about being so high up, he hid it well. Then again, someone like him probably didn't have to worry about accidentally overbalancing. Xander, a longtime Nirvana fan, wondered for a moment over the similarity of the man's features to those of a certain dead alternative rock star, and he distinctly thought, *Kurt Cobain is about to take a swan dive off my balcony.*

Except Kurt Cobain was dead, and the figure sitting on the balcony railing was not him and never had been; Xander knew this without understanding how he knew it. He also knew that the figure next to him was in pain.

Pain was something he could understand.

"So," he said gamely. "Want to talk about it?"

"Not really," said Death.

"Okay," Xander said. "Mind if I stay here?"

"Knock yourself out."

That wasn't too far from the truth; Xander was already feeling lightheaded enough to faint. People weren't meant to be this high up.

As if picking up on his fear, a gust tore across the balcony. Xander clenched the railing and squeezed his eyes shut and prayed for the wind to die. He had Death right next to him, so he didn't think his prayer was that unrealistic.

He counted to ten, realized the wind had, in fact, stopped blowing, and then opened his eyes.

From beneath his mop of blond hair, Death was peering at him.

Xander felt his cheeks heat. Sheepishly, he said, "I'm afraid of heights."

"No, you're not."

"I'm not?"

"You're afraid of falling from a great height and dying on impact."

"Well. Yeah. If you want to get technical." Xander swallowed and absolutely did not look down. "I get that you don't want to talk about why you're sitting on my balcony railing. But can I ask you a question?"

"Sure."

"When you say 'the end of everything,' are you being metaphorical? Are you thinking of killing yourself?"

"That was two questions."

Nonplussed, Xander said, "I'm bad at math."

The blond man smiled, shook his head slightly. "Cheeky. Yes, Xander. I'm teetering on the edge, literally and figuratively." He motioned to the ground far below. "Ten seconds of free fall, then splat. Dead on impact. Very messy." A pause. "Very permanent."

Xander tried not to think about plummeting off the balcony. "You know who I am?"

"I know everyone."

"Okay. Why are you on *my* balcony in particular?"

"That's four questions now. You're right, you're horrible at math."

"I am. I should get a tutor. I'd really appreciate it if you answered, though. Why my balcony?"

Another pause, and then: "We have unfinished business, you and I."

Xander blinked in surprise. "We do?"

Death turned away from him to gaze at the bleeding sky. "Some time ago, you gave me a gift, one that I accepted freely. Because of that, I owe you a boon."

The words both made no sense and made complete sense; some part of Xander recognized them as being true, even though he didn't understand how that could possibly be the case.

"I don't remember giving you anything," he said slowly.

"That changes nothing. The scales must be balanced." Death shrugged again. "Rules."

"Okay," said Xander, his head spinning. "So . . . just to be sure I'm clear on this, before you, ah, finish contemplating the end of everything, you need to give me a boon."

"Aye."

"What sort of boon?"

"Anything within my power to give." A rueful smile. "By the way, the 'can't wish for more wishes' thing is implied. This is a one-time boon. So tell me true: What would you ask of me?"

Xander bit his lip as he considered the possibilities.

A minute ticked by.

Death cleared his throat. "I should mention that this is a limited-time offer."

"How much time?"

Death glanced at his watch, then looked back at the skyline. "Thirty-three minutes."

"Right," Xander said. "Okay. I've got it." He took a deep breath, made sure he had the wording just right, and then he said, "For my boon, I want you to tell me what's led you to come here, now, to do what it is you say you're thinking of doing."

Death whipped his head around to look at Xander. His eyes were the bluest things Xander had ever seen — they were slate blue, peacock blue, a blue that Picasso and Matisse could only imagine in their deepest dreams. They were the blue of the cosmos, of infinite possibility; they held the secrets of the universe.

"This?" Death said, his voice a whisper of malice. "This is how you would waste your boon?"

"It's not a waste," Xander replied quietly. "You matter. What you're feeling matters."

Death laughed, the sound bitter and cold.

"I want to know your story," Xander said. Then, softer: "Please."

For a time, Death said nothing. Then, finally, he spoke, and his voice was the low rumble of a distant storm.

"So be it. You would know my story, Xander Atwood? Then listen."

PART THREE

BITTERNESS

God is growing bitter, He envies man his mortality.

—*Jacques Rigaut*

He turned away from the boy's questioning blue gaze, away from the hope chiseled so carefully, so poignantly, onto his face. As if he could be swayed with a look.

Then again, this boy knew how to sway him. He'd done so before; it stood to reason that he'd use his boon to attempt to do so again.

Xander Atwood. The boy with the chocolate.

His mouth pressed into a tight line. He should have corrected the course years ago, when he'd had the chance. But he'd allowed himself to be moved by a gift given freely, and now he had to pay the gift price. Rules, as he'd told the boy. He'd created the rules in a fit of boredom not long after humanity had invented the wheel, and those rules had long passed their usefulness to him. More often than not, they were as annoying as gadflies coming back to bite. When he'd put the rules in place, he hadn't foreseen the consequences, hadn't anticipated that some humans would use those rules to their advantage.

He had a history of not considering the consequences of his actions.

His eyes narrowed. If only he could break rules as easily as people could. It was yet another thing about humanity that vexed him. So many things about mortals were out of reach.

Frowning, he gazed down. On the street below, people moved. Some walked; others used various modes of transportation—cars, bicycles, skateboards, even wheels attached to sneakers. Some milled outside their buildings, talking or waiting or dreaming while awake. Around them were transplanted trees, artfully placed along the sidewalk in their solitary prisons. Underfoot and unnoticed, strong-willed weeds cracked the pavement. He watched the mortals for a time: people the size of insects, crawling along the surface of the world.

And soon, he began to speak.

"Do you have any idea what forever feels like after the first few thousand years? It gets old." He smiled thinly. "I'm old, Xander. Older than you could imagine."

"What are you?" the boy asked. "I mean, okay, you're Death. Capital D." Lower, he said, "Which I magically know somehow."

"All mortals know, in the back of their minds, who I am. Just as I know everyone, everyone knows me."

"Okay," the boy said. "But what does it mean that you're Death? Is it a role? Are you the Grim Reaper?"

He arched an eyebrow. "Do you see a scythe?"

"Uh. No."

"I'm no reaper, grim or otherwise, though I've been called that, and more. Yamaraj. Yenlo. Azra'il. Thanatos. Joe."

"Joe?"

"It's a fine name. Besides, I didn't come up with it. People did. That's how all this started: you people and your passion. Your energy. Your heat. You were so mesmerizing," he said. "So *warm*. You can't begin to understand how different that is from what I am."

"You still haven't said what you are."

"No, I haven't." He paused, taking in the boy's eager features. "I'm not like you. I'm something else. Something older. Something different. I'm . . ." He floundered. "I don't have the word for it. It's not a human word, not in any language. It's not a living concept. I'm *other*."

The boy nodded his understanding—or, more accurately, his acknowledgment. He asked, "Were you always Death?"

"No."

He closed his eyes, remembering the sound of a door slamming shut—impact, then echoes of contact, then nothing.

"It's been so long since it all began," he murmured. "Even when I look back now, the images are blurry. I came here; that much is clear. I chose to come."

"So you're not from here? You know—Earth?"

He laughed quietly and opened his eyes. "No."

"Where are you from?"

"Beyond. The other side of the door."

"What door?"

"The doorway to elsewhere. A window to another world. From the other side of the door, we could see everything on this side. Think of a snow globe: Your world is inside, and mine is outside."

"You said you came here. How?"

"Interstellar travel on a state-of-the-art spaceship."

The boy's face lit with wonder. "You're joking!"

"Yep."

The wonder gave way to embarrassment. "Oh."

"How do you think I came here? It's a *door*. I opened the door and stepped through. Doors existed long before you did, you know. Chocolate, though, that was all you." He chuckled. "You people have made some brilliant things, but chocolate is among the best."

The boy looked at him somberly for a full minute before he said, "You're joking again."

"Maybe. Stop interrupting me if you want me to tell you my story. Unless you'd like to change your boon to a game of twenty questions?"

The boy blushed and mumbled, "Sorry."

Mollified, he nodded. "Everything from before, everything on the other side of the door . . . most of it is lost to me. That part of my life has been cut off, and all I have left are the tatters from where it was severed." He tapped his head. "Or maybe it's just an age thing. Ancient entity getting senile. But I remember some of it. I remember that my kind were first. I remember that we were easily amused. And I remember that we created something from nothing. We made you," he said, motioning to the boy. "This world, this reality — that was us."

The boy's face paled. "You're saying you're God?"

"I'm saying we were bored. We had a blank canvas and some paint, and we made this reality."

The boy shivered and shut his eyes. "Jesus."

"Heh. No." He smiled, bemused. "Not at all. And the art metaphor isn't exactly right, either. You were a work of art, yes, but you were also a novelty. So many living things, all fighting and struggling and loving and surviving and just *being*. Creating. Like us. You were fascinating." His smile broadened. "I remember watching you take your first steps. I remember when you discovered fire. I remember when you left your first markings on cave walls."

"You *made* us," the boy whispered.

"You made yourselves," he corrected. "That's what was so amazing about you people, all you living things. We gave you the spark, yes, but then you transformed it into an inferno. You created new lives. You redefined the world. You shaped everything around you. It was phenomenal to watch. That's why I didn't want it to end."

The boy's eyes opened again, and now they were bright with fear as well as fascination. He repeated, "End?"

"All things end, Xander. Paints dry and crack. Sparks fade. Infernos burn themselves out. This world, this reality, should have ended long and long ago. The spark of life here had begun to die. My kind were already thinking of the next new thing to make. I don't remember much about us, but I do recall that we're a fickle bunch. Easily distracted. Easily amused." He shrugged. "Easily lose interest."

The boy looked sick.

"But I wanted to see what would become of humanity. Other living things too — horses are admirable creatures, and the platypus is an unsung hero — but I was interested in humanity most of all. I wanted to renew the spark and keep the life cycle going." He paused as he tried to piece together fragments of memory. "I argued for it, I remember that. I pled humanity's case. I lost. It was a death sentence for you, for your entire world. Nothing is forever," he said softly. "That's what I was told, and it's true. Nothing is forever. Even infinity eventually stops."

Around them, the wind blew. The boy, captivated by the story, forgot to be afraid. That was something else about humanity that had always fascinated him: how people could so easily be distracted from their fears. Having a limited perspective had its advantages.

"I still wasn't ready to say goodbye," he said. "So I thought of a way to rekindle the spark for your world. A drastic way. On my side of the door, I alone wasn't strong enough to renew the spark. How could I be? It had taken all of my kind, together, to create your world. But if I were to come *through* the door, step into your reality, be part of it, then I would be strong enough." He shrugged. "At least, that was my theory."

"Theory?" the boy repeated.

"None of my kind had ever done such a thing. There was no way to know what would happen, how the laws of this reality would affect one of us on this side of the door. But I was willing to try. I thought that at best, I would renew the spark and return home. At worst, I would fail and you would die, and I would still return home. But I would try, you see?" He smiled, sighed. "I had to try."

"Um. Speaking for all of humanity . . . I'm glad you did."

He met the boy's gaze. "Be gladder, then, for my ignorance. Because had I known then what my action would cost me, I never would have stepped through the door."

Taut silence as the boy waited for him to continue.

"I let my decision be known. And out of all my kind, only one other stood with me. Only one was willing to test my theory with me. That one agreed to be my companion on this side of the door, as on that side."

"A friend?"

"Yes. No. Both more and less. We were part of each other. Connected."

"Like a . . . what . . . a soulmate?"

"You assume my kind have both souls and mates," he said with a wry smile. "But yes, that term comes close. My soulmate."

"The one you're meant to be with," the boy said, his voice sounding both lost and dreamy.

"The one I had *always* been with. The one who helped define me." He could almost see a face, could almost hear a sound, off-key and distant—a still, small voice like starlight. "We would venture here together, to keep each other company as we rekindled the spark. And together, we would return home and bear witness as humanity discovered its full potential. Together."

The last word echoed and blew apart, lost to the wind.

"What happened?" the boy asked.

Images flickered, incomplete and broken, the memories so faded they were barely impressions in his mind. "I remember standing at the door between worlds," he said. "There was a feeling, an understanding, that what we were about to do would forever change everything. It was a good feeling. It was *right*." He looked at the boy, at the cascade of emotions on his human face. "Have you ever felt that way? Have you ever known that you were about to do something instrumental, and that everything would change because of it, and you still did it because it needed to be done?"

The boy bit his lip, then nodded.

"Then you understand. I thought you people were worth it. So I stepped through the doorway. And then I was here."

Now there was no struggle for him to remember, no need to piece together the past. Everything on this side of the door was so clear that it was blinding.

"The sound thundered across the skies as the door slammed shut. And I realized that I was alone. My soulmate hadn't come through. Whether by accident or by intent, I had been abandoned."

The boy said nothing, but his face spoke volumes.

"And as I realized this, I felt your world pull at me like undertow, dragging me down. I felt its hunger. I heard its maw stretch wide. You called me God," he said quietly, "but there I was, clawing my fingers against the sky, desperately searching for an opening, a seam, a hint of the doorway beyond. Does God get scared, Xander?"

The boy didn't reply.

"Call me a terrified angel, then, stripped of its wings and cast down low. Discarded. Can you understand that feeling, that sense of abandonment and betrayal? That fear of the unknown reaching for you?"

A burst of static from the baby monitor, which almost sounded like the screech of tires.

"I never found the doorway back. I tried. I looked for days, months. Maybe years. It's difficult to tell; time moves slower for me than for you. But however long it was, there came a point when I realized that I was stranded. Everything that I was, everything I'd known, was gone." He remembered a hint of *maybe,* a promise of completion, and he sighed. "My life, my world, everything, out of reach for all time, all because of what I willingly chose."

"I'm sorry," the boy said hoarsely.

"For what? You didn't do this to me. It was me, and only me. I chose."

"But you didn't make your choice alone. The circumstances changed around you."

"So?"

"You're making it sound like it's your fault," the boy said. "It's not."

"Of course it is. I made a choice. I crossed a line from which there would be no return. I could have chosen otherwise, but I didn't. My destiny *is* my own fault."

"But it's *not*," the boy insisted. "You didn't know it was going to turn out like that."

He repeated, "So?"

The boy shouted, "You weren't supposed to be alone!"

The words hung in the air, suspended by fury and denial, and then the wind carried them away.

"The history of the world is not defined by intent but by action. I chose. And I had to reap the consequences of that choice." He laughed softly. "I suppose I'm a reaper after all."

The boy glowered, obviously angry and willfully blind. He demanded, "What consequences?"

He remembered hurling himself at the sky in one last effort to open the door, and then he'd plummeted to the ground like a shooting star. He lay there, exhausted, devastated, unable to move as he felt the grass and ground beneath him shift, felt the creatures in the air and sea and earth around him latch onto his presence. He felt all those things and so much more, felt as they moved toward him, some slowly, some quickly, drawn to him by some unstoppable force.

That had been his moment, he knew now; he could have refused. He could have said *no*.

But he had said nothing, and in doing so, he had sealed his fate.

All manner of creatures, large and small and everything in between, reached out to him, leeched on to him, attached themselves to him and bore their way into him, into the spark that was life itself. He felt them drain him dry, felt himself slowly disappear.

He remembered crushing pain as he felt himself be reborn.

"My presence here was like a beacon," he said, half drowning in memory. "My kind was responsible for the spark of life here, and all living things sensed that. They were drawn to me. They anchored themselves to me. Bonded to me. What was true then remains true now: All living things are part of me, connected to me. Through me, all living things maintain that spark of life."

A pause as the boy considered the words. "You're talking about souls."

"In a way," he replied. "Your soul is your own while you have it, but it comes to life through me. We're connected, you and I, as I'm connected to the people scurrying along the street so far below, to the trees placed as decorations along the block, to the pigeons pecking at crumbs. I'm connected to everything."

"Connected how?"

"I sense you, even though I'm separate from you. And part of you always senses me. We're like a Möbius strip," he said, pressing his palms together and twisting his hands, "forever entwined, yet on separate surfaces. Together for eternity, yet apart."

The boy's eyes widened. "Like Escher's ants."

In the boy's mind, he saw a framed poster that depicted ants crawling along each side of a Möbius strip twisted into a figure eight.

"Exactly like that," he said with a smile. "While you're alive, we're on opposite sides. When you die, we meet along the edge."

The boy chewed his lip. "You said our souls come through you. What does that mean? Come through you how? Do they literally pass through you?"

He smiled thinly. "Back to twenty questions."

"I just want to understand the story you're telling me," the boy said.

"Next time, you should word your boon more carefully."

His face naked, the boy said, "Please?"

Well, it wasn't like there would actually be a next time.

"Souls come through me," he said again. "Before you're born into your body, I send you off. And when you die, I meet your soul before it moves on."

"What happens then?"

"That, you find out when you die. Which, to be fair, won't be long now."

The boy stared at him. "What? But . . . this is about *you*."

"It's never been only about me." He glanced at his watch. "Twenty-seven minutes, Xander. And counting."

Understanding lit the boy's eyes. "We're on the other side of the Möbius strip. What happens to you, happens to us. To all of us. If you commit suicide, all life dies with you."

"Well," he said cheerfully, "that's one way to look at it."

XANDER

Xander felt the blood drain from his face. He was still process-
ing the notion of Death being God, or at least godlike, let alone
some stranded entity that life had leeched itself on to. Religion
by way of science fiction. Fantastical philosophy.

Lunacy.

Part of him was shouting that this was not only impossible
but insane, and part of him was saying it felt right, but all of
him was freaking out over the fact that in twenty-seven minutes, Death was going to kill everything. Xander fought a
crazy urge to laugh. And here he'd thought that running late
for a math test, naked, was the worst of all nightmares. Silly
him.

His head spun, and for a dizzying moment, it felt like he
was falling off the balcony. But no, he was still standing next to
Death, who was still sitting cross-legged on the railing, looking
almost pleased.

(today's the day the world ends)

A fragment of his nightmare sliced through his mind, and
Xander winced as he vividly remembered a man who was not a
man standing tall as death spread across the world. This was his
nightmare coming true, right here, right now. He didn't understand how part of him had known this was coming. Maybe it

had to do with the Möbius strip—when something happened on one side, the other would still feel it, like echoes, or maybe déjà vu. Maybe it was something else entirely. But it didn't matter, not now—not with Death being suicidal and ready to take the world with him. And soon.

(time)

He had to do something.

But what? It wasn't like Xander could stop him—he was just a high school senior, and Death was, well, Death.

Xander's jaw clenched. Someone else should be standing here, figuring out how to prevent the end of everything. Someone more qualified. Someone older. Someone closer to Death or, at least, to dying. Not him. He didn't choose this. The weight of the world shouldn't be on his shoulders.

It shouldn't be him.

He thought he heard a voice in his head say to him, *So?*

And really: So what that it shouldn't be him? No, he hadn't chosen this.

It had chosen him.

Enough. There would be time for self-pity later, but only if there *was* a later. First things first: Figure out how to get Death to not kill himself, let alone the world.

He took a deep breath. *Okay,* he told himself. *Think, think, think.*

He thought they were all going to die.

No, don't think that.

He raked his fingers through his hair as he tried to figure out what he could possibly do to convince Death not to end everything. Xander clung to the railing with his left hand, even though the terror of falling to the street wasn't quite so over-whelming anymore. Old habits die hard.

Again with the dying.

He quashed that thought, smothered it.

Killed it.

He checked himself from rolling his eyes. Fine, he could take a hint. Death was in his thoughts. Then again, how could it *not* be in his thoughts? He had twenty-seven minutes to save the world.

(time moves slower)

Another thought occurred to him, and his eyes widened as he remembered what Death had told him about time. In his story, Death had been looking for the door back to his world, and he didn't know how much time had passed during that search because . . .

Time moves slower for me than for you.

Maybe "twenty-seven minutes" was like the biblical catch-all of forty days being shorthand for "a really long time." It was still twenty-seven minutes—and counting—but those minutes didn't have to correspond to real time. Maybe. He hoped.

But there was more to it than that, wasn't there? Death had insisted on giving Xander a boon before ending it all. What had he called it?

Unfinished business.

Xander grabbed on to that thought, refused to let it go. It swelled from thought to idea to plan in the space between heartbeats: As long as Death was talking, he wasn't killing him-self, let alone everyone else.

Therefore, Xander had to keep him talking. And maybe, just maybe, an answer would present itself.

That hint of *maybe* was a lifeline, and he held on tight.

"All right," he said. "So you wound up here alone. You accidentally became the anchor for life. What happened next?"

"Next?" Death propped his chin in his hands. "Why, I became Death."

"The mayflies were first," he said. "Then the gastrotrichs. The *Arabidopsis thaliana*. The ants and bees and dragonflies. The brine shrimp and mosquitofish. Opossums. Chameleons. Mice. Rabbits. Other living things." He smiled at the boy. "Humans. They died, and then they came to me."

"Did you make them die?" the boy asked.

He clucked his tongue. "It's not like I waved my hands and bellowed, 'I smite thee!' Not that there's anything wrong with that," he added. "Every once in a while, smiting really shakes things up."

The boy stared. "You're joking again."

"Of course I am," he lied. "And no, I didn't make them die. I *could* have. But I didn't. Why would I? Whether it's immediate or eventual, life inevitably leads to death. Life burns itself out, and then I sweep up the ashes."

"By choice?" the boy asked.

Instead of answering the question, he returned to his tale. "Death happened quickest with the mayflies, but soon others died as well. And when their bodies died, their essences returned to me."

"You . . . what, absorbed their souls?" The boy paused. "Mayflies have souls?"

"All living things have an essence, a presence, that's unique to life. And no, I didn't absorb their souls. I reclaimed what was mine."

"I don't see the difference."

He shrugged. "You're only human."

The boy frowned at him, as if he couldn't decide whether he'd just been insulted.

"Here," Death said, "a metaphor: I provide the clay, but living things shape it into whatever they wish. The clay is the spark of life, and the final shape of the clay is the soul. Life comes through me, but souls are your own."

"Okay," the boy said slowly, "let me see if I've got this right. You and your kind made us, popped batteries in us, and then you kicked back and watched the show as we banged our toy cymbals." He arched an eyebrow as he looked pointedly at Death's face. "Here we are now—entertain us."

"Heh. Yes."

"Time passed, and the charge in the batteries began to fade. The toy cymbals slowed, and were going to stop banging altogether. The others of your kind decided not to replace the batteries, but you wanted to put in new ones to keep the toy cymbals playing. So you came here, which was on purpose, and you were alone, which was by accident. And what happened instead of you changing the batteries is you became a battery charger. Yeah?"

"Yeah," he said with a smile. "Close enough."

"Okay," the boy said. "So you charge the batteries before they go into the toys, and you collect the dead batteries when they're done. Right?"

"Rightish."

"So what happens to the dead batteries? What happens when things die?"

"Their bodies rot."

"Their *souls*," the boy said. "What happens to their souls? You said they return to you. What does that mean?"

"You already asked me that. And I already told you that you'll find out when you die."

The boy closed his eyes, sighed loudly, then opened his eyes again. He was clearly frustrated, but he attempted to keep it in check. Kudos to him. "Okay. So you're the battery charger and dead-battery collector." The boy paused. "What's it like, being Death?"

What was it like? None had ever asked him that before.

He remembered those first moments when the dead paraded themselves before him — the mayflies dancing in the air, the gastrotrichs swimming, the *Arabidopsis thaliana* flowering. He remembered the buzz of the dead bees and dragonflies, the sound of the dead ants as they rubbed segments of their abdomens. They all appeared before him, one by one, communicating in their own ways as they acknowledged him and returned their piece of the spark to him before they moved on.

He remembered that initial touch of the dead to Death, soothing him like balm. He remembered the fleeting sense of gratification, of understanding his purpose here in this small world where none was like him and none would ever be like him.

He remembered a blissful moment of being complete.

And he remembered losing pieces of himself once again as more living things were born.

"What's it like?" he repeated. "When things are born, part of me is ripped to shreds. And when things die, those shreds return to me. It's a moment of solace. In that one moment, right after the dead return to me what's mine and just before they move on, I'm more whole. But then something else is born, and I'm ripped apart again."

"Does it hurt?" the boy asked.

"Do you remember the pain of being born?"

"Um. No."

"You're lucky, Xander Atwood. I remember every single birth. I feel it all. And yes, it hurts. It hurts more than you could imagine. But it's a temporary sort of hurt, just as when life dies and returns to me, there's a temporary sort of peace." He traced an eternity symbol in the air. "Life, then death. One leads to the other, and I'm there at the place they meet."

"On the edge of the Möbius strip."

"Exactly."

"Okay," the boy said, nodding. "So you became Death. What then?"

He let out a laugh. "What makes you think there's anything else? I've been Death for thousands and thousands of years."

"But something led you to sit on my balcony railing," said the boy, "and contemplate the end of everything. Something changed."

He didn't reply.

"So you became Death," the boy repeated gently. "What then?"

A breeze toyed with his hair, slapping golden strands against his face. When the wind quieted once more, he replied, "Then I died."

"You . . ." Xander's voice trailed off.

"Died," Death repeated. "Even Death can die. Do you think this is my true form, Xander?"

"Um. Well, no. Not unless you were also the lead singer of Nirvana . . ."

Death smiled, but it didn't reach his eyes. "I'm not human. I don't look human. But when I was stranded here, I took on a human guise. Humanity was the reason I'd come here, after all. I wanted to get more bang for my buck. So: one head, two arms, two legs. No wings. No nothing that wasn't grade-A human."

"You have wings?"

"Do I look like I have wings?"

"You look human."

"And do humans have wings?" he chided. "Of course not. Look what happened to Icarus. Wings are too fragile to survive human vanity."

"Wings would've been cool."

"Aren't you afraid of heights? What would you do, fly two feet off the ground?" Death clucked his tongue. "Trust me, you wouldn't do well with wings."

Xander decided not to push the point.

"I took a human form, but that form didn't last. It couldn't,"

Death said. "All living things burn out eventually. So my body died." Then, softer: "I've died so many times."

Xander felt like his brain had caught fire. He thought furiously, trying to untangle the meaning behind Death's words. Death had died before—many times, he had just said—and yet the world was still here. So was Xander wrong? Was the world not at risk while Death was on suicide watch?

Could he really take that chance?

And even if he could—even if the world was safe no matter what happened to Death—could he just walk away from someone who was hurting so deeply?

Of course he couldn't.

"You died," Xander said, "but here you are. Alive."

"My body dies," Death corrected, "and then I'm reborn in a new form. Sort of like picking a new outfit, one that you'll wear for years. Without washing it. Gets very wrinkled."

"Your *body* dies," Xander repeated. "But that's not the same thing as *you* dying."

"You think so?" Death laughed, the sound harsh and bitter and painful to hear. "Do you remember dying, Xander? Do you remember the agony of feeling life leave your body?"

"Of course not," he said. "I haven't died yet."

Death stared at him with a gimlet eye. "'Of course not,'" he repeated. "Then take my word for it: When I die, it doesn't just hurt. It redefines hurt. Feeling yourself slow as you age is nothing compared to feeling your body suddenly, irrevocably, shut down and fail. So don't tell me that it wasn't *me* who died, that it was merely my *body*. It was me, Xander Atwood. It's always me when I die."

Xander's mouth worked silently, and then he said, "I'm sorry. I didn't realize."

The apology hung in the air. Just as Xander began to think that it was either being ignored or refused, Death nodded once, minutely, a jerk of his chin that was almost imperceptible. And then he continued.

"The first time I died, it was like getting caught in a tornado — I was swept away by a vast power that I couldn't control. It didn't happen all at once. For some time — years, maybe — I'd been feeling colder. No matter how much I stood in the sun's warmth, I couldn't feel the heat along my skin. Have you ever become cold to the point that you no longer feel anything?"

"Sometimes, in the winter," Xander said. "If I'm not wearing a good pair of gloves, my hands will get so cold, I can't feel them."

"It was like that," Death said. "That moment before your skin goes from painfully cold to numb: That's where I was. I didn't equate the cold slowly seeping into my form with my body slowly failing. How could I know? It had never happened to me before. And I had no one to tell me what was happening." Something dark passed behind his eyes. "Just as well. There are things we all have to discover on our own. They either destroy us or rebuild us. And sometimes, they do both."

Xander thought he heard Suzie yelling at him, telling him something he couldn't understand — but the memory slipped away. He shifted his feet uneasily.

"I became cold to the point just before numbness," Death said, "and then I turned numb. And that's exactly when I died: the moment I no longer felt anything, I died."

Awed, Xander said, "What was it like?"

Death closed his eyes. "I had just taken a human, a woman who had died in childbirth. She'd given me her due and moved on. I remember watching her essence depart, remember the feeling of flint in my hand."

"Flint?" Xander asked.

"When living things die, they return to me what's mine, and they give it to me in a pleasing shape. For a time, the most valuable possessions people had were hand axes made of flint." Death smiled, and his face looked almost peaceful. "Over the years, the notion of value changed. Flint was replaced with shells and beads. Then came metal. The first time I saw a turtle coin, I was enamored. You people and your creations," he murmured, his smile broadening. "I still prefer coins."

Xander thought of his lucky penny, tucked deep within his pocket.

"I held the flint axe and couldn't feel the stone in my hand as the spark returned to me. And then the spark caught and flared." His eyes opened, but they focused on something Xander couldn't see. "At first, I was so pleased to feel heat again, I didn't realize the spark had already transformed into wildfire. And then it was too late. It had become a conflagration. It consumed me."

Xander watched the memory of agony play across Death's face, and part of him wanted to reach out and grab his long-fingered hand and squeeze it tight, let him know that he wasn't alone, that it was okay.

But it wasn't okay. He was Death, and when his story was done, he was going to kill himself and take the world with him.

"I felt myself die," Death said quietly. "And just as everything went dark, I was pulled away from the edge of nothingness."

Surprised, Xander said, "So you were saved."

"It was a lifeline," Death said, "but I wasn't saved. I was thrown into the tempest, into the heart of the maelstrom. You said I was a battery charger. If so, that was the moment I got plugged into the outlet. I was caught in a vortex of power, and I was reshaped and cast back to the world, in a new body. I'd been reborn," he said flatly. "Happy birthday to me."

"That's . . ." Xander shook his head and fought the urge to whistle. "That's amazing."

"It was agonizing and beyond my control. It was terrifying," Death said. "You call it amazing, but it was punishment for my hubris, for thinking that I could fix something that the rest of my kind had decided to leave untouched."

"You didn't want to live?" Xander asked, horrified.

"'Want,'" Death repeated slowly, as if he were tasting the word on his tongue. "What does 'want' have to do with anything?"

"When you want something," Xander said, "it has a way of happening."

"Tell that to the person who buys lottery tickets and never wins."

"Something *important*," Xander said.

"I'm guessing that winning the lottery is important to people who actually win."

"You know what I mean," Xander insisted. "If you want something that much, if you work for it and not lose sight of it, then it can happen."

Death was quiet for a time before he said, "I had thought as much, once I found the Slate."

"What's the Slate?"

"It's what gave me hope." Death turned to once again gaze upon the sky, which was now a bruised purple. "Morning of the day of my death and resurrection: Things were born and I was ripped apart; things died and I received temporary solace. Life to death to life again. I walked among humanity, hungry to better understand that for which I'd given up everything. None saw me, unless I wished to be seen. And I rarely did. It was enough that the dead saw me, spoke to me, before they moved on. So I watched humanity define itself and find its place in the world. And soon it was my time to die again. But now I was better prepared. I felt it coming." He paused. "This time, I could fight it."

"Fight dying?" Xander asked.

"Oh, no, not that." He managed a grin. "Nothing cheats death."

"Not even you?"

His grin settled into a tired smile. "Especially not me. But I could fight returning to life. And I did. That time, when I felt myself burn out, I dove for the nothingness that was the absence of life. I told myself that when life itself would reach for me, I would fight it. I knew that if I did so and I was successful, nothing would rekindle the spark, and all life would die out. But I didn't care. I'd been betrayed and abandoned and cast in a role I never wanted, and had suffered such agony that I would do anything to never feel again. I just wanted it to stop." Death met his gaze. "Can you understand that, Xander Atwood?"

Xander remembered a sound like a screech of tires, pushed the thought away. "I think so."

Death nodded. "That was what I planned. I would die, and that would be the end of it. But something happened. Something unexpected." His voice softened. "Something magnificent and brilliant and abysmal and horrifying. Something that changed everything. I found the Slate."

He said the word with a sense of awe; Xander heard the wonder in Death's voice, but there was also a hint of something bleaker—a sense of hopelessness, of loss.

"I was on the brink," Death said. "So cold, so numb. The world had become a frozen wasteland, a winter without end. No living thing had ever been as cold as I. And then heat erupted from deep within me, and I died. This time, as I'd planned, I welcomed the blankness, the nothingness. The end, Xander. It was the end, and it was what I wanted."

Xander's throat was too tight for him to speak, so he nodded.

"And again, just a breath away from oblivion, I felt myself pulled back, as I knew would happen. So I fought it. I denied it. And it passed through me without taking me. Do you understand?" he asked plainly. "I stepped between time and space, and I found the Slate."

Xander's brow furrowed. "You . . . what, shifted into another dimension?"

"Got it in one," Death said, sounding pleased. "The Slate is what exists on the edge of this reality. In it, all possibilities are revealed—all the yesterdays that happened, all the tomorrows that could ever be, everything, right there, shining like crystals of every color." He smiled, truly smiled, and his eyes shone fiercely. "My sanctuary."

Xander could picture it: wave upon wave of shimmering colors, the proud garnets, the lofty aquamarines, the vibrant chartreuses. He saw colors without names and too many colors to name, imagined them all winking in the nexus of imagination and inspiration. A palette of possibilities, winking against a backdrop that was neither gray nor blue, but somewhere in between.

The Slate.

It was all things and no things all at once, both within and without. It was massive and almost incomprehensive and engulfing and terribly private.

"The Slate revealed so much," said Death. "I saw what had come to pass, going as far back as the door slamming shut behind me. I saw the future, so very many futures, most of them so incredibly similar, with only a hair's difference between them."

Xander could picture that as well: crystals shining with yesterdays, shimmering with tomorrows. Stunned, he asked, "How could you see it all?"

"The Slate is outside of time. It could have taken me a hundred million years to view everything, and that would have passed in the blink of an eye."

"Still . . . wasn't it overwhelming?"

"For a human? It would drive you mad. Mortal creatures aren't meant to view the infinite. Your brains would liquefy. But for me? It was enlightening." Death smiled, and when he spoke again, his voice hinted at warmth. "In one possible future, I saw something that changed everything."

"What was it?"

"I saw a hint, just a glimpse, of the one who was supposed to be with me. I even heard a voice, a whisper, meant only for my ears. In that one future, I was no longer alone." Something in his smile turned sadder, turned inward. "My soulmate was with me once more. And hand in hand, we two shared the burden of keeping the spark alive. Together, we flourished and humanity prospered."

"That's amazing," Xander said.

"It was, truly. And it was enough. That hint, that glimpse, was enough to make me want to live. So I left the Slate, and when life pulled at me, I didn't fight it. If there was even a possibility of my soulmate joining me, I needed to see it through. And again, I was reborn, this time with a new sense of purpose."

"Hope," Xander said. "What you saw gave you hope."

"Hope," Death agreed. "It's astounding how something could both be so small and yet so large." He looked at Xander, an odd smile playing on his face. "Hope can lead to wondrous things."

From the baby monitor came the sounds of Lex shifting and babbling.

"Once again, I walked among the living and met with the dead. But this time, I found myself enjoying my role. I threw myself into my work. Just the possibility of my soulmate joining me at one point made my burden easier to carry. I found that I actually liked talking to the dead before they moved on. And I learned how to maneuver your reality's time enough to allow me to not only do my job but also have some serious downtime." He grinned. "Maybe I'm just a cosmic voyeur, but I do so love watching you people. You do such fascinating things."

"You can . . . what, stop time?"

"Eh, time is relative. It was just a question of me finding the balance between real time for me and real time for your world." Death shrugged. "Piece of cake, once I put my mind to it."

"Sure," Xander said faintly. "Piece of cake."

"Over time, I got to see just how creative you people truly are. I saw when you invented cooking. I saw your first man-made shelters. I witnessed your first burials. That was one of my early favorites." Death grinned. "Watching you people mature has been eye-opening. And, at times, cringe-worthy. Look at the Hindenburg. Really. Hydrogen? What were you thinking? Of course it exploded. But you learned. That's what's truly so remarkable about you people: your ability to learn."

Xander tried to imagine everything that Death had witnessed over the history of humanity, and his mind threatened to shut down. It was too overwhelming. It was like trying to count the individual waves of the ocean.

"You've made some fantastic things in your time," said Death. "The wheel. Sailing ships. Weapons of all sorts. Paper. Chocolate."

"That's the second time you've mentioned chocolate."

"It deserves a second mention."

"You want some? We've got a bag of M&M's in the pantry. Maybe come inside with me," Xander added casually, "and join me for some chocolatey goodness while you tell me the rest of your story? A sofa's got to be more comfortable than the railing."

Humor glittered in Death's blue eyes. "Still the boy with the chocolate. No thank you, Xander Atwood. One gift given freely was more than I should ever have accepted. Besides," he said, pivoting around on the railing to better face Xander, "I think you're far more interested in getting me off this railing than you are in feeding me."

Busted.

"It's not just that," Xander said lamely. "I don't do well with heights."

"So you've said."

"Will you come inside?"

"No."

"Um," Xander said. "Okay. So. You were saying that you focused on your work and saw lots of cool things."

Death watched him for a few seconds before he spoke. "Every now and then over the millennia, over my various life cycles, I would take a respite in the Slate." He smiled thinly. "To recharge, if you don't mind me using your metaphor. I'd watch the past with fresh eyes. And when I found myself tired or wondering whether you people really were worth everything I'd sacrificed, I'd view possible futures. And then I'd see that one potential tomorrow, when my soulmate and I are together once more. And that would be enough to get me through. To find my balance. Get closer to Zen."

"A mental health break," Xander said.

"Yes," Death agreed. "That, exactly. For a long, long time, the Slate was the reason why I didn't fight the pull of life at my cycle's end." He sighed. "But it wasn't always enough to help me find my happy place. Hope can be fleeting, especially when between that hope and you is the knowledge of certain agony."

"Pain sucks," Xander said.

"Well put. Pain does indeed suck."

"Do you have any idea how brave you are?" Xander said. "Knowing that you'll have to go through something unspeakably horrible, all to keep everything alive here? You're a hero."

"I'm a fool, Xander Atwood. And being brave can be impossible when there's no one to appreciate your bravery. And that," Death said, "is when I realized that I dearly needed something that humans had. I needed a companion."

"But you said your soulmate hadn't come through the door with you."

"Right. And until that happy day actually happened, I needed someone to temporarily fill the spot. Not as a soulmate, but as a companion. Someone with which to pass the time. Shoot the breeze. Maybe play a game of cards."

Xander could see that; he couldn't begin to imagine how terribly lonely it must be to be Death. "What did you do?"

"I created a companion."

"You . . ." Xander felt his eye twitch. "Just like that? Abracadabra, a companion?"

"Well, it took a little bit more than saying 'abracadabra,' but yes, effectively." Death peered at him. "What troubles thee, Xander Atwood?"

"Nothing. Nothing. I mean, your people created my entire world, right? So I shouldn't be freaked out by you casually mentioning that you created a person." He blew out a breath. "Sorry. Your story is sort of out of my frame of reference, you know? It's just a lot for me to take in."

"No worries. And for the record, it wasn't a person. My companion was a transmogrifier."

Xander blinked, nonplussed. "Okay, you just made that up."

"Well. Yes. I told you as much."

"No, the word. You made up that word."

"Sure. To go along with my creation." Death smiled. "Creative license."

Xander's eye twitched again. He desperately wanted a beer, or something stronger, but A) his parents would notice if their stash of booze was depleted and B) Death was still on suicide watch, so Xander didn't want to leave him alone. "What's a transmogrifier?"

"A locomotive creature that can change its form into either organic or inorganic matter." He grinned, and for the first time, Xander saw a relaxed Death, a slacker, a guy who hung out with you and played video games and talked in vague terms about lofty goals. "Specifically, it's a horse. For the most part. It was as close to a horse as I was to a human. I got the idea from the Botai."

"The who?"

"The Botai. Nomads in the steppes of northern Kazakhstan. For the longest time, the Botai hunted wild horses. And then one day, a hunter didn't kill the horse he'd stalked but instead mounted him, bareback. He twined his fingers through the horse's mane and stayed mounted by pressing his knees against the horse's sides. And for a few glorious moments, that hunter rode." Death smiled. "And then the horse threw the rider and bashed his brains in with its hooves. But that was enough to show the Botai what was possible. Within a year, all of the hunters were on horseback. Want to know what began globalization? The taming of the horse."

"When was this?"

Death cocked his head. "About . . . hold on, I'm counting . . . five thousand years ago."

Xander breathed. "Jesus."

"Still not him." Death's smile faded. "As I said, I'm old. I've seen it all, Xander. I've been there, even if I haven't done that. I've seen the best humanity has to offer. And I've seen the worst. It's been entertaining." He stole a glance at his watch. "And now the show is almost over."

"You haven't finished telling me your story," Xander said quickly. "You created a horse, a transmogri-something."

"Transmogrifier. A fine steed. Horses are such noble creatures. As my steed would happily tell you, again and again."

"Tell me?" Xander blinked. "Your steed talks?"

"All things talk, Xander. You just have to know how to listen. Granted, speaking their language helps." Death paused. "In retrospect, the mistake was giving it a personality."

"Your horse, um, talks back, I take it?"

"It's getting the horse to shut up that's quite the trick." Death chuckled and shook his head. "Oh, that's unfair of me. The steed was a boon companion for many and many a year. Out of all of them, it was the only one that consistently told me what I needed to hear, even if I didn't want to hear it. Not an easy job, by any means." He smiled sheepishly and shrugged. "I'm not always the best company to keep."

Xander repeated, "All of them? So you've had, what, other transmogrifiers?"

"Of course not," said Death. "One was quite enough, thank you. If I would have made more than one, they might have gotten it into their heads that they outnumbered me."

"Then who's the 'them' you're talking about?"

"My colleagues."

"So your soulmate made it through the door?" Xander asked. "With more of your people?"

"I didn't say that."

"Then what colleagues are you talking about?"

A whimsical smile played on Death's face. "The ones I made, of course. You know them as the Horsemen of the Apocalypse."

The boy's eyes widened. "The Four Horsemen of the Apocalypse," he said breathlessly. "From the Book of Revelation! The sun turns black and the moon turns red, the seas boil, the skies fall!" Sheepishly, he added, "Okay, that's either from the Bible or *Ghostbusters*."

"The words in the Bible are about us," he said, "but we're not from the Bible. The first three Horsemen were humans from Laconia."

"Where's that?"

"Greece."

There was a moment filled only with the sounds of the wind and the static crackling from the baby monitor on the floor, and then the boy said, "The Horsemen of the Apocalypse are Greek?"

"Spartan, actually. Specifically, they were helots."

"Zealots?"

"Helots. The forced-labor class. You know." He smiled. "Slaves."

"The Horsemen of the Apocalypse are Greek slaves," the boy said under his breath. "They definitely didn't teach us that in Sunday school . . ."

"The original Horsemen were Spartan slaves, yes. Since then? Well, the Horsemen have come from different ethnicities, from different parts of the world." He smiled toothily. "I'm all about workplace diversity."

"Why did you pick three slaves to be your companions?"

He hadn't. It was the girl who had picked him.

"This was about twenty-five-hundred years ago," he said. "The helots were poorly treated by their Spartan masters. Beatings, rapes, torture—all of that was quite standard. They had hard lives. And though there were whispers of rebellion, none stepped forward to incite the helots to rise up. Until someone did."

He could still picture her face, sweat-slick and thin, her eyes feverish, her mouth curled into a ferocious snarl. He had never seen a human more fetching than that girl at that moment—back bent, hands fisted by her sides, ready to fight for her life.

"The girl was sixteen. That very same morning, her older sister died of starvation—ironic, given that the girl's role was to help in the kitchens and make black broth for the soldiers. And not even an hour earlier, a friend of hers, an albino boy, had died from fever. The surviving girl, in mourning over the deaths of her sister and her friend, didn't show up to serve her Spartan master. Her master didn't take too kindly to her defection."

"She was grieving," the boy said.

"So? It wasn't like she could take a sick day. There weren't any wages for her master to dock. She was a slave, and even though helots had some measure of freedom, they weren't free to live their own lives. She was supposed to work, and she didn't. In his fury, her master beat her to death."

On the railing, the boy's knuckles whitened.

"She didn't go quietly," he said, remembering the sounds of flesh striking flesh. "She fought back, but in the end, it didn't matter. She fought until she couldn't fight, and then she took the blows until she couldn't take them any longer. She died, and her master left her corpse where it fell."

The boy's eye twitched.

"You look sick," he said to the boy. "Don't you know by now just how cruel you people can be? You're liars. You're thieves. Your concern for one another ends at your nose. For all that humans are magnificent, you're also quite horrific. It's a fascinating combination."

"Not all of us are like that," the boy insisted.

"Maybe not. But at one point, everyone is exposed to cruelty."

"Not me."

"No? So you're the sheltered boy, the exception to the rule? You've lived a perfect life, untouched by betrayal?"

The boy clenched his jaw.

"Have you never been treated wrongly? Have you never been hurt by someone you trusted?" He watched his words slam home. "Has that truly never happened to you, Xander Atwood?"

The boy's mouth opened, perhaps to protest, but a memory too vivid to ignore had already begun to play in his mind.

Death knew this, because he had delved into the boy's mind from the very start. He watched the boy's eyes widen as the truth was laid bare before him, and—

A beep shrieked from the monitor, rending the air.

The boy's face blanked.

"Breathe, Xander," Death murmured.

And Xander breathed.

"No," the boy said slowly, as if waking from a dream. "No, that's never happened to me."

He watched the boy for a moment before he continued with his tale.

"After the Spartan master left, I went to greet the newly dead. They were lying there, discarded, their bodies ruined, their essences waiting for release. Just another day on the job."

He remembered standing there in the dusty storage room, watching the three of them hover over their abused bodies; he remembered the girl's head whipping up to face him, her ghostly gaze raking him.

"She was so angry, so enraged over her murder. She all but glowed with fury. She was passion incarnate, and she demanded vengeance."

He could still feel her fists, ill formed and without substance, pounding against his chest as she screamed at him for justice. He could still feel her heat washing over him.

"In that moment, as I stared down at the girl's bloody form, at the bodies of her starved sister and diseased friend, I was moved by her rage. And so, in that moment," he said, "I made them an offer."

Three humans, three different reactions. Fiery Creusa, the younger sister who had been beaten to death, leapt at the chance. She swore herself to him for all time, unequivocally, forever and always. Her eyes had shone like opals as he took her hand.

Dark-haired Philomela, the emaciated older sister, had responded with a measured look and a question on her tongue: What was the price of such an offer? He gave her an answer, and she accepted with a curt nod.

Lysander, the boy with white hair and pale eyes, had watched, and waited. Only after Philomela had accepted did he voice his agreement, quietly, minutely — the barest whisper of acceptance.

It had been enough.

"Life pulls at me," he said, "tears away pieces of me. But I can give pieces of myself willingly. And, if I wish, more than pieces. That was how I created my steed. And that was how I created my new companions. I divided a portion of my own essence into three, one for each of them. I took those pieces and infused them into their bodies. And then I allowed their own essences to return to their bodies, and they were reborn."

The boy's jaw dropped. "You can do that? You can bring people back to life?"

"Of course."

Spluttering, the boy asked, "Then why does anyone have to die?"

"Because mortals are not supposed to be immortal," he said simply.

The boy's mouth moved silently, his frustration all too clear.

"It's as I said before: There are things that aren't meant for mortal creatures. Living forever is one of them."

"What about the Horsemen?" the boy demanded.

"They're hybrids," he said patiently. "And even they aren't eternal. A human can become inhuman, but it's impossible for a mortal to become immortal. It would break you, and you people break easily enough as it is."

The boy looked unconvinced, but he didn't argue.

"The dark sister who had starved to death became Famine. The albino boy who had died from fever became Pestilence. And the fiery younger sister who had died from her injuries, she was War. I gave them steeds, and I unleashed my Horsemen upon the world."

"I thought you wanted them to be your companions."

"And so they were. That doesn't mean they didn't also have day jobs." He grinned toothily. "Everyone's got to earn their keep."

"So . . ." The boy's forehead creased. "The Horsemen of the Apocalypse are supposed to bring about the end of the world. That's the whole 'Apocalypse' part of the name, right?"

"You people and your words," he said, rolling his eyes. "You invest so much meaning into them."

"Words *have* meaning," the boy said. "That's the entire point of them."

"Words mean exactly what the person hearing them wants them to mean. *Apocalypse* is just a word."

"A word that means the end of the world!"

"It's a *word*, Xander. It doesn't cause the end of anything, except, perhaps, my patience."

"But—"

"Listen to you argue." He leaned back against the wind and laughed softly. "What's the point of explaining anything? You hear only what you want to hear. You always have. You can read the most complex meaning into the fall of a stray leaf, all the while ignoring someone screaming at you to get out of the way of the toppling tree. Subjective reality at its finest."

The boy threw his hands wide, his fear of heights long forgotten. "If that's the case," he said, "if I don't believe you're going to kill yourself and take the world with you, then it won't happen. If reality is subjective, then it's all what I make of it."

Death waited.

"Is that what you're saying?" the boy asked, his voice dropping low. "Are you just in my head?"

He smiled. "One way to find out."

They stared at each other, the man who was not a man and the boy who had the world in his hand.

"Release me from my boon," he said to the boy, "and I'll throw myself off your balcony right now. Maybe I'll bounce when I hit bottom. Maybe where I touch down will be ground zero. Or maybe," he said slyly, "nothing will happen because I don't really exist. Maybe I'm a malevolent demon, and what you're seeing is just an illusion. Are you willing to find out? Or will you still go along with what you think is real?"

The boy closed his eyes, took a deep breath, and let it out

slowly. When he opened his eyes again, he said, "This is real. Right here, right now."

"If you say so."

"I do," the boy declared. "You said that *apocalypse* is just a word. Then what's the purpose of the Horsemen of the Apocalypse?"

"They're great bridge players."

The boy glowered at him.

"They help me, Xander. They each have their demesnes. Famine oversees the balance between starvation and abundance. War encourages outlets for aggression. Pestilence is the conqueror of disease and health. They take a lot off my plate."

"So they don't kill people?"

"Directly? They can. They usually don't. People have a way of dying all by themselves."

"But why does there have to be a balance between starvation and abundance at all? Why do people have to go hungry? That's cruel," the boy said. "Dying of disease, dying from war, that's wrong and cruel and stupid."

"Living things die, Xander. It's just a matter of how and when. But if it makes you feel any better, the purpose of the Horsemen is to avoid having *everyone* die of disease or starvation or warfare. They prevent the apocalypse."

The boy frowned, and his forehead creased as he tried to make sense of the words. "What do you mean?"

"My presence acts as a battery charger, as you said. What happens if a battery gets overcharged?"

"Um . . . a short-circuit, I think . . ."

"What happens if your world short-circuits?" He smiled.

"I'll tell you. Disease runs rampant. Crops fail. Earthquakes. Tidal waves. War. In other words, game over."

The boy's face paled, and he let out a strangled "Oh."

"It's always been a balancing act for me." He felt the weight of millennia press against him, and he sighed. "I'm connected to everything, from the mold that causes food to rot to the germs that cause disease, to the people who willingly choose to slaughter one another. I can sway the tides and calm volcanoes. It's a question of knowing when to do so."

"Like firefighters knowing when to let a forest fire burn itself out, and when to put it out?"

"Exactly like that," he said, nodding. "That had been part of my job for thousands of years: finding the balance of life and death."

"But now you had the Horsemen to help you with that."

"Yes."

"So how did the 'Apocalypse' part come into it? I know," the boy said quickly, "I know it's just a word. But it's part of the name. It got there somehow."

"People have to name things, especially those things they don't understand. It gives them a sense of control." He shrugged. "Mortals can't see the Horsemen unless the Horsemen wish to be seen. But mortals recognize us, even if they can't see us. They sense us. In the backs of their minds, they know what we are. And that terrifies them. So they create destruction myths and place us front and center. Thus, we're the Horsemen of the Apocalypse."

"That's sort of unfair."

"Could have been worse. We could have been the Horsemen of Perpetual Cheer."

The boy grinned. "Now, that's terrifying."

The two of them shared a laugh, and for that moment, it was good.

"So now you had companions," said the boy.

He nodded. "I gave them a portion of my power, and they were reborn as Horsemen. The world trembled at their coming. That's not hyperbole, by the way. Unleashing part of my power caused a massive earthquake. Completely leveled Sparta," he said. "War, the Red Rider, took advantage of the chaos and incited the helots to rise up against their remaining masters. That wound up paving the way for the Peloponnesian War. She couldn't have been happier."

"All of that," the boy said, his voice filled with wonder, "from what you did?"

"Yep." He smiled fleetingly as he remembered War leading the helots into battle, her scream of defiance and violent joy tingeing the air red.

"So many people died," the boy said.

"You make it sound like a tragedy," he replied, clucking his tongue. "It's just a matter of perspective. Like I said, Xander, everyone dies. It's just a matter of how and when."

The boy said nothing for a long moment as he digested the words. Finally, he asked, "Once you had your companions helping you with your job, did that make things better for you?"

"For a time," he admitted. "I talked with them, far more than I ever had with other humans. I watched the world with them. I enjoyed their company. Well. For the most part. There were times when one or the other of them would be quite frustrating. But they did make things better for me."

"Because the Horsemen were your friends," said the boy.

He felt himself tense, though he didn't know why.

"Of course not," he said. "Famine was too awed by me to ever be something as familiar as a friend, and Pestilence was too engrossed with his work and, frankly, with Famine."

Undeterred, the boy asked, "What about War?"

He remembered her hand in his, so warm that it heated him from within. Her energy, her heat, thawing him, making him feel something close to alive.

"She and I became . . . close."

"So she's your friend," the boy pressed. "Right?"

The tension grew, and now it hinted at anger. "That War is long gone," he said sharply. "All three of them died. For all of their new power, they were still just people. They died, and I offered their power to others."

"What others?"

"Too many to count."

Flashes of red and white and black as he pictured the faces of the different Riders across the years.

"When the first three Horsemen died, I took their power and placed it into specific tools. A set of scales for Famine. A sword for War. A crown for Pestilence. And then I gave those tools to other humans, who then became Horsemen."

"Dead humans?"

He arched an eyebrow. "Can a dead human wear a crown or wield a sword? No, only those first three were brought back to life. And that took too much out of me to do again. Plus, earthquakes. So every other Horseman-to-be from that point on was either dying, about to die, or thinking of dying. Teenagers, mostly."

"And yet, we're not even allowed to vote. There's irony for you."

"Adults have already become the people they're going to be. But teenagers are first discovering who they really are, what they can do. I'd rather give massive power to someone who can grow into it and learn how to use it instead of giving it to someone who's more rigid." He smiled tightly. "Less tendency for teens to go power-crazy or just crazier than adults."

"Are there Horsemen out there today, now?"

"Sure. Famine broods over calories, and Pestilence whispers to scientists to nudge them into finding cures. War is passionate as ever."

He traced his fingers along his mouth, imagined the feeling of War's lips against his, of her fist against his face.

He was so numb.

"Then talk to them," the boy said.

He didn't reply.

"Tell them how you're feeling," urged the boy. "Tell them that you're suicidal, that you want to end it all. They're your companions. They understand you better than anyone else. They can help you."

"Help me?" he echoed coldly. "No, Xander Atwood. No, they wouldn't help me."

"Of course they would . . ."

"Do you know what they're doing right now, as I prattle on and on about the life of Death?" He smiled a skeletal grin. "They're talking about how to stop me."

XANDER

Death's eyes gleamed as he gazed upon Xander. "What do you think of that?" he said, his voice cold and brittle. "The three other Horsemen are gathered right now, plotting against me."

"How could you know that?" Xander asked, trying to ignore the way his heart was racing.

"I see everything. I'm connected to them, more so than to anything else. Part of me animates them, makes them what they are. I feel the wind on their flesh, the sun on their heads. I smell their sweat. I hear their accusations. Oh, the things I hear."

"What . . ." Xander's voice cracked. "What do you hear?"

"True things. Painful things." His eyes narrowed. "That's how they would help me, Xander. They use their words to flay me."

"But they're your companions," he said desperately. "Your friends."

Death leaned forward in a sudden motion, startling Xander into taking a step backward.

"Friends?" Death hissed. "You mean the people who talk behind your back, who say things about you? Who betray you? Are those friends, Xander Atwood?"

Ted's face, looking wane and exhausted and so very haunted.
Suzie shouting at him, telling him—

"No," Xander growled. "Friends have your back. You can turn to them, no matter what. That's what they do," he insisted. "Friends are there for you, always!"

A smile crept along Death's mouth. It was an upsetting smile, one completely devoid of humor and bordering on ugliness.

"Friends can break your heart," he said softly, poisonously. "Which is why I don't have one. Excuse me for a moment."

With that, Death vanished.

Xander stood on the empty balcony, his mouth opening and closing and opening again. A strong gust of wind whipped past, snapping him out of his daze. He grabbed the baby monitor and hightailed it back inside his apartment, shutting the balcony door behind him.

He let out a shaky breath and wondered if he was losing his mind. A glance at his watch showed him that he'd been standing outside for almost thirty minutes.

"Okay," he said, trying to convince himself that it was, indeed, okay. "Okay."

He didn't believe it was okay at all.

Feeling lost and alone and hopeless, Xander wandered down the hall, heading for the nursery. One look at his baby brother would settle him, ground him, remind him of what was real. Because, honestly—Death? That was a bit much, wasn't it?

Of course it was.

He must have imagined the entire thing. Vividly. Because Death wasn't some anthropomorphic personification, let alone some stranded alien entity or a grounded angel. Death happened. People lived; people died. Period.

Okay, he told himself as he opened the nursery door. He'd

check on his brother, and then he'd try Riley again. Maybe even give Ted a call, see what he was up to. Xander, the man with the plan.

Feeling renewed, he walked over to the crib and smiled as he peeked inside.

The smile froze on his face, then cracked as his mouth twisted into a rictus of disbelief and horror.

Lex was gone.

Outside the apartment, the wind howled.

PART FOUR

INTERVENTION

Everything intercepts us from ourselves.
                    —*Ralph Waldo Emerson*

War paced along the beach, her footprints marring the sand. The wind tore against the ground strongly enough to kick up dirt and silt, pelting War with sediment. She barely noticed. On one side of her, a massive cliff reached up, covered with green vegetation that seemed to mock her with its brightness. On the other side, the Pacific Ocean stretched out and out, the rolling water striped in ribbons of blue.

She hated looking at all that blue. It made her think of *him,* of his eyes that were once so unfathomable.

Snarling, she continued her march along the narrow strip of beach. Her warhorse kept out of her way, amusing itself by hunting rats in the undergrowth. Normally, she would have told the horse not to kill, but at the moment, she didn't really give a damn. She was in a black, black mood, so she let her steed get its jollies by taking out as many rats as it wanted.

Around her, the wind howled.

War stomped her boots into the damp sand, leveling it, leaving impressions like ruins. As she marched, her fingers clenched and released, clenched and released. She was itching to summon her Sword, to feel its perfect weight in her hands and swing it far and wide. She wanted to split the sky and hear its screams; she wanted to hew the earth until it wept.

She wanted the world to bleed.

War breathed in through gritted teeth and refused to draw out her Sword. There would be time for blood after.

She could always find time for blood.

Missy Miller hasn't cut herself in years, not since she truly accepted the Sword of War and all that it meant. The lock box with her razor is still sequestered in the safety of her bedroom; even though she never intends to use it again, she can't bring herself to throw it away. It's a part of who she is, or who she was—it's a reminder of how far she's come.

Breathing deeply, taking in the taste of salt and dust, she continued her circuit of the beach. Waves slapped at the shore and receded and then returned, their rolling crashes echoing her own rolling fury—she fumed, she quieted, she fumed once more.

Finally, she couldn't bear the wait. She reached out with her mind and demanded, *Where are you?*

A feeling like a stifled sneeze, and then a reply: *Just over Peru. Be right there.*

A smell of burned chocolate, and another reply: *I see New Zealand coming up.*

Move your asses, she growled.

This time, there was no reply.

War hated being ignored. She folded her arms and seethed.

She still gets angry, sometimes so angry it's like she loses herself in a sea of red. And there are other times when her control is a precarious thing, and the lock box becomes so very enticing. But overall, she's found a balance between bottling her rage and letting it fly free. More than that, she's found a way to be both Missy Miller and the Red Rider of the Apocalypse. Part of it is having a few years of experience under her belt, but most of it is listening to her gut, knowing when it's time to put away the Sword and settle back with her college books and weekly phone calls with her family.

And part of it is knowing that no matter what she does or who she is, he's *there for her.*

Moments later, the White Rider and his steed touched down on the beach, the horse running along the sand and coming to a jerky halt not ten feet in front of her. She tapped her foot as he patted his horse's neck and murmured that the steed shouldn't worry, that he would be right there on the beach and he promised he'd come back. The horse blew against his gloved hand, a nervous reply that meant a range of things from "Okay, gotcha" to "Don't leave me" to "I'll be brave."

War rolled her eyes. The white steed suffered from separation anxiety. She had no patience for anxiety.

Her own horse, fiery red and strong, agreed with her as it broke the back of yet another rat.

War couldn't complain about her horse eavesdropping, since she had just done the same with the White Rider and his steed. Even so, she didn't like it. At the moment, she didn't like much of anything.

"Red," said Pestilence, the White Rider, as he walked up to her. He had a confident stride and an easy smile, though his eyes were guarded. His outfit was snow white, but sand billowed around him as he walked, speckling the white with dirt. His thin silver crown caught the sunlight oddly, seeming almost invisible and then winking hypnotically. A broad white patch marked his hair, but whether that was from his tenure as the White Rider or simply a fashion statement, War couldn't say; her own hair was short and spiky and tended to be various shades of red.

She liked red. No matter how much she hated everything else, she would always like red.

"White," she replied, nodding once.

Neither of them offered to shake hands.

WEAK, War thought, but then pushed the thought away. That wasn't her; it was the voice of the Sword. It had very distinct opinions, and she did her best to keep those opinions out of her brain. If it were up to the Sword, she would have set the world on fire long ago.

"Thanks for agreeing to meet," she said. The three of them rarely got together, other than when work had them cross paths. She liked Pestilence well enough, though he was too much of a pacifist for her taste. As for Famine, War tolerated her. Barely.

"I was glad you suggested it," Pestilence said. A pause, and then: "Have you heard from him?"

Her lip curled into a sneer. "Since this morning? No. You?"

"No."

"This is bad."

"Very bad."

He's so very good for her, in every way — he listens to her, he gives her advice, he supports her when she tries new things. And then there's the other way he's good for her, how his touch does such things to her. At first, she hadn't known whether it was the Sword that kindled her attraction to him — the Red and Pale Riders had long been partners, on and off the battlefield. But soon, she didn't care how her feelings for him had begun; they're her feelings, and she treasures them.

She treasures him.

Both of them turned to the east to watch the Black Rider and her horse approach, sliding across the sky like an oil slick.

"Could she move any slower?" War growled.

"Be nice."

"I am being nice."

"Be nicer."

"Take your advice and shove it where the sun doesn't shine. Please," she added sweetly.

"Much better."

The black horse finally landed on the beach. Famine, the Black Rider, slid off her mount and fished something out of her coat pocket—a sugar cube. She offered the treat to her steed and another to the white horse, which had come prancing up to the black. The white steed accepted the snack and sneezed its thanks, and then it and the black horse nuzzled as they chewed. Famine patted her steed's neck, then walked over to War and Pestilence. She was head to toe in black; a gloved hand kept her broad-brimmed hat from flying away in the wind. She approached the other Riders stiffly, as if she were saddle sore. Then again, it wasn't like she had much padding to cushion her, so maybe riding her steed was painful.

Whatever. It wasn't War's problem.

Her face hidden in shadow, Famine nodded at the other Riders. "White," she said to Pestilence, and then, cooler: "Red."

"About time," War muttered. At Pestilence's pointed look, War forced herself to grin. There, she was all about the good cheer. "Thanks for coming." See that? She was practically drowning in diplomacy.

"Where's your steed?" Famine asked, darting a glance up and down the beach.

War shrugged. "Somewhere on the island. Killing rats."

"You're letting it kill?"

Her eyes narrowed. "Don't tell me how to handle my steed. Besides, the rats don't belong here. The Polynesians brought them when the rats stole aboard their ships."

"Infesting them," said Pestilence, nodding.

"Gorging on their grain," said Famine. "And after the settlers abandoned the island, the rats remained, dining on a smorgasbord of newborn birds."

"Destroying the ecosystem," said Pestilence.

They all knew this because the parts of them that were Horsemen had experienced those events, and they themselves remembered it as a sort of race memory. The Riders' collective conscience. If War were still in high school, she would have rocked her history class.

"So yeah, I'm letting my steed get its jollies by taking out as many rats as it wants," War said. "I like birds. Especially with a side of fries."

Famine's nostrils flared, but she didn't rise to the bait. "You wanted us to talk. So? Let's talk."

And War couldn't think of a thing to say.

He listens, but he doesn't say much, not about himself. He hasn't even told her his name. When she asks, he says that Death is always personal, so whatever name she chooses for him, that would be his name for her. At first, she thinks this is incredibly romantic. But

over time, she comes to see this as sad. To try to better understand
him, she doesn't call him by name, any name, not ever. He's simply
Death, the Pale Rider.

And she is his handmaiden.

Pestilence cleared his throat. "Have you heard from him?"

There was no need to clarify whom the White Rider meant.
Famine shifted her feet. "Not since this morning."

"Us, either," said Pestilence. "What was he like when you
saw him last?"

The Black Rider's jaw worked silently, as if she were grind-
ing her teeth. "He was cold," she finally answered. "But that's
nothing new."

"Were you on the job?"

"At a wedding."

"Let me guess," War said. "The bride starved herself to fit
into her wedding gown."

"It's not your concern," Famine snapped.

Ooh, she must have hit a nerve. "Touchy touchy."

"Back off, Red."

"Look at that," War purred. "Famine found her backbone.
No, wait, that's just your spine. Sticking out prominently. Because you don't eat."

Famine's mouth twitched. "I said back off."

War grinned, and the Sword said, *"MAKE ME."*

"Ladies," Pestilence warned. "We don't have time for this."

War took a deep breath and let it out slowly. She knew she
was being bitchy, but only part of that was actually her. Most
of it was from the Sword. The Red Rider had a long history
with the Black Rider. Neither of them liked each other. And it

usually ended with one of them killing the other. The Sword tended to bring out War's ugly side, especially when Famine was nearby.

SHE DESERVES IT, the Sword said.

"He's right," War gritted. "Sorry. I'll behave."

The Sword mocked her. She ignored it.

Famine nodded curtly. In the shadows of her face, her eyes glittered. No, there was no love lost there. War's fingers drummed restlessly against her arms, and she told herself to let it go.

"You said he was cold," Pestilence nudged.

"He said things to me." The Black Rider's mouth pressed into a thin line. "Cruel things. True things, if harsh."

War snorted.

Famine sniped, "What?"

"He's *always* harsh. Cutting." War smiled tightly. "Sometimes, he's funny. Sometimes, he's dark. But he's always harsh. Ruthless. Brutal."

"This isn't about you," said Famine.

"I didn't say it was."

"No," said Pestilence. "It's about him. Frankly, he scared the hell out of me today." He told them how, in some flyspeck village in some backwater country, Death had completely eradicated malaria.

"He slaughtered disease," War said. "I'm impressed."

Pestilence shot her a look. "Do you have any idea how reckless that was? What I had to counter that came to take malaria's place?"

"He threw disease off balance," Famine mused. "He stepped into your territory."

"That's not like him," Pestilence said.

"At all," War admitted.

"And then all the crows died." He described the birds, black and frozen, falling from a tree.

"My God," War breathed. "That's . . ."

"Bad," said Pestilence.

"Bad," she agreed.

"You're overreacting," Famine said. "He's acting a little oddly —so what?"

"A *little?*" said Pestilence.

"So some crows died. That doesn't mean anything other than some crows died."

"What about the malaria?"

"Yes, well," she said, shrugging. "He made a bad decision. Like that's never happened to you. He's just a little off today. That's all."

Pestilence's eyebrows arched in surprise. "You really think that?"

"Of course. We all have our days." Famine glanced at War. "Some more so than others."

War spluttered, but Pestilence held up a gloved hand. Seething, she bit her tongue and ignored the Sword's suggestion to cut Famine down where she stood.

"This isn't just having an off day," the White Rider said. "This is sea-change different. When have you known him to just let things die like that? Or to blow away the balance of disease? Even when plagues ravage entire countries, he sits back and lets things run their course. You know why? Because disease isn't his demesne. He's said as much to me."

Beneath the brim of her hat, Famine's face was inscrutable.

"The Spanish flu killed off almost a hundred million people," he said. "He didn't stop it. He could have, but he didn't."

"Neither did you," Famine commented.

"That was before my time. And don't change the point. If he didn't step in to stop something like the Spanish flu or the Black Plague or AIDS or even Alzheimer's, why on earth would he kill off malaria now?"

"Change of heart," Famine said coldly.

War rolled her eyes. "Oh, for God's sake . . ."

"That wasn't some quick-fix miracle cure," Pestilence said, his voice rising. "What he did was rash."

"You're both making too much out of this. So he's acting different. Maybe even rash. That doesn't mean anything," Famine insisted. "He's allowed to be moody."

"This isn't just some temper tantrum," Pestilence said.

The Black Rider pulled her coat tighter around her and didn't reply.

Missy tells him that she loves him, but he doesn't reply—not with words. He holds her and loves her, and makes her feel so very alive.

But he never says those three words to her.

She still tells herself that it doesn't bother her.

"Don't you see what's happening?" Pestilence looked at Famine, then at War, who grumbled and turned away.

"You do see it," he said softly. "Don't you?"

War refused to reply. She knew what he was insinuating, but she refused to acknowledge it.

"See what?" Famine asked peevishly.

"This morning," the White Rider said, "when he visited me,

he gave me a gift. That's when he destroyed the malaria, and then he told me my work was done."

Famine grew still.

"Did he give you anything?"

"At the wedding," she said slowly. "He had a bouquet of flowers, and he gave them to me."

Blood roared in War's ears. "*He* gave *you* flowers?" She could count on no hands how many times Death had given her flowers.

Uneasy, Famine said, "They dried up as soon as I touched them."

"You get flowers," War snarled at Famine, "and you get a day off," she said to Pestilence. "Me? I got the shaft."

A beat, and then Famine asked, "Is *that* what they're calling it these days?"

"He cut me off!" War gnashed her teeth. "That was *my* gift: He cut me off from him. I can't feel him." She remembered him leaning over her, the press of his lips against hers — the sudden chill as he stole her heat. "He was right there, a breath away from me, but it was like there was a wall between us."

Famine frowned. "I don't understand. He . . . what, took away your empathy?"

"Only with him. But isn't that enough? He shut me out. *Me.*" War ignored the sudden sting in her eyes. Softly, she said, "He hurt me so much."

"Ask yourselves now," said Pestilence. "Has he ever, *ever,* done anything like this before? Not just in your experience, but in your Rider's?"

"He's always cold," Famine said.

"Harsh," said War, shivering.

Pestilence said, "But he isn't rash. Out of all of us, he's the one who's patient. He's the one who understands the importance of waiting." He looked at Famine. "He's acting rashly, for the first time in forever. He's gotten colder, crueler." He turned to War. "He's gotten distant, has even cut off the one person who could truly understand him. He's giving us gifts. Don't you see what's happening here? He's suicidal."

The words rang true, and not just because the White Rider obviously believed them.

He spoke the truth. War could see it, could feel it.

She turned her back on him so that she wouldn't punch him in his fat mouth. But already, the Sword was laughing and laughing and laughing as images of blood ran freely in her mind—her blood, the blood of others, it was one and the same.

"Don't be ridiculous," Famine said. "He can't be suicidal. He's Death."

"Oh, so you've never been hungry?"

The Black Rider didn't reply.

"I'm telling you," Pestilence said. "He's suicidal. And that's not the worst of it."

War rubbed her arms. "No?" she said, not looking at him. "What could possibly be worse?"

"Have you noticed the weather?"

That threw her. "What about it?"

"It's gotten colder. Windier." Pestilence paused. "Angrier."

War got it. Eyes wide, she turned to face the White Rider. "You can't mean . . ."

He nodded, once, his mouth set in a thin line.

Famine let out an exasperated sigh. "It's just the weather."

Pestilence insisted, "It's *him*. When he gets cold, the world follows."

"You're insane. Winter happens. Wind happens."

"But it happens more erratically when he's like this," Pestilence insisted.

"How do you know that?"

On his brow, the Conqueror's crown gleamed. "Because I know."

"He's right," War whispered, her words half lost as the Sword clamored for blood. "Oh God, he's right."

Famine spluttered, "Right about what?"

"This isn't just about him being suicidal," Pestilence said grimly. "He's suicidal, and he's taking the world with him. If we can't stop this — if we can't stop *him* — then it's going to be hell on earth."

"You're being dramatic," said Famine.

"I wish I were," Pestilence replied. He took a moment to quash the nausea that suddenly flooded him—the White Rider antacid special, much better than the pink stuff he used to chug. "You have no idea just how bad it's going to be."

A SHEET OF WHITE, the King wailed.

Yes, he growled silently. *I know, shut up.*

You can't tell them, the Elder whispered.

I have to.

What will the knowledge do, other than break them?

What other choice did he have? The three of them were coworkers, and like it or not, what was happening now was part of their job. Granted, it was firmly in the "Other Duties As Assigned" column, but still, the responsibility was theirs.

To his left, War stood in profile, rubbing her arms as if to ward against a chill. Her cherry red coat looked almost cheerful in the sunlight, but her face was a study in solemnity—tight jaw, pinched mouth, a troubled look in her eye. She, at least, understood what was to come.

Of course she does, said the Elder. *She's his handmaiden. She should be ecstatic. The Last Ride is coming.*

You don't know her, Pestilence chided. *She's not like that.*

She's War. Of course she's like that.

Acid bubbled in Pestilence's stomach again. He swallowed thickly, tasting bile.

Billy Ballard is delivering his grandfather's eulogy, pretending his stomach isn't about to rebel. He talks about the man who had become his father figure, the man who taught him how to ride a bike and throw a baseball and how to always find his way home. He talks about his grandfather's slow slide into Alzheimer's, and how over the last couple of years of his life, Gramps had shown re-markable resilience. Medicines and prayers and everything in be-tween go only so far, he tells the mourners—the sick still must have spirit. They have to want to be healthy. They have to want to live. And his grandfather fought tooth and nail for life. He had enough spirit that three years ago, he even stood up to Death himself.

The mourners think he's being metaphorical. He lets them think that.

He tells everyone that even though his grandfather lost the battle against Alzheimer's, he held on to his dignity until the very end. He's never been prouder of the old man.

He won't say goodbye, he tells the mourners. As long as they keep his grandfather's memory in their minds, part of Gramps will live on.

To his right, Famine hid in shadow, from head to foot. She was thinner than he remembered, and clearly anorexic, even though her long coat and baggy pants hid it well. He'd tried to talk to her about it, once. That had gone poorly. Even before that ill-fated conversation, he'd tried to become closer to her over the years—hunger and disease tended to work hand in hand—but she always kept her distance. She was far more guarded than any of the previous Black Riders. More wounded, perhaps.

Lady Black, whispered the King.

Once, yes. That playful name was from the time when Famine and Pestilence had been closest, during the first thousand years that the King had reigned as the White Rider. But the time of Black and White together almost intimately was long gone. Now he had Marianne, and Famine had . . . whoever it was that she had.

Three years ago, Billy Ballard had kissed the girl, and she had kissed him back. With tongue. Since then, he and Marianne have been together. It's only gotten better after high school. Now they're freshmen in college—same state, but different schools; he'd gotten a full scholarship to his, and her parents had handpicked hers. They talk every day and see each other almost every weekend. They do the party scene; they do the quiet scene. They learn more and more about each other as they slowly discover who they are. Eighteen, and learning about how far first love can truly go.

Eighteen, and learning about life.

"He's not suicidal," Famine said.

"He is. All the signs are there. And more than that," Pestilence said. "Can't you feel it? Deep down, in the part of you that makes you what you are, that makes you the Black Rider . . . can't you feel that something's wrong?"

Famine gripped the brim of her hat and said nothing.

"Can't you feel it in your gut?"

War barked out a laugh. "That's just hunger pangs she's feeling."

"Red," he sighed. "Please. For this once, can the two of you let it go?"

"She started it."

Famine snorted. "Oh, please . . ."

"Well, you did. Okay, not *you,* but the Black Rider did."
War's eyes glittered like diamond chips, enticing and sharp.
"You had to goad her on, didn't you?"

"Enough!" Pestilence shouted. "This isn't about the two of
you!" He glared at them both. Famine, hidden within shadow,
was still, but War laughed softly, lushly.

"Listen to you, so commanding. The Conqueror in truth as
well as name. Will you lead us," the Red Rider asked, "when
the time comes for the Last Ride? Will it be your Bow lifted
high that acts as our banner, signaling the end of the world?"

As I said, the Elder sighed. *How could War not wish for the
End?*

"You know it's not like that," he said, to War and the Elder
both. "There won't be a Last Battle, no climactic explosion
with the world falling to ash in our wake." He saw it so clearly:
the end of the world, arriving on a sheet of white. "It will be so
much worse. If there's no Death, then there's no life."

"If there's no light, there's no darkness," said War. "Blah
blah."

See how casual she is about the end of everything? the Elder
asked.

She's hurt, Pestilence replied. *When Death cut her off, that
scarred her. And more: that scared her. She's lashing out in anger
and fear.*

That doesn't forgive what she says.

No, he agreed, *but it makes it understandable.*

"It's more subtle than that," he said. "It's not like if he dies,
bang, out we go. We're still here. But there won't be any new

life." He paused to let that sink in. "No babies, from any species. Once everything alive now finally dies, that's it. We're the last generation."

Silence, other than the screaming of the wind.

"Think about what that means," he said, his hands imploring. "People talk all the time about making things better today, for tomorrow. But there won't be a tomorrow, not like that."

"Even if I believed you," said Famine, "which I don't, I doubt it would be as bad as all that."

He quashed the urge to shake sense into her. "It would be the end of society. There would be no point to anything."

"It'll be nihilism," War said slowly. "People will stop thinking about things like right and wrong, won't give a damn about anyone but themselves. It'll be one huge going-out-of-business party, with no one caring about the consequences."

He couldn't tell if she was disgusted or excited, and he didn't want to know.

"Anarchy," he agreed. "Many will die in the crossfire. More will die by choice. Whoever's left will do whatever they need to do to make their lives tolerable. There won't be any such thing as law or morality. It's the end of society."

Famine shook her head. "You're wrong."

"I'm not. Even if the last generation lives to eighty, ninety, a hundred, what then? Who will take care of them? Help them as they age and weaken?"

"Scientists would come up with something," she said curtly. "A cure."

"For what? You can't cure death," said Pestilence. A memory that wasn't his, of a father kissing his daughter good night one final time, her diseased face the color of plums. "Believe me," he said gruffly. "I know."

"Cloning, then," Famine snapped. "They've done it with sheep."

"It won't work," Pestilence said. "That's what's about to happen here: the death of the future. Life won't continue, not in any form. No cloning. No cures. No innovation. No *nothing*."

"Well then, robotics. Or some other scientific marvel. People work well under pressure."

He stared into her shadowed face, and he said through gritted teeth: "It. Won't. Work."

"'This is the way the world ends,'" War murmured. "'Not with a bang but a whimper.'"

"You're crazy. Both of you." Famine shook her head. "He's not suicidal. The world isn't ending, not now, not anytime soon."

Stunned, he blurted, "Why won't you *see*? Why are you being so willfully blind?"

"Why don't you believe in him more?" she countered. "After all he's done for you, for us, how could you think so little of him?"

"It's not about *believing* in him," he shouted. "He doesn't need our belief! He needs us to stop him from doing something that affects everything forever!"

His voice echoed and was lost to the wind.

"If he really needs us," War said softly, "then he shouldn't have treated us so badly."

Pestilence glared at her. "He's not himself!"

"That makes it less true?"

"You can't hang the fate of the world on one bad thing that he did to you! Listen to you! You're acting like he did this to you out of some personal vendetta, and you," he said to Famine, "you're sticking your head in the sand and pretending everything is fine! My God," he shouted, "grow up!"

War's lip pulled up in a fierce tic, and he could see her hands trembling like a junkie's. Her urge for violence was a physical need, one he could easily sense—it radiated from her like sickness.

A moment later, a horse's scream tore through the air, and then the red steed was right there, its black eyes narrowed to slits, its ears flat against its skull as its tail swished viciously back and forth.

Pestilence stood very still.

He knows the bullying will eventually stop. High school had been hard, but since he'd started standing his ground, the attacks had come less frequently, had been far less vicious. By senior year, they were nothing more than nasty comments from people he couldn't care less about. Now, in college, he still gets the look from some people, the one that used to make him duck his head and pray he would turn invisible. And he still gets the comments, sometimes.

But he can handle it. He believes in himself far more than he ever had before. And that confidence shows. He has new friends. He has a full scholarship. He has Marianne.

He has his life. So he can ignore stupid comments by stupid people.

And for the times when he can't, Bill Ballard stands his ground.

Pestilence steeled himself, and he hoped the warhorse couldn't hear the wild beating of his heart. Or smell the sweat on his forehead. He was afraid, but that fear didn't control him.

He wasn't that person anymore.

Just as he was about to summon his Bow, the other two horses appeared, the black flanking the red, the white steed standing in front of him, blocking him. Protecting him. Though his horse wasn't brave, right now it was ready to fight for him. Neither the white steed nor black made a sound, but their intent was clear: Back the hell off.

"Call off your beast," said Famine.

"My *beast* could eat yours for lunch. Then again, there's not much meat there." War patted the red horse's haunch. "I'm fine," she said, quieter, calmer.

Not for the first time, Pestilence was struck by how gentle she could be with an animal that would gleefully rip out a person's throat. Specifically, *his* throat.

"Go back to the rats," she murmured to her steed. "Kill them all for me, would you?"

The warhorse snorted once, then launched itself in the air, looping down into the vast jungle of vegetation that made up most of the island. Only after it retreated did the other two steeds visibly relax.

For that matter, that's when Pestilence relaxed as well. War could be . . . unpredictable. And her steed could be murderous. He had been ready to stand his ground, but he preferred not to fight. He scratched the white horse in its favorite spot, right behind the ears.

"Thank you," he said. "My brave steed."

The horse blushed — or would have, if it could blush — and nickered softly.

Famine spoke similarly to the black, and then the two horses went off together to run up and down the shore. Pestilence watched the two for a moment, and he envied their ability to live in the now. No worries about the future; no past pains that lingered.

Eddie Glass, the school bully and his personal tormentor, had graduated among the last in their class. Bill has seen him exactly once since then. He'd been home for winter break, walking by the old pizzeria, and he glanced in the window to see Eddie acting like the king around a court of thug wannabes. In that one look, Bill knows everything there is to know about Eddie Glass, who was clinging desperately to high school memories while Bill himself had moved on.

Bill would pity Eddie Glass, if he bothered to think about him at all.

"You okay?" Pestilence asked War.

"I've been better," she admitted. "This is a messed-up situation. I'm a little emotional."

"And pound cake is a little fattening," muttered Famine.

War shot her a look, then sighed. "I'm sorry. My steed was just reacting to my anger. It's a good steed," she said fondly, proudly.

"They all are," Pestilence said, and then something occurred to him. "Did either of you see the pale horse when you last saw him?"

War and Famine both shook their heads.

"I think something happened with his steed," Pestilence said, remembering Death's offhand comment about needing a horse that left him to his own affairs, and that good help was hard to find. "I think he got into an argument with it."

War glanced in the direction her warhorse had gone. "You're right," she said tightly. "He needs us."

Famine stood, unmoving and impassive, saying nothing.

Pestilence wanted to scream at her, but that would just send the horses back, spoiling for a fight. And time was running out —he was sure of it. He could feel it deep inside, in the part of him that housed the spirit of the White Rider.

The end was coming.

Cold, wailed the King. *So cold.*

And it was. In the past few minutes, the temperature must have dropped by ten degrees.

"Look," Pestilence said, trying to keep his desperation in check, "if we try to help him, and it turns out that he's fine, just feeling a little grumpy, then no harm, no foul. But if we don't try to help him, and he's not fine at all, then we're doing the worst thing possible: nothing. You asked how I could think so little of him, but I can't think of anything worse than leaving him to suffer alone." He tried to read her expression, but the darkness beneath her hat gave nothing away. "Does he deserve that?"

A long pause before Famine said, "No."

He released a breath he hadn't realized he'd been holding. "Then are we agreed?" he asked, looking from one Rider to the other. "That we need to figure out how to help him? And, if needed, how to stop him?"

War smiled toothily. "You bet."

The Black Rider wrapped her arms around herself, like a straitjacket of shadow. "I don't see how. If he really wants to die, then we can't stop him."

"Bullshit," Pestilence said. "He's still alive now. That tells me he doesn't want to die, not really."

"Then maybe we should wait."

War laughed harshly. "For what? A suicide note?"

"We can't wait," Pestilence said.

"Fine," Famine said. "But what do we *do?*"

"Yes," said a cold voice from behind him. "What do you do?"

Pestilence felt the breath catch in his throat. In his head, the King screamed and the Elder cowered. He turned slowly to face Death, the Pale Rider of the Apocalypse.

FAMINE

Famine heard Death's voice just before he appeared out of no-where, tall and pale and so very angry. His long blond hair whipped about his head in a frenzy, as if the wind were trying to rip it away and reveal the skull below. The green and white striped pajamas had been replaced with a ratty sweater and jeans busted at the knees. His hands were hidden in his pock-ets, but the casual stance couldn't belie the rage that burned in his eyes like blue fire.

Her heart danced crazily in the safety of her ribcage, and she realized that she was afraid.

It's five years ago and Tammy Thompson is so afraid as she's standing over the bathroom sink. Her insides twist violently as cramps rack her body, and she's thinking that maybe, just maybe, she took too many laxatives.

But she had to, she had to, they had stopped working, they weren't helping her at all, so she had to take more and more. And now her stomach hurts, it hurts, God, it hurts and there's a weight on her chest and it's so hard to breathe and she thinks she might be dying.

This is the first time she hears his voice, like some angel from up high calling to her, asking her . . .

"Is this how you spend your free time?" Death asked, smiling a terrible smile that made her think of a piranha pondering lunch. "Talking about me behind my back? Wouldn't it be nicer if you took up a hobby? Golf, perhaps, or a nice game of chess?"

"How did you find us?" Pestilence asked. If he was afraid, it wasn't obvious. He astounded Famine, whose fear was building by the second.

Something was going to happen—she sensed it, like milk on the verge of turning. Something bad.

Death's smile stretched to inhuman proportions. "No matter what pains you take to be secluded, you can't hide from me. Wherever you go, I go as well. You could have flown to the moon, and I would have known." He shrugged. "No surprise parties for me, alas. Takes some of the fun out of life, but hey, 'fun' is only the beginning of a funeral."

A lump worked its way into Famine's throat. No matter how she swallowed, she felt as if she were choking. The rage in Death's eyes suffocated her, stole her breath.

It's so hard to breathe and she thinks she might be dying. This is the first time she hears his voice, like some angel from up high calling to her, asking her if she is ready to die.

"Because ready or not, you're dying, Tammy," he says, his voice like chocolate-covered strawberries, so sweet, so addictive.

She sees him reflected in the bathroom mirror, a tall man with long blond hair and penetrating blue eyes; she knows who, what, he truly is, and the knowledge chokes her.

"Your heart is about to go into cardiac arrest," he says, not unkindly. "Is this what you really wanted?"

She flinches from the question. She's crying and shaking and the weight on her chest has gotten heavier, like an elephant is slowly crushing her.

And he says . . .

"I've been listening to you talk." Still smiling, Death began to walk around them, circling them lazily, his bare feet leaving no footprints in the sand. "Oh ye of little faith."

His gaze seared Famine, and no matter how she tried, she couldn't look away.

"It's not like that," War blurted.

"No?" Even with the wind gusting, Famine heard Death's soft laugh. "Why don't you explain it to me?"

Pestilence replied, "We're worried about you." He sounded perfectly calm, immensely reasonable. Famine couldn't understand it; her own thoughts were a panicked mess, a tangle of present and past.

"Worried? About me? I'm flattered."

"Don't be," War seethed. "Pestilence thinks you're suicidal."

The White Rider sighed, exasperated. "Not the way I wanted to approach this . . ."

War ignored him. Glaring at the Pale Rider, she said, "I think he's right."

"Do you, now?" Death paused in his circuit, considered War and then Pestilence, measuring them both with his gaze. Then he cocked his head in Famine's direction. "What of thee, Black Rider?"

She felt herself flinch from his unforgiving blue eyes.

She flinches from the question. No, she doesn't want this. She's crying and shaking and the weight on her chest has gotten heavier, it's like an elephant is slowly crushing her.

"I know," he says, "it's painful. Hearts are fragile things, so easily broken. Yours is breaking now, Tammy. You're about to die, alone, here in the bathroom, and your sister will find you, cold on the floor." He smiles at her fondly, as if he knows her. "Your death will ruin her life. Your parents will stop talking, and their marriage will end in an acrimonious divorce. That's the thing about death—it's never just about the dying."

Guilt stabs her, or maybe that's just her stomach tearing itself to shreds. She tries to speak, but all that comes out is a whimper of pain, so she looks into his eyes and tells him silently that this is a mistake . . .

"I said he was mistaken," Famine whispered hoarsely, her eyes still trapped by Death's gaze. "He has to be mistaken. You can't be suicidal. You're . . . you," she finished lamely.

"That I am," Death agreed, inclining his head in a mocking bow. "As I've been since time began."

"You're you," Pestilence said, "but something's changed. You're not acting like yourself."

"I never *act* like myself," he replied, all winter cheer and frostbite. "I *am* myself. The only acting I do is when I put on a human face. And after so much time wearing it, the fit is rather poor."

"You're hurting," War said. "Your pain's bleeding you dry."

"We know that something's wrong. We want to help you, but we can't if you don't talk to us," said the White Rider.

Famine would have spoken, would have told them how futile their efforts were, but her tongue had turned to ash.

She tries to speak, but all that comes out is a whimper of pain, so she looks into his eyes and tells him silently that this is a mistake, that she doesn't want to die, but she can't bear to be so fat so fat *every time she looks in the mirror she despises what she sees and she just can't look anymore.*

"It's no mistake," he says. "You overdosed, and now you're dying. All those laxatives. My goodness, Tammy. I know there were times you felt that life was shit, but did your death have to be shit as well?"

Her mouth full of marbles, she says, "Please."

"Please," said Pestilence, his arms out as if to appease, "talk to us."

"And what would you have me say? Shall I tell thee of my dashed dreams, perchance?" Death slid a glance at War. "Shall I speak of lost love?"

The Red Rider's gloved hands balled into fists. "You pushed me away!"

He laughed coldly. "Whoever said I spoke of *thee?*"

War's face blanched, and then two hectic spots of red stained her cheeks. A fine tremor worked its way up her arms. She growled, "You bastard!"

"Indeed. I'm the bastard child of this world and mine, orphaned on the day I was born." He threw his arms wide, and for a moment, Famine glimpsed dark wings unfurling. "None is like me."

"Please," the White Rider implored. "Tell us what's hurt you."

"Please," she says.

"Please what?" he asks, curiosity coloring his words. "What would you have of me? A quick death? I'm afraid that's out of the question. You brought this upon yourself, Tammy Thompson. I'm happy to keep you company until you breathe your last, and from there, well, that's the great unknown, isn't it?" He laughs softly. "Is *that what you're asking? Do you seek my company? A friend at the end?"*

"We're your friends," Pestilence said. "Anything you have to say, we're here for you."

"Friends," Death repeated, rolling the word on his tongue. "My boon companions. I made thee long and long ago for this very thing: to have companionship. So tell me, my Riders: Are you my friends?"

Famine wanted to tell him that yes, she was his friend—she wouldn't leave him, wouldn't abandon him the way that she herself had been abandoned by someone she had trusted with her deepest secrets. She wanted to say all that and more, but when she opened her mouth to speak, her voice failed her.

"I want . . ." Her voice fails as another spike of pain rips her apart.

"Wouldst thou live?" he asks.

Unable to speak, she nods.

Unable to speak, Famine nodded.

"Of course we're your friends," said Pestilence. "We always have been."

War sniffed loudly. "What he said. We're here for you. Even when you're insufferable. Even when you're cold. We're here." Softer, pleading: "Please. I love you. I *love* you. Don't cut me off like this. Let me help you. Let us help you."

Famine had frequently seen War's sharp humor, as cutting and merciless as the sword she wielded. Famine had often seen War's rage. Never before had she witnessed her tenderness. The Red Rider was crying silently, tears glazing her cheeks.

If Death was moved by her appeal, Famine couldn't tell.

"You truly want to help me?" the Pale Rider asked, his voice like rotting fruit—overripe and poisonous. "Is that what you want?"

"Is that what you want?" he asks. "To live? You need to say it, Tammy."

The elephant presses its foot into her chest, and she gasps.

"Time is not your friend, I'm afraid. Say it now, if you would say it at all."

"Yes," she whispers. "I want to live."

"Yes," Famine said over the lump in her throat. "Yes, we want to help you."

Death looked at Famine, looked at all of them, his own face unreadable.

"Well then," he said slowly.

"Well then, Tammy Thompson. For thee." On the counter of the bathroom sink, a small white box appears. "Open the box, if you would live."

Hands shaking, she reaches for the package. When her fingers touch it, the box turns black as ink. She's beyond being startled, though, so she opens the box and sees a copper charm, in the shape of an old-fashioned set of scales, gleaming on a piece of black silk.

"All you have to do is take the Scales and agree to be the Black Rider. Will you do that, Tammy? Will you agree to something you don't understand and learn what it means as you go? Or will you set the box aside?"

Either way, she's going where Death will lead. So she picks the way that will let her take another taste of life.

Tammy Thompson grabs the charm, but now it's a large balance made of brass or maybe bronze, big enough for her fingers to wrap tightly around the handle at the top. And suddenly she can breathe—the elephant has fled, the pain is gone, and the whole world waits before her like a banquet. She tastes the hunger of humanity, samples it and finds it delectable.

"*Thou art Famine, the Black Rider, blight of abundance,*" he declares. "*Go thee out unto the world.*" Then, warmer: "*Rock on.*"

Feeling a new appetite awakening within her, she turns to face Death. "*What happens now?*"

"*Now you ride.*"

"Well then," Death said slowly, "it's finally time to ride."

Famine couldn't breathe.

"Oh, no . . ." That was War, her voice small and scared. "No, no, no . . ."

"The four of us?" Pestilence asked, no longer sounding confident — if War was scared, Pestilence was battling terror. "Together?"

"Together," Death agreed. "But not the four of us. It's time."

There was no dramatic speech, no grand gesture.

There was no time for goodbyes.

Something clawed into Famine, hooked into her deeply, caught the part of her that made her the Black Rider . . .

. . . and pulled.

She screamed as the Horseman was torn away in one long strip, peeled from her like wallpaper. Her screams mingled with those of the others, their voices weighing heavily in the air.

It was the last thing they did together.

With one final pull, the essence of the Black Rider tore free. She let out one final, agonized shriek, then she collapsed to the ground. She tasted sand and grit, smelled the stink of her own sweat and more.

And then the elephant pressed down on her chest.

"Oh God," a girl screamed, "oh God oh God I'm *bleeding*—"

"Help us," a boy shouted. "Please!"

She tried to speak, but the elephant muffled her voice.

From far away, a cold voice replied, "I have helped you, William. More than you know. And now it's time for me to ride."

One final wave of pain broke over her, and then Tammy Thompson was falling, even though she was already on the ground.

PART FIVE

THE BOY WITH THE CHOCOLATE

Because I could not stop for Death, He kindly stopped for me.

—Emily Dickinson

XANDER

On the night the world ended, Xander Atwood lost his brother.

He stared at the empty crib, not understanding what he was seeing—the baby had to be there; he couldn't sit up, let alone crawl, so how could he have gotten out of the crib? Panic hit him like a fastball in the chest, slamming him with a terror so complete that for three seconds, he couldn't move, couldn't breathe, couldn't think of anything other than *Come back come back you have to come back Lex come back here right now!*

Just as the horror receded enough for him to find his voice, his brain caught fire. He doubled over and let out a choked cry as he clutched his head. Agony, overwhelming and terrifying, turning his blood to shattered glass and slicing him from the inside out.

And then, a beep. On the heels of that, a small, still voice, telling him . . .

—there's a voice whispering his name and telling him to kiss them all goodbye because today's the day the world ends and he screams as the shadow reaches for him because he knows that when the shadow touches him that's the end of everything and it can't be it can't he won't let it he *won't*—

Breathe, Xander.

He gasped in a strangled breath, and—

—and he saw his baby brother, sleeping peacefully in his crib.

Xander felt panic build up inside him again, slower this time, like he was chained to the bottom of a well that was being filled with water from a garden hose: He was going to drown, and there was nothing he could do but watch and then try to hold his breath.

Breathe.

He inhaled deeply, then let it out and shook his head. Lex was right there in the crib, where he was supposed to be, where he'd been all along. His eyes had been playing tricks on him, that was all.

Feeling stupid, Xander walked out of the nursery and closed the door. Then he ran down the hallway and into his bedroom. He needed the safety, the stability, of his bedroom. His sanctuary. All he'd meant to do was grab his phone, check to see if Riley had gotten back to him and then flop onto his bed and play video games, but something caught his eye, something subtle, almost intangible, something that he couldn't quite put his finger on and yet he knew was there.

Something was different.

Frowning, he scanned his bedroom. On the walls, which were painted a steel blue that looked almost gray, his paintings from years of art classes hung in frame after frame, dotting the room with shimmering colors: proud garnets, lofty aquamarines, vibrant chartreuses, too many colors to name. Over his desk, the Escher print of ants crawling along a Möbius strip stood sentry. His parents had given that to him when he'd first become interested in art. At least, he was fairly certain that's how he'd gotten it. When had it been—ninth grade? Tenth? Last month? He couldn't remember.

Just as he couldn't remember when he'd gotten the two blue nudes.

He stared at them, the Matisse and the Picasso posters, framed side by side just over his headboard, and he swallowed thickly as he tried to convince himself those pictures had been in his room for years.

The same pictures that had been at Marcie's house, in the tiny office off the main hallway.

Xander closed his eyes and took a deep breath. It was just stress, that was all. Stress was messing with his memory, messing with his head. Keeping his real college plans secret, then waiting and waiting and waiting to hear from Stanford, and then figuring out when to tell Riley and his parents what he'd done—that had been hard, especially while still keeping his grades up. On top of that, he hadn't slept well in months, thanks to his strange dreams and his baby brother waking him up at ungodly hours of the morning.

Yes, that was it. He was stressed. That was why he was having trouble remembering some things, why his eyes had tricked him into thinking that Lex hadn't been in his crib—

(of course little Lex was in his crib his parents' baby was safe in his crib)

—and why he'd been losing time, like what had happened at Izzy's during the game and then on the car ride home with Ted —

(Izzy's voice, saying she's sort of stunned Xander was actually talking to him, and Xander asking him who, and Izzy saying)

"Enough," Xander said aloud. Because it was enough. He was just zoning out from sheer exhaustion. Xander glanced at the blue nudes and let out a rueful laugh. Do not operate heavy machinery. Do not drive while under the influence.

A sound, like a screech of tires.

No, there was no sound, not like that. Certainly not thirty stories up, deep in the bowels of his bedroom. He was just hearing things. That happened to his mom a lot—she'd swear the baby was crying, even when Lex was fast asleep.

"Just sleep deprivation," his dad would say, and then his mom would smack his dad upside the head, because that man could sleep through anything.

Just sleep deprivation.

Just stress.

Xander glanced at his desk, where his phone rested on top of his open sketchbook—the picture in progress, showing four horses and the end of the world. He checked, but Riley still hadn't gotten back to him. Xander tucked his phone into his pocket and stared at the four horses—no, at the three horses and the one horse that was not a horse, for a man who was not a man—and then he ran his fingers through his hair, pushing it away from his face. He really needed some sleep. Then maybe he'd stop hearing things.

Because right now he was positive he was hearing music.

He cocked his head and listened. Yes, there it was: A snatch of music rode the air, leaving behind an impression of sadness and resignation.

Frowning, Xander walked out of his room and down the hallway, following the sound as he headed toward the living room. It was a guitar's distinctive strumming that he heard; the music was a slow, sad tune that he knew well — one of his favorites, from his favorite album, a song that never failed to pull at his heart.

In the living room, the door to the balcony was wide open.

On the balcony, a guitarist was leaning against the railing, not minding how the wind was tugging at his long blond hair and grabbing the ends of his baggy sweater, not minding how easy it would be to topple over that railing and fall thirty stories and end in a smear on the street.

Air whooshed out of Xander as he watched Death play the guitar.

Real. Everything from before had been real.

Death was here because he owed Xander a boon, and then he was going to kill himself and take the world with him.

As if he'd been waiting for an audience, Death began to sing. His voice was haunting and completely familiar — and not just because he was a dead ringer for Kurt Cobain.

Xander finally remembered.

DEATH

The boy finally remembered — part of it, anyway. It was a start. The rest would come, and soon; once the first memory slid into place, the rest tended to follow quickly.

Especially when there was a little mood music.

Smiling, he continued to play the guitar.

XANDER

Xander Atwood was six years old the first time he met Death.

He'd been stuck in the lobby of his mom's tennis club, waiting for her to finish her lesson, and he was bored silly because there was no one else around. So he decided to build a fort using the cushions from the sofa. That's how he found a treasure trove of three quarters and five nickels—more than enough for him to hit the vending machine. He bought two chocolate bars and returned to the waiting area to eat his snack.

This time, he wasn't alone: a blond-haired man was sitting on the sofa, strumming a guitar and singing quietly. When he noticed Xander, he winked.

"You play good," Xander said.

"Thanks."

"You sing good, too, but not as good as you play the guitar."

The musician grinned. "Music comes first and lyrics come second, or so I've heard."

"What're lyrics?"

"Words that make up a song."

"Oh."

The blond man kept strumming the guitar, and he starting singing again. Xander listened. He felt like the musician was telling a story with the song, but Xander didn't understand what the story was about. The man kept singing that something was in the *way, but he never said what the something was. Even so, listening to the song made Xander feel sad enough to cry.*

When the guitarist stopped playing, Xander somberly offered him one of his two chocolate bars.

The man smiled at him. "What's this for?"

Xander tried to express himself properly—the song had made him ache inside, like he'd lost his favorite toy or maybe even like his parents were never going to come home again and he was all alone forever—but he didn't have the words. So he shrugged and said, "You played good."

The musician's blue eyes glinted. It made Xander think he was laughing without making a sound.

"Thanks." The man accepted the candy. "A sweet gift from the boy with the chocolate."

"Will you play more?"

"Another time." Still smiling, the musician placed the guitar inside its case, then put the chocolate bar on top of the guitar. "I've got to get back to work."

Xander frowned. "You don't work here?"

"At the moment, I do."

Just then, a cluster of people ran through the lobby and raced to the tennis courts. Xander couldn't read all the words on their jackets, but he recognized the snake-and-staff symbol on their patches. They were 911 doctors.

"Thanks again for the chocolate," said the blond man as he closed his guitar case.

"Are you gonna be back here?" Xander asked.

"Oh, sure."

"So maybe I'll see you."

"I'm sure you will," Death said with a smile. Whistling, he picked up his guitar case and ambled over to the tennis courts.

Xander watched him go, then went back to making a fort out of the sofa cushions.

Three minutes later, the 911 doctors charged through the lobby again, this time pushing a table with wheels. An old woman was strapped to the table, and there was a mask covering her nose and mouth. Xander watched the group rush out the front door of the tennis club.

The guitarist didn't return.

Soon, Xander's mother was ushering him out the door, babbling about life and death and the natural cycle and wouldn't he like some ice cream?

Ice cream, surely. But not chocolate. That was the day Xander Atwood stopped eating chocolate, even though he couldn't tell you why.

He'd just lost his taste for it.

On the tennis court, he finished his work (Drea LuPone, 67, massive stroke) and wondered what to do about the boy with the chocolate.

Next to him, the pale steed snorted. "Either correct the course or let him live. Just please do a steed a solid and stop obsessing."

"I don't obsess," he murmured. "I ponder."

"You say tomato . . ."

"Hush. I'm pondering."

"You're obsessing. You stayed in the lobby just to talk to him, when instead you could have been down here working."

"What? I let Drea live a few minutes more than she otherwise would have. She appreciated it; she was quite the competitor."

"Don't you win by default when you die on the court?"

"Only if you get the point."

"So you met him. Talked to him. Have you decided to correct the course?"

"Nope."

"Nope, you haven't decided, or nope, you're not going to course-correct?"

He grinned and patted his steed. "Come on —there's a world of people who are waiting to die."

The pale horse sighed. "You think you're being mysterious, but you're really just a slacker."

"You say tomato . . ."

Xander remembered meeting Death all those years ago at his mother's tennis club, remembered listening to him play the guitar and then giving him a chocolate bar. Was that how all of this had started? With something as innocent as a gift given freely?

Could a single act have such repercussions?

(none saw me)

Xander almost had it. For just a moment, he saw not the human façade but the truth taking flight, a glimpse of wings beating against the sky. He thought he could hear, somewhere beneath the music, the sound of a beep—a steady rhythm, a backbeat to the melody of the guitar, to the harmony of Death's voice.

"I formulate infinity," Death sang, "stored deep inside of me."

Xander felt like he was standing on the precipice of something huge, like his feet were dangling over the edge of the Grand Canyon. All he had to do was take that proverbial leap of faith, and then he'd see the truth. Or he'd plummet to his death.

It was a long, long way to fall. He stepped back from the edge and focused on the song.

Death's long fingers moved deftly across the guitar, making

music as if that was what he'd been born to do. Though Xander
had long known the lyrics to "Oh Me," this time he heard a
poignancy to the words that he hadn't been able to appreciate
until this moment.

When the song ended, he waited until the last chords were
lost to the wind, and then he said, "You still play well."

"It's not me, you know. It's the form I'm using. He was a
musician, a singer."

"I'm aware," Xander said dryly.

"It's his talent, not mine. I have no such ability. My kind
don't have things like music or song," said Death, removing the
strap from around his shoulders. "But when I take the form of
the dead, I can use their abilities."

"It's pretty cool."

"It's an echo," he said, shrugging. "Nothing more."

"Well, your echoes rock. Your singing's gotten better."

"It's the same," Death said. "That doesn't change. I don't
change."

"Everything changes."

"Not me," the Pale Rider said as he placed the guitar on the
balcony floor. "Never me."

"Of course you change. I just said that your singing got better."

Death smiled. "That's just your perception. Subjective reality, remember?"

"Sure, I remember," Xander said. "This is the part where
you ask me if I'm willing to take a chance that this is all in my
head, right? Well, don't bother."

Beneath his tangle of windswept hair, Death's eyes gleamed.
"But wouldn't that prove, once and for all, that none of this is

real? What if my death is the act that pierces the veil covering your eyes?"

"How noble," Xander said, folding his arms across his chest. "Listen to you, making your death out to be some incredible sacrifice. Is that what you want? To be the sacrificial hero of the story?"

"You called me a hero earlier, after accusing me of bravery."

Xander felt his cheeks heat. "Yeah, well, you called yourself a fool."

"And so I am. But we're all the heroes of our own stories," Death said cheerfully. "Even when we're also fools."

"But this isn't a story. This is life. It's *your* life."

"The life of Death," the Pale Rider boomed, sweeping his arm wide. Ted would have appreciated both the bombastic voice and the grand gesture. Hell, Ted would have taken notes. Death chuckled. "There's a sort of symmetry there, don't you think?"

"Yeah," Xander said, "and it's bookended nicely with the death of life. Which is what you said would happen when you die."

"No, Xander. That's what *you* said would happen. And I said that was one way of looking at it."

"You're mincing words," Xander gritted.

"Am I, now? I've been told that I'd make an excellent lawyer."

Xander frowned at him, at those twinkling blue eyes and that casual smirk that made him see red. *This isn't about me,* he told himself. *Don't get angry with him. He's hurting, and he's lashing out.*

That's what people do when they're hurting.

"But I'm not a person," said Death.

Xander blinked at him, then blinked again. "Mind reading's rude."

"Can't help it. You're a screamer."

"Excuse me?"

"Your thoughts. You don't just think them. You scream them. Your thoughts are so big, so loud, they fill the world." Death made a show of tugging his ear. "Kind of deafening."

"I'll stop screaming my thoughts if you stay out of my head."

"Don't make promises you can't keep."

Nonplussed, Xander said, "I'll try to stop screaming my thoughts."

"I can work with that," Death said. He glanced at his watch. "For a little bit, anyway. Four minutes left, Xander."

Four minutes to convince Death not to kill himself. Four minutes to save the world. If time mattered. Which it might —there was no way to know, not until it was too late.

"Then tell me the rest of it," Xander said, trying not to panic. He'd think of something. He had to. "Finish the boon. What made you come to my balcony tonight?"

"You already know the answer: the chocolate bar. You gave me a gift, so I owed you a gift price."

"Yeah," Xander said. "About that. You said that people can't see you, not unless you want to be seen. But I saw you, back when I was a kid. Why did you let me see you?"

Death looked immensely pleased. "What do *you* think?"

Suddenly uneasy, Xander darted his gaze away. "I don't know."

"Don't you?"

Xander shook his head. He didn't know, and now he didn't

want to know. He was standing on the edge again, and he felt himself losing his balance. He shut his eyes tight.

Death said, "I was there in the tennis club to correct the course."

Xander didn't want to ask.

Xander had to ask.

He whispered, "What does that mean?"

He could hear the smile in Death's voice as he replied, "It means you died, Xander."

Xander Atwood died when he was nine months old.

He'd been feverish, so his mother put him into a tepid bath to help cool him. After the bath, she towel dried Xander and set him down on the floor so that she could get him diapered. When he didn't move at all, she knew something was wrong.

When he didn't respond to her touch, she started to scream.

Xander's father raced in, told her to call 911, and then gave the baby mouth-to-mouth. By the time the paramedics arrived, Xander was breathing fine.

Tests revealed absolutely nothing: Xander had simply stopped breathing. It had been the longest sixty seconds of his parents' lives.

For the next two months, his mom and dad slept in his bedroom, on the floor, terrified that the baby would stop breathing again and they wouldn't hear it.

By the time Xander was thirteen months old, his parents were both back in their own bed, but they kept their door wide open—a habit they didn't break for many years. That habit would come back to bite them when Xander was ten and he walked in on them having sex, but that was far in the future. For now, it comforted them to know that if something was wrong, they would hear it.

They never found out why Xander had died that day.

And when something wound up being very wrong, they didn't hear a thing . . . not until it was far too late.

DEATH

Every second of every day, 1.7 people die. That's the average. Some-times, more than one person dies at once; other times, it's just one person.

The second that Xander Atwood died as a baby, it was one of those "just one person" times.

During that particular second, Death was a little busy.

Time isn't linear for one such as Death, not unless he chooses to let it be so. Every moment is an eon; every second is an eternity. It's part of what allows him to do what he does. It also makes it un-fathomable when one such as Death is in pain. Mortals can com-fort themselves by saying the pain will pass—it only feels like forever. But for creatures such as Death, that agony literally is for-ever.

Dying takes a little longer.

It's a door slamming shut, the resonant thunder booming until it dwarfs all other sound. Deafened, he feels himself falling.

There's a moment of panic, as always, a moment that stretches into infinity in which he's terrified that this is all there is, that oblivion will grip him like a lover and rock him into nothingness. In that moment, he clings desperately to the He Who Was. He wants to hold on. He wants to be.

He knows what he must do, and the knowledge crushes him. The holding on isn't nearly as agonizing as the letting go.

He lets go.

The pain swallows him as he is erased. It takes one second and it lasts until the stars explode and the universe spirals into the void.

And then, he is rewritten.

Reborn.

He reaches out, and the universe takes his hand and anchors him. He Who Was is now He Who Is.

The first new breath is searing; the second, less so. By the third, it's simply routine.

It's simply life.

The moment transforms from present to past—a tense shift, a time shift, and then he returned to the here and now. He opened his eyes—new eyes, but still blue, always blue—and the first thing he saw was the pale steed.

"Well," he said, and "well" again, fascinated by the sound of his new voice. "Well, that part's done."

"Groovy," said the steed. "Buy a horse a cheeseburger?"

XANDER

Xander didn't feel his legs give out. One second, he was standing in the doorway between his living room and the balcony; the next, he was on the ground, his back against the door frame, his legs splayed out in front of him.

He'd died.

He saw it in his mind, clear as HDTV: him as a baby, lying naked on his nursery floor, not breathing, his mother screaming, his father performing mouth-to-mouth.

He could feel borrowed air inflating his lungs, feel it hissing out like a busted tire.

A sound like a screech of tires . . .

"No," he whispered.

"Yes."

He blinked up at Death, who was still sitting easily on the balcony railing, his elbows propped on his knees, his chin in his hands.

"You were nine months old, and you died. No official cause," said Death, "though my money's on SIDS, and it was only for a minute. But you were dead, Xander Atwood."

"Then—" Xander's voice cracked, and he worked some moisture into his throat and swallowed before he tried again. "Then why am I still here?"

"What you mean to ask is why didn't I take you at that

moment." Death shrugged. "You happened to die at an inopportune time."

The world had shifted five degrees to the left when Xander hadn't been looking. Dizzy, he repeated, "Inopportune."

"I was in the throes of my cycle beginning anew."

Xander tried to make sense of the words, but his head was spinning and his heart was screaming and things like logic and rationality had taken a back seat the moment Death had appeared on his balcony. "So . . . I got a second chance because you were busy?"

"You could say that. The second you died, I didn't exist."

He blinked, and blinked again, and all he could say was, "Oh."

"As I said, it was an inopportune time." Another shrug. "You sort of slipped off my radar. When I figured out what had happened, I put you on my to-do list."

Realization dawned. It was less a light bulb turning on than it was a neon spotlight in Xander's brain.

"Correcting the course," he said. "You were at the tennis club that day to kill me, because I was supposed to be dead. Right? That *is* what you meant," Xander said, his voice rising, "isn't it?"

"So dramatic." Death clucked his tongue. "Not like you hadn't already died. Well. For a little bit. Yes, that's exactly what I meant, well done. Gold star for you."

"But you didn't kill me."

"No."

"Because . . . I gave you a chocolate bar?"

Death's mouth quirked into a lopsided smile. "I was moved."

"My life was saved by a chocolate bar."

"Of course not," Death said. "You were kind to me. That's what led me here today: your act of kindness. The chocolate was just a bonus."

If Suzie were with him, she would have said that chocolate was *always* a bonus.

Xander looked up at the Pale Rider, who was looking back at him pointedly, as if he were waiting for something. Behind those blue, blue eyes, Xander saw emotions sparkling like crystals catching the light—a wink of compassion, a glittering of gratitude. But more than anything, he saw exhaustion staring back at him and, beneath that, a hint of fear.

Death was afraid. Xander would have bet his life on it. Which, Xander supposed, was appropriate when one trafficked with Death.

The Pale Rider was afraid to die.

And that meant Xander could save him. He just had to figure out how.

He cleared his throat. "Thanks," he said, and then immediately felt sheepish, because the word was nowhere near enough. "For, you know. Not correcting the course."

A shrug. *"De nada."*

"It's not nothing," Xander said. "It matters. Life matters. You matter."

Death rolled his eyes. "Here we go again . . ."

"If life didn't matter," Xander said, louder, "then death wouldn't be a big deal. But it is. You are. Don't you see that?"

Another shrug.

Okay, Xander told himself as he climbed to his feet. Time to backtrack. "What happened?" he asked. "You were lonely, so you created companions, first your steed and then the

Horsemen. And they helped, you said. For a time, at least. They helped. But something must have happened. When did they stop helping?"

Death smiled thinly. "It might have been around the time when they were talking about how to stop me."

"Is that where you went before, when you popped out of here? To talk to them?"

"No. I went to kill them."

Xander spluttered, *"What?"*

"I went to kill them."

"You *killed* the Horsemen of the Apocalypse?"

"The steeds too. Really, it's not such a big deal. I am Death, after all. Besides, it's not like I murdered them. I just took back what was mine. More whole again, for the first time in thousands of years." He spread his arms wide and glanced down at his billowing sweater. "Does it look like I've put on weight?"

Xander had only thought his head had been spinning before. Nauseated, he said, "You really killed them all?"

"Technically." Death lowered his arms. "I reabsorbed the parts of them that made them Riders. So yes, I killed the Horsemen. The human parts were theirs, so those remained."

"The people who had been Riders—they're still alive?"

"For now." He glanced at his watch. "Ticktock, Xander."

"You didn't kill them," Xander said, his heart racing. "You could have, but you didn't."

Death shrugged. "Not a big deal."

"It is. You care about them," Xander said. "You love them."

"Love," Death repeated, turning the word into something profane. "You humans are so quick to use that word, as if saying it makes it so."

"Saying it, no. Feeling it, believing in it, yes. Love makes us do amazing things."

"Love makes you do stupid things."

"That, too, sometimes." Xander thought of the Amazingly Perfect Riley Jones, the one for whom he'd changed his future, and for a second he thought he heard Suzie yelling at him to wake up already. "Love can mean everything."

"Love can cause more pain than you ever imagined."

A sound like a door slamming shut, or maybe a screech of tires.

Quietly, Xander said, "And love can make that pain bearable."

Death laughed softly. "How romantic. Now who's the hero of the story, Xander? Does true love solve everything? Does love really mean a happily ever after?"

"It can," Xander insisted.

"Just because you love someone," said Death, "that doesn't mean you're loved in return. And even if you are, that doesn't mean the one you love will always be with you. Your love can leave you, abandon you, and then all you have left are pieces so jagged they slice you when you try to grasp them."

For the first time in years, Xander suddenly, vividly, remembered his first love, and he shuddered because Death was right: Being in love was no guarantee of happiness.

Ashley Davidson had taught him that lesson long ago.

XANDER

Some people say that love and death are connected. Xander got to experience both when he was twelve.

He fell madly, completely in love with Ashley Davidson the first time he saw Ashley smile. He would spend hours thinking about Ashley's eyes, the way they were so black that they looked almost blue. In his seat in the back of the classroom, he would quietly dance to the music of Ashley's voice. He'd cast surreptitious glances toward Ashley during PE, trying not to look at Ashley's legs but not being able to help himself. He wrote Ashley's name again and again, whispered it to himself at night. Thinking of Ashley made Xander's heart do amazing gymnastic feats in his chest. It didn't matter that he lacked the courage to tell Ashley how he felt: His love for Ashley transcended words. He was content.

And then Ashley died.

Everyone had known that Ashley had been sick, the sort of sick that adults talk about in hushed tones even when they think the children are out of earshot. Everyone had known that Ashley didn't choose to be bald but instead had to be because of the chemo. Instead of complaining about it, Ashley turned it into a fashion statement and wore brightly colored bandanas, a different one every day. That had been fourth grade. In fifth grade, Ashley traded bandanas for hats: large-brimmed ones, bowlers, baseball caps, cowboy hats, floppy hats, even an Abraham Lincoln stovepipe hat. But in sixth grade, Ashley had made it to school only one day, the first day of class. Xander remembered someone teasing Ashley for daring to bring in a classroom snack the way that the elementary school kids did. Ashley had blushed, and had looked so tired, and Xander wanted to say something funny to make Ashley smile that radiant smile again, but he couldn't think of the words. So he said nothing to Ashley that first day of middle school.

And he never saw Ashley again.

It wasn't quick. Everyone knew that the cancer had come back, and many people even knew the name of the specific disease, but Xander refused to learn it. If he didn't acknowledge the illness, it didn't really exist. Ashley would return one day, healthy and happy, and Xander would once again be content to steal a glance and hold a song in his heart. But then September became October, and October led to November, and still Ashley didn't return.

The day before winter break, he got a phone call from his friend Teddy. And that's when he found out that Christmas had been canceled for Ashley. Permanently.

Xander stopped eating because his chest felt too hollow.

He got a new iPod for Christmas, as well as a prescription for Lexapro.

Soon he was eating regularly again, and his psychiatrist got him to start drawing as a way to get his feelings out. He made it through winter break in a haze of video games, medication, and sketchbooks.

At the end of the school year, a tree-planting ceremony was held in Ashley's honor. Xander stared at the sapling and tried to picture Ashley's face, but all he saw was a baby tree.

The lesson of Ashley Davidson would stay with him forever: Just because you love someone, that doesn't mean they won't leave you stranded.

Loving someone exposed your heart and left you ripe for disease.

Loving someone ate away at you until you were a husk, starving for even a sip of affection.

Loving someone cut you to pieces.

In the end, loving someone completely could be the death of you.

Xander knew this implicitly. And yet, years later, he still fell madly in love with Riley Jones.

And that was the beginning of the end.

DEATH

He couldn't love, not really. That's a human emotion, and though he was many things, he wasn't human. That's what he told himself the first time he gazed upon War seated atop her steed, and he felt something deep inside of him shift, subtle yet tangible—a connection that he couldn't deny.

He wouldn't love, he told himself as the girl who had been Creusa stained the world in red. Love was a feeling he hadn't experienced since the door had slammed shut behind him. Love wasn't for one such as he.

He couldn't love her, he said gently after War moved to kiss him for the first time. Her lips parted in a wicked smile and she said she didn't need love, not when she had passion, and then her lips were on his and her heat thawed him. Not love, no, but something hotter.

It wasn't love, he realized as he watched War and Famine snipe at each other in the way that sisters do. Each Horseman had been formed around a piece of himself, and War had sprung from the piece that contained a memory, a feeling, of another—a still, small voice that could move stars. Not love, but the memory of love. An echo, false and, ultimately, doomed to fade.

It was an impression of love, he decided as he witnessed the first murder among the Horsemen. The Black Rider had taunted the Red, had told her that while Famine and Pestilence were forces that happened to people, War was dependent on people for her existence. "You need them," Famine had said sweetly. "For all that you rage, you need them. You despise that about them, and about yourself. You're starved for attention." She smiled, then, and let out a ripe laugh. And that's when War split her apart like rotten fruit —the first act of destruction between Red and Black, which would play itself out in various ways over the millennia. Yes, an impression of love, Death thought as he walked over to the fallen Black Rider, and that was right, because mortals were so very impressionable.

It wasn't love, he told himself when the girl who had been Creusa eventually died. He bound the essence of War into the idea of a sword, and he wrapped it in red cloth and sealed it in the Slate. It was a slice of affection and, at times, a cut of passion.

And yet, when he offered the Sword to another, he again felt that connection, that hint of memory, that whisper of a feeling that once had meant so much to him.

He returned to the Slate, where he searched through the tomorrows until he found the one that sated him, made him whole, and there in the midst of everything and nothing, he made his peace.

There would be a time when the one he waited for would find him. Until then, he had echoes and memories—and a Horseman who claimed to love him until the skies blackened and the seas boiled.

It wasn't love. But it would do.

For now.

Xander remembered Ashley Davidson, and he bit his lip as he felt that loss so completely, so overwhelmingly. It was like he was twelve all over again and he'd just gotten the news. He'd lived for Ashley's smile, and that had been stolen from him by a cancer whose name he'd never learned.

"It doesn't matter," said Death.

Xander blinked and looked at the Pale Rider, who was still perched whimsically atop the balcony railing, his long blond hair flying crazily in the wind. "What doesn't matter?"

"Even if you do find love," said Death, "so what? In the end, it doesn't matter. Everyone leaves you."

"No," Xander said, denying Death's words but thinking of Ashley Davidson, remembering how hollow he'd felt when Ashley died, as if part of him had been scooped out and would never be filled again.

"They do, every single one. No exceptions to the rule, Xander. They say they'll be with you forever, but they're lying, either to you or to themselves."

Now Xander wasn't thinking of Ashley Davidson but of Riley Jones—that laugh, that smile, those kissable lips.

He suddenly, desperately, needed to know if Riley had texted him back.

"At best," Death said, "people die and leave you behind. At

worst, people leave you long before they die or even take a step out the door. Either way, the result is the same."

Xander whispered, "No," but the sound was lost as an image bloomed in his mind: Riley standing on the back deck at Marcie's house, black braided hair streaming in the wind like some pirate's banner, dark eyes fixed on him, and what Xander saw in those eyes made his skin crawl and his stomach knot and suddenly he was afraid—no, more than afraid, he was terrified because it all had come to this . . .

A beep shattered the image, the sound disembodied, overwhelming. Xander, so grateful that the false vision was gone, didn't wonder where the beep had come from; if he felt a ghost squeeze his hand, he discounted it as a trick of the wind.

He breathed in; he breathed out.

"Everyone leaves you," Death said, "and you die alone."

"No," Xander said again, louder, as he remembered that this wasn't about him and Riley, wasn't about him at all. "The people you love don't just stop caring."

"Of course they do. Something else always comes along. You're like magpies, always looking for the next bright and shiny thing."

"That's not true," Xander said.

"Really?" Death smiled coldly. "You think you know? You don't. I've been around, Xander, and I've literally seen it all. People make promises and give assurances, but those are just words. And the thing about words is they're easy to ignore, and far easier to break. You people have littered the world with broken promises."

Xander is at Marcie's party, and for a moment he thinks he sees something, something horrible, but no, it's just Ted and Riley—

"Not everyone is like that," Xander insisted. "There are good people out there, friends who always have your back. When they promise something, you can believe them. You can trust them."

"Trust?" Death's shoulders bobbed with silent laughter. "Trust is even easier to break than a promise. Trust always gets broken. It's a rite of passage. That was the first lesson I learned here, when the life I'd come to save leeched itself onto me and drained me dry. Pay attention, class. Life means betrayal."

Xander tried to speak, but there was a lump in his throat and all he could think of was how he wasn't thinking about what he absolutely hadn't seen at Marcie's party.

It didn't happen. Seeing was believing, and he hadn't seen it. It didn't happen.

"It's not anyone's fault," said Death. "It's part of who you are. At a cellular level, you're all programmed to do what you need to do to survive. And that means when the time comes, you'll lie, you'll cheat, you'll steal, you'll do anything you need to do in order to survive. But don't take it personally. It's only human."

"That's not true," Xander insisted. "It's not just about survival. It's how we *live.* And we don't live alone," he said, his voice rising. "We find people we care about, people we *trust,*" he said, shouting now, "ones who're *there* for us and *help* us and *make it all worthwhile!*"

His words echoed until they were lost to the wind.

"You throw trust at me like a weapon," said Death, "thinking you're striking me with some profound truth. But in the end, trust exists only until it's not needed. And then it breaks as quickly as a person's spirit."

They stared at each other, Xander breathing heavily and Death not breathing at all.

"What happened to you?" Xander asked softly. "What hurt you so badly that it shattered your trust?"

Silence, thick and suffocating.

"What brought you to my balcony?" Xander asked, more urgent now, feeling in his gut that this was the heart of the matter and it was now or never, baby, now or never. "Something must have happened, something big enough that it made you want to kill yourself. Something changed."

A muscle worked along Death's jaw, but he didn't answer.

"Finish the boon," Xander demanded. "What changed?"

When Death finally replied, his voice was empty and bleak, and he didn't meet Xander's gaze.

"I told you of the Slate," he said, "how it had become my sanctuary, the one place to which I could retreat and rest."

Xander nodded, but Death wasn't looking at him. In a monotone, the Pale Rider continued.

"I told you how there, in the heart of the Slate, I could see all yesterdays and tomorrows, how I could entertain myself forever by remembering the past and observing possible futures, then step back into my role here, refreshed, ready to continue my work." Quieter now, as if confiding a secret. "I told you of the one thing for which I was waiting, the one tomorrow out of all possible tomorrows that meant everything to me. I told you of that glimpse of my other, there in the distance, beckoning to me."

Silently, Xander waited.

"I told you how that and that alone had been enough to keep me chained here, cycle after cycle, giving everything that

I am to something that had been taking advantage of me for so long that my presence had simply become a given. I told you all of this."

"Yes," Xander said quietly.

"What changed, you asked." Death turned to face him, to stare at him with those haunted, empty eyes. "My tomorrow changed, Xander Atwood. My future, the only future that mattered, was erased."

Death's voice was so very flat, but its absence of emotion made it all the more difficult for Xander to hear.

"My hope," said Death, "my very reason for being, was suddenly gone. The one you called my soulmate will never come through this side of the door. My waiting has all been in vain. That *maybe* will never be."

Xander's mouth went dry. The thought of him being without Riley during four years of college had been enough to make him gamble his entire future; he couldn't begin to imagine waiting for thousands and thousands of years just for a possibility. He rasped, "How do you know?"

"I looked," Death said. "I checked and rechecked all the possibilities, from the most obvious all the way to the barest hint of a maybe. And it wasn't there. It wasn't there," he said again, sounding lost.

"When was this?"

Death shrugged, one-shouldered. "Recently. Today, yesterday, last week—does it matter? It happened. I returned from the Slate and for a time, I wandered. It was my steed that made me aware I had been blighting the land in my wake. And I killed the dolphins. That was a mistake, but it didn't matter. Nothing matters, not anymore. The Slate showed me that."

"It showed you a future you didn't like," Xander said, treading carefully. "That doesn't mean that nothing matters."

"It means exactly that," Death said. "I've been either banished or abandoned, and either way, I've been forgotten." Quieter now, and filled with a subtle poison: "My vigil here has been for naught. My soulmate is gone forever."

"Are you sure?"

"*How do I know? When was this? Am I sure?* Your questions grow tiresome," Death said coldly, sitting up straight on the railing, wearing his costume of a blond man in a baggy sweater and ripped jeans, looking completely inhuman. "The Slate showed me the truth of things."

"But—"

"You asked, I answered. The boon is done."

Panic welled up in Xander, squeezing his bowels, his chest, his throat until he thought he was going to vomit his fear all over Death's bare feet. The Pale Rider was about to take his final ride, off the balcony and down thirty stories.

Time had officially run out.

(dolphins)

"Wait, I don't understand," Xander said quickly. "How could an entire future just not be there anymore?"

"Something happened, something irrevocable, something that affected this particular future." Death's eyes glittered darkly. "I could scour all paths of all the yesterdays and determine exactly what it was that changed everything for me, but why bother? Knowing changes nothing. A butterfly flapped its wings and my world crumbled. My other is gone. All I've done has been pointless."

"Of course it hasn't," Xander said, trying to stay calm. How

could he get through to Death? "Your presence here has affected billions and billions of lives. That's not pointless. You let
us live."

"I should have let you die."

"But you didn't."

"I didn't," Death agreed. "And that cost me everything."

"It cost you, yes, but look what it gave you." Xander moved,
lunging across the balcony and grabbing the acoustic guitar.
He held it up by its neck, an offering to an angry god. "It gave
you music."

Death's nostrils flared. "It made me a thief."

"It gave you music," Xander said again. "Call yourself a thief
if you want, but that doesn't change that it's *you* taking the
guitar and strumming the strings. It's *your* voice raised in song.
It's you."

"It's pointless. Everything here is pointless."

"But it's not," Xander insisted. "When you were telling me
about what it was that drew you here in the first place, you kept
talking about our creativity. Our heat, you called it. You said it
was fascinating to watch. The wheel. Stupidly high buildings.
Chocolate. Music. It's all because of you."

"I didn't make those things."

"You being here let us make those things, and so much
more. Don't you see?" Xander said, imploring. "Everything we
do here is because you've kept the spark alive. We're alive because of you. It's the most amazing gift anyone, anything, could
ever have. And we celebrate that gift every time we make something. Every time we create, that's because of you." He offered
Death the guitar. "We make music because of you."

The Pale Rider didn't move to take the instrument.

"Look at everything we've done in the past hundred years," Xander said. "No, in the past fifty years—the past *five* years. Look at the songs we've written, the music we make and listen to on the radio, in concert, on television, on the Internet, on our iPods. Don't you want to see what happens next?"

Death sighed. "Yes. But I'm tired, Xander. I'm tired, and I know the pain that's to come, and the thought of it is unbearable. The only thing that's buoyed me was the knowledge that there would be a time when, finally, I wouldn't be alone. But that time will never come. I'm done, Xander. It's time for me to ride."

(the dolphins)

"Please," Xander said, lowering the guitar. "Don't do this."

"Your concern is touching, but it's also self-serving. You care only because of the Möbius strip." Death smiled tightly. "Survival, Xander. You'll do whatever it is you need to do, even if that means wasting your time with me."

"It's not a waste!"

"You take my words and twist them, put meaning into them until they're nice and pretty, then give them back to me wrapped in a bow. It's so human."

"Listen to me," Xander said urgently. "Talking to you, spending time with you, that isn't a waste. You *matter*. Not just because of what your job is, what you've been roped into doing for thousands of years. You matter because life matters."

"I'm not alive."

"Of course you are. Maybe not in the same way as me, but you're alive. You're here. You're part of everything. And that's literal, in your case. I understand that you're in pain," Xander said, more gently now, "that you've been hurt worse than I could ever begin to imagine, that you believe the one thing that made everything worth it is gone. But how you're feeling now, that's not forever. Maybe it feels like it is, but it's not."

"How do you know what's forever and what's not, Xander Atwood? Have you watched the centuries flow and ebb?"

"No," Xander admitted.

"Then don't presume to tell me what forever feels like."

(the dolphins were a mistake)

Something nagged at Xander—a thought, an idea, but he didn't quite have it. He tried a different tack. "Maybe what you need is to step away for a bit, get your head clear. Get another perspective, you know? Everyone needs a mental health break every once in a while."

The Pale Rider chuckled and shook his head. "*Death Takes a Holiday*, you mean? Where would I go, Xander? Where could I possibly go that life wouldn't leech on to me?"

"The Slate—"

"Has shown me how futile everything is. Why would I go there?"

(the dolphins were a mistake he made a *mistake*)

"Because maybe you made a mistake," Xander said breathlessly.

Death grew still.

"Maybe you saw something in the Slate that wasn't really there," Xander said, his words coming in a rush. "Or maybe something was there that you just didn't see. A trick of your eyes. Stress. Sunspots. Whatever you want to call it. Maybe you made a mistake!"

"I don't make mistakes."

"Of course you do. It happens to everyone."

"Not to me."

"No? Why don't you ask the dolphins?"

Death blinked.

Xander saw a world of meaning in that blink, everything from surprise to disbelief to anger. Whatever else the blink meant, it proved one thing: Xander's words were having an impact.

Death was listening to him.

"What if you're wrong?" Xander asked, keeping his excitement in check. "What if that hint of *maybe* is still there, and you just didn't see it? What if there still is a tomorrow where your soulmate finally joins you?"

"I looked," Death said tonelessly. "I looked again and again. That future is gone."

"But what if another one took its place? Maybe that specific possibility is gone, but what if now there's another one, somewhere, where your soulmate finds you? Maybe in that one, the door opens again."

Death frowned.

"You said your kind has made other realities," Xander said. "Maybe your soulmate has just been searching in the wrong ones. Maybe you'll figure out how to send up a smoke signal. Maybe one of the others of your people will find you. Maybe you'll find them. Maybe humanity will help you get a message to your soulmate. Maybe *lots* of things. There are so many maybes, I don't know how you ever could have seen them all. But I'll tell you one thing I do know: If you check out now, none of those maybes will ever happen."

Something flashed behind the Pale Rider's eyes, a thought too quick for Xander to follow.

This was it—Xander knew it, felt it in his gut. This was the moment where Death's hope was either renewed or completely obliterated, and it all came down to how much Death was willing to believe.

He had to convince the Pale Rider to take a leap of faith.

He had to show Death that he was more human than he realized.

"Can't you at least admit that it's possible?" Xander implored. "That maybe, just maybe, you were so set on seeing that one specific future that it might have changed and you missed it? That there's still a chance your soulmate and you will be together again?"

A long pause as the Pale Rider considered and the world hung on a thread.

And then Death said, "It's possible."

Xander wanted to cheer. Instead, he calmly replied, "The only way for that future to happen is if you're there to meet it when it arrives."

"All this time," Death said slowly, "I've seen one image, one tomorrow, burning brightly in my mind. That was my one hope."

Xander nodded. He understood. "The thing about hope is that it changes over time. It changes as we grow."

"I don't grow."

"Maybe you do. Maybe your specific hope has just taken on a different shape."

Death's empty gaze lost focus, and his frown lifted into something less stern, less disbelieving.

"Look again," Xander coaxed. "Open your eyes and really look. And maybe you'll find that new tomorrow."

"Maybe," Death said, tasting the word. "Maybe," he said again, and this time he nodded. "Maybe you're right."

Xander risked a smile. "Maybe I am."

"'Open your eyes.' It's good advice. Perhaps I'll take it." Death hopped off the railing—and onto the balcony, not over the side and falling thirty stories below, thank God.

Xander's knees loosened with relief, and he sagged against the wall. Which was right by the railing. Which was the only thing separating him from plummeting to his death. He felt lightheaded, and he thought he was going to be sick. Apparently, now that the crisis was passing, his fear of heights had come back with a vengeance. He inched away from the railing and tried not to vomit.

"Well then," Death said, sounding almost chipper as he picked up his guitar. "I have to clean up a mess I made. But now that I'm off the railing, Xander, maybe you'll finally get off the ledge."

Xander, his back firmly against the wall, blinked up at Death. "Um. What?"

"You've shown me a truth." The Pale Rider slung the guitar strap across his shoulders. "I didn't consider the possibility that I'd made a mistake, or that my hope still existed in a different form." He strummed a few notes. "What about you, Xander? When will you be ready for the truth?"

Xander tried to ask, "What truth?" But his throat closed and his chest was too tight and his head began to pound.

Death began to play the opening to "Heart-Shaped Box." Xander knew that song well. He knew all Nirvana songs well. He loved Nirvana, had once dreamed of growing up to be like

Kurt Cobain, of making music that called to a generation, except Xander didn't have a musical bone in his body.

Xander had lots of dreams.

The song transitioned to the chorus. Death sang about the cost of priceless advice, his voice bordering between petulant and smug.

Xander whispered, "What truth?"

Death must have heard him even over the music, because his long fingers hovered over the strings. As the last chord echoed, he smiled at Xander, patient, knowing.

Waiting.

"The truth you've known for a long time," Death said, "but haven't been willing to see."

A sound like a screech of tires, followed by a piercing beep.

Xander clapped his hands to his ears and doubled over, and all he could think was *No* and *No* and *NO*.

A still, small voice replied, *Open your eyes, Xander.*

Ted's voice, tinny and distant: *Come on, Zan. Open your eyes.*

But when Xander finally opened his eyes and looked up, Death was gone.

PART SIX

INTERLUDE

But meanwhile time flies; it flies never to be regained.

—Virgil

BILL

Bill pressed his shirt tightly onto Missy's slashed wrist. She was shaking and horribly pale, but he thought that was more out of anger than shock.

"I'm going to kill him!" she screeched, clasping her arm.

"Wait your turn. And lie back down."

"I don't want to lie down! I want to get off this island and kill the bastard!"

"You'll be meeting that bastard real soon now if I can't stop the bleeding," Bill said through gritted teeth. "So unless you want that conversation to be very one-sided, lie. Back. Down."

She glowered at him, but she did what he told her. Small favors. He applied pressure, and she fumed.

"You weren't this demanding when you were the White Rider."

"You weren't this bullheaded when you were the Red."

That actually got a tired smile from her. "You just didn't know me very well."

The blood was soaking through the shirt. "Damn it. Hold this—yeah, right there," he said, pressing her hand against the makeshift bandage. He quickly removed his belt and tied it around her upper arm, turning it into a tourniquet. He pulled the ends taut, and Missy hissed.

"Sorry," he muttered. "Direct pressure wasn't enough. Had to go for the main artery. We have to get the bleeding to stop."

She swallowed and nodded, then turned her head away.

Bill folded her wounded arm, then placed it on her chest, her hand by her chin. "Don't move," he told her. "I have to check on Famine."

"Tammy," Missy corrected.

"Tammy," he agreed, and then he pulled himself up and went to the fallen woman's side. She'd collapsed as soon as Death had removed their Horseman mojo, but Missy had also begun screaming about blood. Bill had made the call to help Missy first—she, at least, was still alive, and for all he'd known, Famine could have been dead.

No, not Famine. Tammy.

He knelt by her side. She was horribly thin—clearly an-orexic—and she wasn't breathing. Cursing under his breath, he placed the heel of his hand flat on her chest, just over the lower part of her breastbone, then placed his other hand on top and interlocked his fingers. Keeping his elbows straight, he pressed down and began to pump. He counted out loud as he pumped, one and two and three and four, pressing on every number and relaxing with every "and." When he got to thirty, he tilted Tammy's head back, lifting up her chin, then pinched her nostrils shut. Bill took a deep breath, locked his mouth over hers and exhaled slowly into her.

Her chest inflated.

Good; no obstruction of her airways, at least. Bill would take all the good news he could get. He breathed into her again, then went back to the cardiac compressions, counting out loud with every press.

Missy called out, "Bill?" Her voice was weaker than before. "What's going on?"

He pumped as he replied: "Tammy's. Not. Breathing. Giving. Her. C. P. R."

She cursed, loudly and colorfully.

Bill kept going with CPR. After his third round, he ran over to Missy to check her wound. She was still bleeding. She was going to lose her arm.

No, she was going to die.

Tammy was going to die.

The three horses were probably already dead.

Bill wanted to shout his fury to the heavens. Even after Tammy and Missy died, he would still be stranded on an uninhabitable island, with no cell phone service, no one knowing where they were, all because the three of them had wanted to talk in private. They should have known that there was no place so secluded that Death wouldn't know what they were doing. Now everyone was dying, and Bill was completely screwed. How would he go? Starvation?

No—he'd die from exposure. It would have to be disease for him, wouldn't it? How else would a former Pestilence die?

He wished to God that he had the Elder's voice in his head, telling him what to do. He'd even have taken the King's insane ramblings. But they were gone; all of the voices of the previous White Riders were silent.

He couldn't even remember what they sounded like.

Bill exhaled sharply and told himself that it was enough. There would be time for self-pity later, but only if there *was* a later. First things first. He rewrapped his sodden shirt around Missy's wound, then folded her arm back over her chest.

"Lie still," he said, pretending his voice hadn't cracked.

Missy smiled and closed her eyes. "You're cute when you're commanding."

He ran back to Tammy, who still wasn't breathing, and got back to performing CPR.

Missy's voice, warbling: "It was an accident."

Bill, counting as he tried to get Tammy's heart to work again, didn't reply.

"I'd been cutting. First time in months. Was too upset to hold the blade right. Got sloppy. Just like he'd promised." Missy let out a tired laugh. "He told me my family would think I'd committed suicide. That's sort of funny now."

Yeah, Bill thought. *Hysterical.* He kept working on Tammy, kept hoping that she'd start to breathe on her own. Kept believing that what he was doing wasn't futile, because really, what else could he do?

"Think he's gonna do it?" Missy asked. "Is this the end of everything?"

"It will be if your bleeding doesn't stop," Bill said harshly. "So shut up and try not to bleed out, okay?"

She laughed again, weakly, sounding like an old woman instead of someone maybe pushing twenty-one. "You make it sound like it matters. We're dead. We're all dead. He's gonna kill himself, and take the world with him."

"Oh, ye of little faith."

Bill's head jerked up from the sound of that voice—so cold, yet infused with mirth. Death stood there on the shore, holding his guitar and smiling at them as the wind made his hair dance.

"You're back," Bill said.

"I am."

Beneath Bill's hands, Tammy's heart began to beat again. She took in a dusty breath, and then another. Bill rocked back, momentarily stunned, then he growled, "Missy's arm. The blood loss."

"Already done, William."

He scrambled up and ran over to Missy. First he helped her remove the belt from her arm, and then he removed his bloody shirt. The long gash on her forearm was already healed, the pink line one of far too many other lines on her skin.

"What about Tammy?" Bill said, not looking at Death.

"Sleeping."

"The horses?"

"Have moved on to greener pastures. All of them were old, far older than horses should live."

His steed was gone. His poor white horse, so nervous and yet so very brave, had been taken from him. No goodbyes, no farewells, no chance for him to thank the horse for being his companion and helping him on his crazy journey as the White Rider.

Bill swallowed his rage enough for him to ask, "Changed your mind about dying?"

"Yes." A laugh, as if Death were bemused. "Apparently, I *can* change. I've come to realize that what I hope for may still, in fact, be viable."

All Bill could think was that Death had the audacity to laugh. He'd taken something vital from them all, taken it without asking, and he'd killed their steeds and left the three of them abandoned and hurt, and now he had the audacity to laugh. It wasn't a cruel laugh, either — just a simple expression of amusement.

Death had callously maimed and discarded them, and now he found that amusing.

Bill had never wanted to hurt someone so much in all his life, not even when the school bullies had made him their chew toy.

Missy's voice, low and shaky: "Still dizzy. Help me up?"

Bill offered Missy a hand, and soon she was on her feet.

"Thanks," she murmured. Then slowly, deliberately, she staggered up to Death and punched him squarely in the mouth.

Missy's fist hurt — hitting Death had been so much easier when she'd been War — but she refused to ruin the moment with something as lame as saying "Ow." She gritted her teeth and bore the pain. That was okay; she and pain were old friends.

He touched his mouth — no blood, no loose teeth, no *nothing,* damn him — and laughed softly. "Some things will never change. You still default to violence."

She snarled, "And you're still a bastard." She'd meant it to come out as a shout, but all she could manage was a harsh whisper. Stupid blood loss.

From behind her, Bill rasped, "How could you do that to us?"

Death looked at Missy, then past her to Bill, to where Tammy lay on the sand. He said, "I was helping you."

She held her aching hand and glared at him. "You killed our steeds and ripped us apart and left us here to die," she seethed, "and you think that's *helping?*"

He shrugged. "It would have been better than the alternative at the time."

"Which was what?"

"Feeling me die."

That shut her up.

"Understand me," he said, his voice cold, passionless. "I

meant to die. And not some temporary death, either—no momentary blip off the radar, then all systems go. This wasn't just
coming to the close of a chapter, only to start one anew. This
was going to be for real. Forever. Nothing you said or did could
have stopped me. I was focused on my own destruction."

"Dramatic, much?" She aimed for heat and got barely a sim-
mer. "You were suicidal. We get it."

"You don't. You three were still Horsemen, still directly connected to me. The best that would have happened is I would
have died and you three would have immediately followed. At
worst, I would have died, and you would have burned out,
leaving you mindless husks. So I severed the connection." He
paused. "I caused you pain. For that, I apologize."

Missy's eyes narrowed. "Is that supposed to make it all better? Make our pain stop? Or maybe that brings our steeds back
to life? Oh, wait," she said, snapping her fingers. "It doesn't do
any of that. Screw your apology!"

"You're angry."

"You think?" She jabbed a finger in his chest. "You ripped us
apart! You killed our horses, you son of a bitch! You don't get to
just pop over here and say you apologize!"

He looked down at her finger, which had gone cold. "It was
a poor choice," he said, gently removing her finger from his
chest. That one touch was enough to send shocks of chill up to
her elbow.

"Damn right it was," she muttered.

"I'm sorry I hurt you," he said softly.

She wanted so much to read more into his words, his tone,
the expression on his face. But he was so very cold, and he'd

hurt her so very much. So she folded her arms across her chest and said, "I thought you were going all kamikaze and taking the world with you."

"Oh, I was. Probably."

"Probably?"

"Well, maybe. Don't look at me like that," he said. "It's not like I know. I've never died permanently before."

"What do you mean, you've never died permanently?"

Behind her, Bill said, "What do you mean, you don't know?"

"Questions, questions. You people and your questions." He shook his head. "I die quite a lot, Melissa. My forms burn out, and then I'm formed anew—unless I choose not to be re-formed. And then, well, that's the question, isn't it?"

Missy's jaw dropped. In the back of her mind, where War used to play, she thought it made perfect sense—of course he didn't always look the way he looked now. But even so, she was shocked to hear him casually mention that he died. A lot. But before she could give voice to her thoughts, Death was already sliding a glance at Bill.

"I don't know what would happen to me if I chose not to be re-formed after I died," he said. "As I mentioned, it's never happened to me before."

Bill said, "But . . . you know everything."

"I know many things, William. Maybe even most things. But not everything. I certainly don't know what happens when I die."

"How could you not know? You're *Death*."

"I know what happens when *you* die. I know what happens when living things die. But I'm not a living thing, not like you.

When something that's eternal becomes finite . . . well." He smiled tightly. "That's one for the philosophers, don't you think?"

"I . . ." Bill floundered. "I was positive all life would die when you died."

Death laughed softly. "A little white bird tell you that?"

"Um. Sort of."

Missy had no idea what they were talking about, and she didn't care. "So you really had no idea what would happen to you? Heaven, hell, somewhere in between?" She smirked. "Nirvana, maybe?"

"I don't exactly have a user manual for this role, Melissa. I've had to learn what happens as I go."

"Boy," she said dryly, "that sounds familiar . . ."

"Why do you think I've let the Horsemen learn the hard way? Personal experience has shown me that works the best. And you're such quick learners."

She lifted her chin. "Here I thought it was because you were a sadist."

"In some ways," he said, looking over to where Tammy lay. "Yes, I might have taken all life with me when I died. I might not have. But it's moot. I've decided to live."

"Because now you have new hope," she said lightly, pretending that she didn't care. So what that she'd loved him and he'd thrown her away? She was used to the ones closest to her hurting her the most. Her wrist throbbed, but she ignored it. "Well, good for you. Enjoy that hope. Before you leave, how about you magic us off this island? You sort of took away our only means of transportation."

"Yes, and I apologize for that. It may please you to know that the horses are happy."

She glowered at him. "My horse was happy when he was killing rats."

"And now the warhorse has discovered a different sort of happiness. All of the steeds have."

"Even yours?" Bill asked.

"That's a . . . unique situation," he replied, looking at Bill. "And it's one I will attend to shortly. But yes, Melissa," he said, turning to face her again, "I will take you back. I'll take you home, if that's your wish. You'll return to your lives. But first, there's something I have to do."

She rolled her eyes. "Priorities."

"You could say that." He smiled at her, and she was struck by how empty it was. His smiles always used to have layers of meaning—humor, anger, curiosity, so much more. There used to be a sense of whimsy to him, even when he was darkly serious. But now he was empty, cold.

And seeing him that cold slashed her like a razor.

Her snark failed her. Mouth dry, she asked, "What do you have to do?"

And Death replied, "I have to die."

Bill's shoulders tensed painfully. His first thought was this had been just a tease, just some warped game Death was playing with them. But then he realized what the Pale Rider was saying, and it was enough to steal his breath.

Death died. A lot. And now it was time for him to die again and be re-formed.

There was so much he wanted to say, but all he could manage was an ineffectual "Oh."

"You can't be serious," Missy shouted hoarsely. "You just said it was moot because you decided to live!"

"And I have, Melissa. And that means first, I have to die."

"It's like the harvest god," Bill said numbly, remembering school lessons from long ago. "Born in the spring, rules in the summer, sacrificed in the autumn, dead in the winter. Then born again in the spring."

"A little less frequently than that," Death said. "But yes, that's close."

"That's *stupid*." Missy was crying, but Bill didn't think she was aware of the tears streaking her face. "You can't die!"

"I can," Death said, his voice surprisingly gentle. "I don't want to. It hurts, more than you could know. More than I ever want you to know." He lifted his hand and caressed Missy's cheek, once, just a small touch, but it was enough to double her tears and set her shoulders shaking. "But this form is done, Melissa. It's held together with the cosmic equivalent of duct tape, and it's still falling apart."

Bill had known that Death was hurting, but he'd had no idea there had been physical pain as well. All he could say was, "I'm sorry."

Death flicked a humorless smile.

"There has to be another way," Missy said, anger and sobs turning her words into weapons.

"There isn't."

She cocked her fist as if to punch Death again, but he caught her hand and held it, stroked it with his thumb. She looked up at him and said nothing, but she must have thought something loudly, because Death's smile softened.

"I know," Death said.

Even though Bill couldn't hear Missy's side of the conversation, he felt like an eavesdropper. He turned his back on them and went to Tammy's side. The woman who'd been the Black Rider was still unconscious, but at least she was breathing easily. Sleeping, Bill assumed, as Death had said. Bill took Tammy's hand and held it, tried to will strength and health into her frail body. He wished he could help her be healthy. He wished he'd been able to know her better when they were Riders. But Tammy had been Famine and Famine only; there had been no hint of the person she'd been before she'd taken the Scales.

"It'll be okay," he told her, knowing she couldn't hear him, but he said the words anyway because they needed to be said.

"This part is bad, but it's going to pass. You'll get through this. We all will. And then, well, there's a whole world out there." He squeezed her hand. "You'll see. It'll be okay."

And he knew that his words were true. It would be okay.

This isn't okay, Missy thought angrily. *There has to be something else, some other option.*

There isn't.

She knew he was right, and she hated him for it.

You don't hate me, Melissa, no more than you hate yourself. But I'm sorry to cause you so much pain.

Shut up. She buried her head in his chest and hugged him fiercely. *Just shut up and hold me.*

Cold arms wrapped around her and held her tight.

You stupid, sorry excuse of a Horseman, she sobbed. *I don't want you to die.*

I know.

And then the floodgates opened as her thoughts came out in a jumble, one atop the other. *I'm sorry. I'm so sorry. I wish I was enough for you, that I could be your hope. I wish there was something I could do to make it better. I wish you didn't have to do this, wish you didn't have to hurt so much. I wish.* With her next thoughts came images in her mind, so vivid it was like she was looking at snapshots in a photo album. *I wish we could be together, you and me, doing stupid things like eating ice cream in the summer or climbing up on the roof of my parents' house and counting the stars at night. I wish we could hold hands and walk on the grass and watch the sunrise. I wish you could really understand what it means to be in love. I wish I was the one who could show you about being in love. I wish you were happy. I wish I could make you happy. I wish. I wish.*

"Missy," he murmured. "You do all that already."

She sobbed louder.

Every time you've held my hand, he said to her, *I've felt the heat of your skin even through your gloves. I've felt you, Missy. All this time, it's been your passion that's enamored me. As I've slowly grown colder, it's been you striving to keep me warm. To show me what it's like to be human. Every time you laugh, every time you hurt, I feel it. I understand it a little more. Every time we've kissed, you've heated me more than you could know. Maybe that's what love is for me, Missy—that feeling of heat. It's quieter than passion but louder than contentment. It's . . .*

Love, she said, hugging him tighter.

And though she wasn't looking at his face, she could hear his smile when he replied, *Love.*

"I love you," she whispered, "you stupid, sorry excuse of a Horseman."

A feeling like frost on her chin as he tipped her head up and gazed at her. And finally, she saw something beyond the empty blue of his eyes.

She saw love.

That's what she told herself: It was love shining in the depths of his eyes. Maybe she was lying to herself, because how could one such as Death understand something as human as love? But if it was a lie, she didn't care.

"Thank you," he murmured. And then he kissed her, softly, chastely, on the lips.

When he pulled away, she could still feel him pressed against her; his chill had seeped into her and threatened to freeze her heart. So she did the only thing she could do: She pulled him back to her and kissed him properly, fiercely, telling him with that kiss just how much he meant to her, how he'd saved her long before he'd almost killed her—how being with him, working with him, had shown her more about life than she'd ever thought she would have known.

It was a good kiss.

Afterward, she looked into his eyes and saw herself reflected there.

"Thank you," he said again, warmer this time. He touched her cheek once more, then stepped away. He cast a glance at the guitar he'd dropped on the sand, and he picked it up, slinging the strap around his shoulders.

"One for the road," he said.

Then he played the opening to his final song. Missy had known what it would be, what it had to be, and as Death sang "All Apologies," she began to cry again, silent hot tears that stung her eyes. This was his true apology—to her, to the other Riders, to everyone and everything.

And she forgave him.

She listened as Death said goodbye to the world in the only way that he could, and when he was done, she wiped away her tears. When he offered her the guitar, she took it from him.

"This won't take long," he said.

"For us, maybe," Missy said. "What about for you?"

He smiled at her and didn't reply.

Bill's voice, cracking at the seams: "Is there anything we can do?"

Death's smile broadened. "Thank you, William, but you already have. See you soon."

Then Death bowed his head, stepped sideways—

—and vanished.

It was only a second that he was gone. It was the longest second of her life.

A slap of wind, hard enough to rock Missy backward. And then a man appeared next to her, wearing a flannel shirt and blue jeans, his hair wavy and gray. His eyebrows were arched and almost wicked; his smile, sardonic. He seemed both older and ageless, and was so very different from how Missy had always known him. Yet something about him was still the same.

His eyes, she realized as she stared at that weathered face. His eyes were the same bottomless blue eyes that she'd seen the first time she'd met him years ago on her doorstep. Death's eyes never changed.

"Wow," Bill said. "It's really you?"

"It's really me." The voice was different—deeper, more resonant, an actor's voice rather than a singer's—but the infectious grin was absolutely all his. He held his hands out and did a pirouette. "Good?"

Missy's voice didn't want to work, so she nodded.

"It's different," Bill said. "But yeah. It's good."

He came to a halt, his arms out, as if waiting for applause, and then he chuckled and stuffed his hands into the pockets of his jeans. "Always takes some getting used to," he said, but Missy didn't know if he was referring to himself or to them.

Before she could stop herself, she marched up to him, pulled his head down to hers, and kissed him.

And *kissed* him.

It was a very good kiss.

When she finished, she looked up at him and smiled. "It's really you."

"Told you so."

"You're warmer," she said, brushing her fingers over his lips. "Warmer than ever."

"Perk of a new cycle. New form, new warmth."

"Um." That was Bill. "So. Sorry to interrupt. But what happens now?"

"A question for your question." Death winked at Missy, then gently pulled away until he was standing between her and Bill. "Want a job?"

Missy heard a gasp, and she didn't know if it was hers or Bill's.

"I could re-form the Horsemen," Death said amiably. "Four Riders of the Apocalypse, together again, working to keep everything in balance. Life, death, the occasional game of bridge." He waggled his eyebrows. "Interested?"

Missy exchanged a look with Bill. Even though they couldn't read each other's minds any longer, they both turned to Death at the same time, and together they gave him their reply.

The Pale Rider smiled. "I had a feeling that's what you'd say."

BILL

Marianne Bixby opened the door to her college dorm room, and she grinned. "Hey! Wasn't expecting you."

Bill smiled sheepishly and held up a carton of mint chocolate-chip ice cream. "Had an urge."

"For ice cream?"

"That too."

She opened the door, and he walked inside. "Roommate?" he asked, tossing the ice cream onto her desk.

Marianne shut the door and grinned at him. "Out for the night."

"Classes?"

"Not until tomorrow afternoon. Well, look at you," she said, doing just that. "I thought it was just the lighting outside, but it's not. You dyed your hair!"

He hadn't. But he wasn't surprised that the white streak was gone. "You like it?"

She cocked her head and considered. "Yeah. It'll just take some getting used to. Why'd you do it?"

"Needed a change. Speaking of which . . ." He smiled hugely as he spread his arms wide. "I'm a free man."

She arched an eyebrow and smirked. "If this is a breakup, it's got to be the worst one on record . . ."

"I quit my job."

"Mister Impulsive!" she said, giggling. "The hair, the job —"

"The ice cream."

"Oh, I was getting to the ice cream." She wrapped her arms around him and kissed him lightly on the cheek. "I'm glad you quit. You were working too much."

"Tell me about it."

"So until you get another one . . . more time for me?"

He hugged her, breathed her in. Smiling, he murmured, "All the time in the world for you."

"Love you," she whispered.

"Me too." And then Bill Ballard kissed his girl — kissed her and kissed her, and she kissed him back.

The ice cream melted.

Neither of them cared.

"I can't believe you quit your job," Sue Miller said. "I thought you loved your work."

Missy sighed and slumped down in her chair. "Me too." She was glad that her sister had been home when she'd called. Four years ago, the notion of her voluntarily talking to Sue would have been insane. But the two had grown close in the last few years. Missy had found a new appreciation for her sister, especially once Missy had gone to live on her college's campus. The magic of living in separate time zones had done wonders for their relationship. "But the hours were crazy, and the work could be murder."

"You gonna take time off? Or are you looking for something else?" A pause, in which Missy could practically hear Sue leering. "Or is your mysterious boy toy gonna morph into your sugar daddy?"

"Yeah," Missy said. "Um. We sort of broke up."

Sue shrieked, "You *what?*"

Missy held the phone away from her ear. When the echo faded, she said, "Thanks, I wasn't half deaf until now, always been meaning to try it . . ."

"What *happened?*"

"Well, addendum: We're not *over* over," Missy said. "Just sort of on a break. For now."

"His suggestion? Or yours?"

"Mine." And that had been even harder than telling him that she wouldn't pick up the Sword again. But it was the right decision. "He's going through some personal stuff right now," she said, trying to be nonchalant. "Changes, you know? He needs some time to himself, to figure things out."

"But . . . I don't get it. Don't you love him?"

Missy sighed, and the sound was bitter. "Yes. Too much, even."

"Then shouldn't you be with him? Help him figure out whatever it is he needs to figure out?"

"I want to. But I can't. This is something he's got to do alone. And when he knows what he really wants, then I'll be ready to hear it."

"What if what he wants isn't you?"

Missy stared at the acoustic guitar leaning against the wall. "Yeah, well," she said lightly, "that's why we're on a break. Just in case. I love him, but I'm not going to waste my life waiting for someone to wake up and realize how amazing I am. If he wants me, he knows where I am. Until then, there's a whole sea out there."

She hoped with all of her heart that in the end, he would want her. That would mean he'd finally tell her those three words he'd never said to her, not once. He'd hinted at it, touched on it, but never truly said it. And as much as she loved him, she couldn't give her heart to someone who couldn't say that he loved her. That was like bottling her heart in a glass jar — and that was something she wasn't willing to do. Not anymore.

"Listen to you," Sue chirped. "So practical! You sound almost grown-up."

"Yeah," she said tiredly. "Yay, me."

"Missy . . . are you okay?"

"I've been better," she admitted. Her wrist throbbed, and she rubbed it absently.

"Are you . . . ?"

"No," Missy said. "I'm not. Not that."

"Because if you are," Sue said quickly, "you can tell me. You know that, right? You can tell me."

"Sue," she said. "I promise. I'm not cutting."

A long pause, and then Sue replied, "Okay. Good."

"Good," Missy echoed.

"Wow," Sue said. "No job. No boy toy. One more year of college, then you're out in the cold, cruel world. So tell me, Melissa Miller—what're you going to do with your life?"

"I have no idea. Guess I have to figure it out." Missy couldn't help it: She laughed. "That's kind of exciting."

Beneath her bed, the lock box with her razorblade grew dusty.

For Melissa Miller, it was a personal victory.

TAMMY

Tammy is sitting in front of the vanity mirror in her bedroom, brushing her hair. She smiles at her reflection. For the first time in forever, she likes what she sees. She's not too fat. She's not unhealthy. She's normal. She looks younger than her age, maybe seventeen, still in high school with her whole life waiting for her. Her bedroom is sunny, filled with daylight, and she hums to herself as she keeps brushing her hair.

Her mother is in her room with her, going through her closet to weed out the things Tammy doesn't wear any longer. Clothing flies from the closet, landing in a heap on Tammy's bed. Sweaters, tops, dresses, pants, all sorts of outfits slowly blot out the bright comforter.

All of the pieces her mother pulls out are black.

Her sister is sifting through the pants and sweaters and other discarded clothes, grabbing what she likes. Tammy doesn't mind. She doesn't need those clothes any longer. But then her sister lifts up a long black coat and holds it up to her, smoothing out the sleeves, and she coos over how good the coat looks.

Tammy stops brushing her hair.

"Not that," she says. "That's not for you."

Her sister pouts. "But you're not wearing it anymore."

Tammy holds the brush, and for a moment she imagines it lengthening and expanding until she's holding an old-fashioned set *of scales, shining brass or maybe bronze, and she feels the hunger of the world pressing heavily against her.*

"It's still not for you," Tammy says.

"Then who is it for?"

The voice is a rich, booming baritone, and steeped in humor. Tammy turns around in her chair and sees a gray-haired man in a checkered shirt and blue jeans sitting on her bed. Even before she sees his blue, blue eyes, she knows who he really is.

"You've changed," she says, surprised.

He shrugs easily. "So I've been told. How are you, Tammy?"

She looks down at her lap. "Confused."

"Understandable," he replies. "When we last met, I was on a runaway train. I hurt you, badly. I'm sorry about that."

She doesn't trust her voice, so she nods.

"I need to know what you want, Tammy."

She lifts her head and meets his gaze. "You mean, do I want to be Famine again?"

He smiles and says nothing.

"No," she says, comprehension dawning. "You mean, do I want to live?"

"Do you?"

She turns away from him to stare into her mirror once more. "I don't know."

"I can't make the decision for you. Well. I could kill you," he says cheerfully. "But that's not the same thing."

"I'm tired," she says.

"I know."

"And I'm scared. I'm scared all the time."

"I know."

She closes her eyes. "Do you want me to live?"

"Tammy," he says kindly. "I want everyone to live. But you have to meet me halfway. You have to want to live too."

"But I stopped living so long ago," she whispers. "When you offered me the Scales, I was dying."

"Yes."

"And when I was Famine, I turned my back on my human life. I walked away from it. My family, my friends, everyone—I lost them all, because of what I did." Her breath hitches. "I have nothing to go back to."

"People can surprise you, Tammy." A chuckle, and then: "They certainly surprise me. And I've been around for a long, long time. What do you say, Tammy? You willing to give it a shot?"

She's terrified.

She wants to say no.

But a still, small voice whispers that maybe, just maybe, people can surprise her and she'll find her own reason to keep on living.

Before she can talk herself out of it, she says, "Yes."

"Well then, Tammy. Open your eyes."

And Tammy Thompson opens her eyes . . .

. . . and she waited for the room to come into focus. It took a minute, but shapes finally settled down and colors snapped to attention. Gray textured ceiling; soothing gray walls. Tammy recognized the sense of sterility and knew she was in a hospital even before she noted the tubes snaking out of her arms. She felt like her body had been wrung out like a sponge. No, that would have been a step up—she actually felt like used chewing gum stuck on the bottom of someone's shoe. She took a shaky breath and was surprised that it didn't hurt.

"Tammy?"

She tried to sit up, but that was a spectacular failure. She barely managed to rotate her head on her pillow to look at the person who'd spoken.

Her reply died in her mouth.

Sitting on a chair next to the hospital bed, Lisabeth Lewis smiled at her. "Hey," she said, smiling tiredly. "You're up. Your mom and sister went to get some food, but they'll be back soon."

"You're here," Tammy croaked. Her mouth was painfully dry, but it hurt less than looking at the one person whom she'd trusted with everything and who had left her stranded in an uncaring world.

"I'm here," Lisa said, still smiling and looking so very sad. "I heard what happened, and I couldn't not come. You're going to be okay. The doctors here are going to help you get healthy."

She meant, help Tammy get fat.

Lisabeth Lewis, of all people, was preaching to her about being healthy. The same Lisabeth Lewis who once admired her because she'd been able to stick a finger down her throat and vomit up her food.

The same Lisabeth Lewis who'd cut Tammy out of her life.

"You left me," Tammy said. "You *left* me. We were best friends, and then you just . . ." Exhausted, she closed her eyes. "You hurt me so much."

"I know," Lisa said quietly. "I had to make a clean break, to get healthy."

To get fat.

"I could've done it better," Lisa admitted. "I did what I had to do, but I was selfish about it. I should've talked to you. I should've told you that I couldn't be your friend. When I got out of the clinic, I should have called. I didn't. That was wrong of me. That was shitty of me. I'm sorry."

Tammy wanted to be angry. She wanted to be bitter. And she was both of those things, but tangled in there, too, was a sense of relief, of respite, as if part of her that had been clenched tight for years was finally beginning to loosen.

"Was that when you stopped eating? When I left?"

Tammy whispered, "Yes."

"I'm sorry," Lisa said again. "I'm so sorry. If I could take it back, I would."

People can surprise you.

"If you want me to go," Lisa said, "I'll understand." When Tammy didn't reply, Lisa said, "Please, tell me what you want."

I need to know what you want.

Tammy took a deep breath and opened her eyes again. She looked at Lisa—no longer thin, and much more beautiful than Tammy had ever seen her—and she said, "I don't know what I want. But I'm glad you're here."

Lisa smiled, and she reached over to take her hand. "Me too."

He'd gotten better at separating part of himself. This time, there was barely an earthquake. A number of humans would chalk it up to climate change. And that was as good a way to put it as any.

The pale steed snorted and stamped its newly made hoof. "Really? You unmade me, and now I'm back?"

"And better than before."

"Please spare a steed and don't break into song." The horse glared at him, in the way that horses do. "Unless you don't do that anymore. New cycle?"

"Yep."

"Humph. You all done feeling sorry for yourself?"

"Yep."

The steed took in his new form. "Not going to do spontaneous manic monologues about your past, are you?"

"Nope. At least, not for a while. The urge might overtake me."

"You realize I'm angry with you, right?"

He patted his steed's neck. "You have every right to be. I'll strive to make amends."

The horse blew out a satisfied breath. "For starters, buy a steed a cheeseburger. Getting remade makes a horse hungry."

"Any particular place?"

The horse considered. "The one with all the health-code violations."

"That narrows it down . . ."

"You know the one. The meat is questionable and the bread is soggy, but oh, those fries . . ."

"Ah. Yes, I know the one. Shall we?"

"Just like that? What about work? All those souls to see?"

He shrugged, smiled. "They can wait."

PART SEVEN

CREATION

The primary imagination I hold to be the living power and prime agent of all human perception, and as a repetition in the finite mind of the eternal act of creation in the infinite I Am.

—*Samuel Taylor Coleridge*

By the time his parents got home, Xander was a mess. His head was pounding like there was no tomorrow, and he kept hearing a high-pitched beep shrilling in his mind like an alarm clock on helium. When he'd first noticed the beeping, he'd looked to see if one of the smoke detectors was on the fritz, but no, everything was fine.

Everything was fine.

So he ignored the weird intermittent beeping and rubbed his head, but when that did nothing to ease his headache, he went for the aspirin. And then for the beer. He'd known that his parents would give him hell about the drinking, but he'd spent part of the night talking to a suicidal Death. He thought he'd earned a drink.

When his mom and dad walked in, Xander was curled up on the den sofa, staring blankly at an old episode of *Doctor Who* as he thought about Ashley Davidson. It had been six years ago that he'd learned Ashley had died. Xander's first beer of the evening had been a toast to his first crush; the second was to the Amazingly Perfect Riley Jones.

Who still hadn't returned his text.

That had been why Xander had chugged the second beer. And left the empties on the coffee table. Along with the packages of pretzels, chips, and peanuts. And all the crumbs. He

had a third beer to drown the unsettling feeling he'd been starting to get about Riley. Now he was pleasantly buzzed, and
thinking about poor dead Ashley and how first loves were always doomed, and then his mom was yelling at him.

"Xander Atwood!"

He knew he was in trouble when his mom bellowed his last
name along with his first, but he couldn't bring himself to care.
Ashley was dead, Riley wasn't returning his texts, and he'd been
schmoozing with Death. He had enough on his plate already;
he just couldn't be bothered to think about his mom. Who was
now shouting:

"Have you been drinking?"

Sort of rhetorical, given the empty cans littering the table.

His mother hissed in a breath, and he realized he'd said his
thought out loud. Oops.

"Oh my God," his mom proclaimed, "you're *drunk!*"

He muttered, "'Course not. Only had three beers." It took a
good five or so to get him plastered.

"Son," his dad said in a very fatherly voice, "I think you
should go to bed."

So Dad was good cop for the night. Okay, Xander knew
how to play that game. He grinned up at his father. "Sure, Dad.
Just wanna finish this episode first."

"I said you should go to bed," his dad replied, sounding less
and less like the good cop. "Now."

"Jeez. Keep your voice down," Xander said, wincing. "You
wanna wake the baby?"

His mother and father exchanged a look.

"The baby," his dad repeated.

"Uh, hello? Lex?" When his parents just stared at him, he

said, "You know, the screaming ball of joy currently inhabiting the crib in the nursery?"

His dad said, "Son . . ."

Xander rolled his eyes. "Man, you two go out on a dinner date, you forget about all your responsibilities. Nice. Very role modelish."

"You're drunk," his mother snapped.

"Yeah, you already said that."

She bared her teeth. She had very white teeth. "Go. To. Bed."

"Yeah, yeah, whatever." Xander started to pull himself off the sofa, but his father yanked him up by his shirt collar and got right in his face.

"You don't talk to your mother like that!" his dad snarled. "I don't give a damn if you're drunk or not, but you will speak to your mother *with respect!*"

Xander squirmed out of his father's grip. "Fine!" He barreled past his mom and out of the den. Jesus, his parents were so uptight! He stomped down the hallway, not caring if he woke the baby. That would serve his parents right. Let them calm their precious baby Lex, get him to stop screaming and go back to sleep.

A sound, like a screech of tires.

Xander slammed his bedroom door behind him and flung himself onto his bed. He heard his parents arguing—man, they really didn't give a crap if they woke Lex—and he felt only a little guilty that they were shouting at each other about him. The walls were thin, and his parents were loud, so he was able to get the gist of it, even with his door closed. There was a lot of backing and forthing, but it all came back to his one-hit wonder, the gift that kept on giving: He'd screwed up with Carnegie Mellon.

Well, yeah. Reneging on early acceptance wasn't something he'd recommend.

The room had started spinning, so he shoved his pillow over his head.

As he began to doze, one thought pecked at him like the proverbial early bird hunting for the elusive worm: He didn't remember telling his parents about how he'd changed his college plans without their consent. He must have, because why else would they be shouting about it now? So they must also know about Stanford.

Which was why he couldn't understand why his mother was sobbing over how he'd thrown his life away.

Whatever. He'd worry about it tomorrow.

In his pocket, his lucky penny waited.

Xander woke in the middle of the night, startled and disoriented. He could have sworn that Lex was crying, but as he listened, the only sound he heard was his own frantic breathing.

Xander stared at the digital clock on his nightstand, then he burrowed under the blanket and tried to go back to sleep. No good; he just couldn't shake the feeling that someone was crying.

Uneasy, he yanked the blanket back down. He listened again, thinking that he'd hear his mom go into Lex's room for her nightly calm-the-baby motions, but he didn't hear a thing.

In the apartment, no one moved.

His head began to hurt, a steady, almost rhythmic throb in his temples. Xander stumbled out of bed and into the bathroom, where he popped two aspirin and washed them down with a few handfuls of water. He looked at himself in the mirror, stared at his dark reflection there in the unlit room, and told himself to get a grip. It was oh-my-god o'clock in the morning, and he had to get his butt back to bed. Tomorrow was a school day.

Tomorrow was *the* day.

He'd see Riley and find out why he hadn't gotten a return text. It was probably nothing — maybe Riley's phone had run out of juice — but part of Xander wouldn't rest easy until he knew for certain that everything was fine.

Everything was fine.

And he'd also find out why Ted and Suzie and Izzy were acting so weird around him; ever since Marcie's party —

(open your eyes, Zan)

— the three of them had been off-center. Different. If Xander didn't know better, he'd almost think they were talking about him behind his back. Something had changed. He just didn't know what.

He walked out of the bathroom and paused outside the nursery. It was painfully quiet.

Deathly quiet.

(today's the day the world ends)

Xander blinked as the thought triggered a memory — no, a dream from last night. He had been standing on the balcony, trying to talk Death off the railing. Or something like that. It was a little fuzzy now. Maybe he'd remember it come morning.

He had a sudden, overwhelming urge to see Lex, to brush his fingertips across the baby's cheek, just a soft touch to let Lex know that his big brother was there and all was right with the world.

Xander opened the nursery door and stuck his head inside.

And he saw a storage room.

He blinked and blinked again, and then he felt panic welling up inside him as the nursery firmly remained a storage room. No changing table atop a bureau; no rocker-glider. No nightstand with a lamp and his mother's paperback novel lying dog-eared and well worn.

No crib.

Xander must have cried out, because his parents' bedroom door flung open and his mother came crashing into the hallway.

"Zan?" she said, sounding frantic. "What's wrong?"

"Where's the baby?" he shouted. "What happened to Lex?"

His mother stared at him, wide-eyed, mouth gaping, and then she closed her eyes and took a deep breath. "Xander. Honey. You're having a nightmare."

"Lex is gone!" he shrieked, flailing his arms. "What happened to my brother?"

"Xander! Listen to me!" His mom grabbed his shoulders and pressed down, something she used to do when he was a kid and having a tantrum; now, as then, it automatically quieted him. "It's just a bad dream!"

He whispered, "Where's the baby?"

"Xander," his mother said. "Son. Open your eyes."

(open your eyes, Zan)

"Look," his mother said, pivoting him until he was right in front of the room that was supposed to be a nursery. His mouth worked silently as he looked at the piles of boxes and storage bins gathered haphazardly on the floor. In the back corner, shadows gathered until they pulled into the shape of a man, reaching for him—

—and the shadow reaches for him and he knows that when the shadow touches him that's the end of everything and so he screams again—

and Xander screamed and stumbled backward.

"Xander," his mother said firmly, her hand pressing down on his shoulder. "It's just a dream. Look, Son. Look."

(open your eyes)

So he looked, and he saw shadows, only shadows. There was one man in the apartment, and that man was still fast asleep in his parents' bedroom, because nothing short of a nuclear blast could wake his father.

His brother was gone.

"Son," said his mother. "This is just a bad dream. Go back to bed now. Time for a good dream, Xander."

"It's only fair," he said, remembering the promise from his childhood: After the bad dreams came the good, because that was only fair.

His mother nodded and steered him back to his bedroom, then she rose up on her toes to kiss his forehead. "Good night, Zan."

Feeling lost and so very small, Xander said good night and shut his bedroom door. He threw himself into bed and waited for sleep to come.

It didn't.

Xander shoved his pillow over his head and made himself remember holding Lex — his fragile baby brother, with the soft spot on his head that still hadn't closed.

Except Lex was gone, erased as if he'd never been.

Xander was losing his mind.

He turned on his table lamp and grabbed the spiral sketch-book and pencil that waited on the nightstand. He had to get the images out of his head and onto paper; maybe then he'd be able to get some sleep. But when he tried to draw, his hand shook so badly that he couldn't keep the pencil point from dancing on the paper's surface.

Disgusted, he tossed the sketchbook onto his nightstand. It landed with an indifferent thud. The pencil missed the table completely and disappeared somewhere on the floor.

He settled into his bed and pulled his covers high. Aloud he said, "Time for a good dream."

Sleep was a long time coming.

When it finally did, Xander didn't dream.

It was the beep that woke him — shriller than an alarm clock, more insistent than a fire alarm. It was a sound that resonated through him, that was part of him, a sound he couldn't ignore or tune out. It called to him, beckoning, and he had no choice but to answer.

Xander opened his eyes.

He was in bed yet not in bed; he couldn't understand it, other than he had to be waking in a dream. He sat up and swung his legs over the side of the bed, and he listened, waiting.

Beep.

He looked around, trying to determine from where the sound had sprung. There, on his nightstand, his sketchbook lay discarded, abandoned; beside it, his alarm clock was silent. Next to his clock, a pile of coins glittered—his change, emptied from his pockets. Farther down, his overflowing bookshelves threatened to spew paperbacks onto his carpet—works by Kurt Vonnegut and Spalding Gray and Neil Gaiman and Terry Pratchett and Piers Anthony and Tom Stoppard and so many others, stories that had captured him and taken him far, far away, whether they were true stories or only mostly true or not true at all. There was his desk, with his computer and cell phone and philosophy textbook, buried somewhere amid the mound of drawings and papers and sticky notes. On various shelves, framed pictures winked, showing him and Ted, him and Suzie and Izzy, him and his parents—fragments of his life captured forever in a moment, frozen. Around him, the walls were decorated with fantasyland maps and Escher's Möbius ants and, in the center, the two blue nudes: the enraged Matisse and despairing Picasso. So many other things that defined him and yet were just trinkets, trifles. Things.

Muffled, yet adamant: *Beep.*

It came from outside his room.

Xander stood up and wondered only for a moment why he was wearing his blue button-up shirt, the one that made the blue in his eyes really pop, as well as his jeans and sneakers, but he had more important things to do—specifically, he had to find out what was causing that sound.

He walked out of his room . . .

. . . and into his philosophy and film studies class. He stood in the doorway, blinking, and he said, "What? What? What?"

"The late Mr. Atwood," said Ms. Lewis, shaking her head. "At this rate, you'll be late for your own funeral."

As if in a dream, he slid into his seat next to Ted and replied, "Wouldn't you want to be?"

Ms. Lewis sighed loudly, then turned her back to finish writing on the board.

"You're only half as clever as you think you are," Ted murmured.

"Which is still twice as clever as you."

"Ouch. You practice that comeback as much as you practice smiling in front of a mirror?"

Xander should have known it was a mistake to share that tidbit with Ted.

"Seriously," Ted whispered, "why bother? If Riley hasn't noticed you by now, it's not gonna happen. Let it go."

"It's good to have goals," Xander said, and then he frowned. Something wasn't right. He was dating Riley—had been with Riley for two months at this point. He and Riley were in love. Everything was fine.

Everything was fine.

He listened to Ms. Lewis pitch the upcoming school musical, read her comments on his report about *Rosencrantz and Guildenstern Are Dead,* and listened again as she explained the theory behind solipsism.

As Ms. Lewis got the DVD of *The Truman Show* set up, Xander distinctly felt a sense of déjà vu.

The lights went off, and he heard it, even over the swell of background music, rising, building until the sound carried like a scream:

Beep.

It came from outside the classroom.

Xander rose from his seat. When Ms. Lewis didn't stop him, he headed toward the door. His fingers over the doorknob, he paused and looked back. No one noticed that he'd left his seat, or if they did, they weren't commenting about it or trying to stop him.

Déjà vu gave way to fear.

That was foolish, he told himself. There was nothing to be afraid of. Everything was fine.

No, he couldn't quite convince himself that everything was fine, but even so, he opened the classroom door and took a step . . .

. . . and grabbed a paintbrush. "Light adds depth to colors," he said to Suzie. "It changes them, sometimes subtly, sometimes drastically." He squeezed raw umber onto his palette and added a few streaks over Suzie's patches of brown. "See?"

Suzie complained that he was being finicky, and he replied that details matter, especially the small ones. He led her around to his section of the prop tree, and he showed her where he'd painted a few objects into the bark: War's sword, gleaming brightly; Pestilence's silver crown; Famine's scales.

Around them, hundreds of coins winked.

In Xander's pocket, his penny weighed a thousand pounds.

"Come on," he said uneasily. "I'll tell Deb that you want to paint part of the wall."

As he got Suzie set up with a roller, she asked, "Hear anything from Carnegie Mellon yet?"

He shrugged. "You know how it goes. I'm doing the hurry-up-and-wait thing."

"Thought you applied early admission."

He had. He'd actually received the acceptance letter, but he hadn't said anything about it to anyone — not his parents, not his friends. Not yet. "I'm sure I'll hear soon."

"Well, some places have sent them out already," Suzie said. "Stanford, for instance. Riley got an acceptance letter today."

"Riley told you that?"

"Sure," Suzie said, casting him an odd look as she dipped her roller into paint. "We've only been friends since third grade. Riley sort of tells me everything. Why?"

"No reason," he said, feeling like the world was out of focus. Something was off, something wasn't right, no matter how he tried to convince himself that everything was fine.

"You going to Marcie's thing on Saturday?"

"Yeah," he said, thinking if Riley got a letter today, then maybe there was one waiting for him already. "We're going to the party."

Suzie said, "We? We who?"

"You know," he said, hearing the words coming from his mouth. "Us. You. Me. Izzy. Ted."

She looked at him like he had drool pooling at the corner of his mouth. "Presumptuous much?" Then she grinned. "Well, you're right. Of course we're going."

"Wouldn't miss it for the world," he said, thinking that he had time, didn't he? There had to be time.

But then there was another *beep,* and he was already moving on. He stepped away from the Art Squad and turned a corner . . .

. . . to find himself in his room, a letter in his hand.

He read the letter, and then read it again, and again until the words blurred and were no more than smears of ink.

He wanted to crumple the paper into a ball, crush it until it was hard and unyielding and then hurl it at his closed bedroom door, see if it would leave a mark. But all he could do was let the letter slip from his numb fingers.

He watched it make its way to the carpet in a fluttering, lazy circle, somersaulting twice before it landed.

He sat down hard on his bed and stared at the piece of paper littering his floor. It was just a thin piece of paper, with one paragraph's worth of words. And that paper, with those words printed onto it, was enough to change the future.

He couldn't pretend anymore—nothing was fine, nothing would ever be fine again.

Nothing. He was nothing.

Something in his chest tightened, and his eyes stung. He felt himself falling, even though he was still sitting on his bed with his feet planted on the floor—he was falling into someplace dark where he couldn't breathe . . .

A small, still voice: *Breathe, Xander.*

Xander breathed.

And then, a shining thought, almost blinding in its intensity.

Riley.

Yes, he could tell Riley everything. Tomorrow, at Marcie's party, he'd tell Riley what he'd done. And Riley would help him figure out what to do.

Tomorrow was the day.

(open your eyes, Zan)

From somewhere outside his room, a *beep*. It resonated, reverberated, and Xander leaped up from his bed and charged over to his bedroom door as if the sound were his salvation. He opened the door . . .

. . . and sauntered into Marcie's house. Everyone had shown up for the party. No surprise there; Marcie's shindigs were famous for being parent-free and alcohol-heavy. As Izzy had said on the way, Marcie's parents were either incredibly cool or incredibly oblivious. And Ted voted for incredibly cool. Suzie, who didn't drink, abstained from voting.

The party blared around them, with music blasting from hidden speakers and people resorting to screams to be heard. As a result, the volume was just under migraine-inducing. Xander barely noticed; he was too busy doing a circuit of the house, seeing who was where. He needed to find Riley, tell Riley what he'd done, have Riley tell him, in turn, what he should do. Riley would make everything fine again.

But before that could happen, Xander needed liquid courage.

A pit stop into the kitchen for the first beer of the night, and then Izzy and Ted peeled off to join other groups. Xander stayed with Suzie until she found a handful of others who dominated the high end of the GPA spectrum. Suzie happily joined in their passionate debate about their local U.S. senators. Xander waited until she was firmly entrenched in the conversation, and then he slipped away.

He had to find Riley.

There was Deb and fellow art geeks, which gave way to the thespian crowd, where Ted was working on getting smashed.

Izzy was elbow to elbow with the varsity soccer girls and guys.

Xander saw them all, hanging with their friends, schmoozing easily. They were fine without him.

Everything was fine without him.

He finally spotted Riley, who was with the others from the track and field team. Xander let out a relieved breath. Before he headed over there, he needed to replenish his empty beer. Besides, he could get one for Riley, too, and casually offer the fresh drink as he joined their group. Riley would take the beer and grin at him — oh, that infectious grin — and then the two of them could slip away, maybe to that small room just down the hallway, and they could talk.

Maybe even more than talk.

Yes. *Yes.* Everything was going to be fine.

Xander went into the kitchen, tossed the old bottle, and grabbed two more, but when he walked back to where the track team was gathered, Riley was nowhere to be seen.

Everything was fine.

Everything.

Sipping from both bottles, Xander wandered his way to the small room, some sort of home office, and closed the door behind him. He needed a little me time. He went through the beers in the quiet of the small room, slowly working his way toward a decent buzz. When he was done, he'd talk to Riley, and Riley would tell him what to do, and then the two of them would start their happily ever after. He deserved one, didn't he? After all he'd done? The risk he'd taken?

Of course he did.

Everything was going to be fine.

He was nudging the last bit of backwash from one of the bottles when someone opened the door to the small room, slurred something about trying to find a bathroom. Xander pointed her in the right direction and went to find Riley. No more waiting. It was time.

After one more beer.

He threaded his way back to the kitchen. The house was packed sardine-tight with partiers, everyone hovering around the booze like they were ready to body slam anyone who dared to take the last one. Xander managed to snag a can of the cheap stuff—the only kind left—and then went to find Riley. But there were so many people, all pressing against him, that it was impossible to find anyone he knew. It was impossible to think.

Clutching his beer, he retreated to the small room again. He closed the door and leaned heavily against it. His heart was pounding, and now he was sweating like he was running a marathon. He popped his beer and chugged it, desperate to find some sort of calm. He let out a deep belch, followed by a shaky breath.

Everything was going to be fine.

He pushed away from the door and walked around the room, attempting to gather his thoughts. But there was a buzz in his brain and a beep on the horizon, and he was running out of time. He knew it in his gut: He was running out of time.

(today's the day the world ends)

Something slammed against the door.

Xander whirled, startled, and saw two people stagger into the room, close enough to get drunk off each other's breath.

Eating each other's faces.

Xander's vision tunneled to a pinpoint and the world gave way to a sea of red as he watched Ted and Riley kiss sloppily, their hands groping and slick.

The empty beer can slipped from Xander's fingers. It hit the wood floor and bounced once, then rolled lazily along the floorboards until it came to a stop by Riley's feet.

"Zan!" Ted blurted. "There you are!"

Riley swayed and grinned, saying nothing.

Xander stared at the one he loved, at that empty drunken grin, at the mouth that he dreamed of kissing, and all he could think was *No* and *no* and *no.*

Riley's grin melted into a frown. "Teddy, your boy there looks sick."

Teddy.

Teddy.

"Bastard," Xander growled.

Ted held out a hand. "Come on, Zan. Don't be like that."

Xander barreled past them and out of the small room. He couldn't see, couldn't think. He stumbled his way through the house until he came to the back deck. Blundering outside, he took heaving gasps of air, but it still felt like he couldn't breathe. People gave him space, or maybe he pushed them out of the way. He didn't know; it didn't matter.

Nothing mattered.

Someone was calling him, shouting his name, but he didn't want to hear it.

"Zan!" Ted's voice, penetrating like a spike through his brain. "Xander, come on! Don't be like this!"

Xander staggered around to glare at his best friend, who dared to smile his smug trademarked smile, as if this was all some kind of joke. And it was—Xander had been played the fool. The joke was definitely on him. He jabbed a finger at Ted's chest.

"You *ass!*" he snarled. "You know, you *know* how I feel about Riley! You've known forever!"

"I know," Ted agreed.

Xander shouted, *"How could you do that to me?"*

"Do what to you, Zan?" Ted, no longer smiling, looked tired and angry and out of patience. "Stand on the sidelines and wait and wait for you to man up and make your move? How long was I supposed to wait, Zan? You've been mooning over Riley for freaking years. *Years.* And I was good, Xander. I waited for you to finally do something about it. I supported you, man! I wanted you to do it! But you just couldn't. You didn't. And then tonight, when Riley kissed me . . ."

"Kissed *you,*" Xander spat.

"Yeah, kissed *me.*" Ted sighed, exasperated. "Even six months ago, I would've told Riley no. Hell, *two* months ago. But Zan, school's out soon. Real soon. We've got summer, and then college. Riley's got Stanford. You've got Carnegie Mellon. Come on. It hasn't happened yet, so when was it gonna happen?"

"I gave up Carnegie Mellon for Riley! I gave it all up! I threw it out to go to Stanford, just to be with Riley!"

A muscle spasmed along Ted's jaw. "I . . . I didn't know."

Xander pulled his hair until his scalp screamed. "Because I was *waiting!* Waiting for that damned acceptance letter to finally come! Waiting and waiting, Ted. You thought you were waiting for me? You wanna know how long you were supposed to wait? All I needed was that one letter, that one yes, and then I was gonna tell everyone. I was gonna tell Riley."

"Zan," someone said. Suzie. From behind him. But Xander didn't turn around, didn't want to face her, face anyone.

"But then I got my letter, *Teddy.* I got it yesterday. And you wanna know what it said?" Xander laughed bitterly. "They don't want me. Stanford said no. I gave it all up just to be with Riley, and now that's not happening, and you're in the back room making out with the one I've been in love with for years!"

"That's not his fault," a cold voice said.

Xander knew that voice.

Xander dreamed about that voice.

He turned and stared helplessly at the Amazingly Perfect Riley Jones. Riley stood there, hands fisted, eyes narrowed, that beautiful mouth pulled into a frown.

"I kissed him," Riley said. "And he kissed me back. I never asked you to give anything up for me. You're friends with Suzie-Q and Teddy, but me? You're no one to me."

The words punched Xander in the gut, punched him until he thought he was going to puke. "I gave up everything for you."

"Who asked you to?"

Xander couldn't breathe.

"What, you want me to say, Aw, how sweet? How romantic? You kidding me?" Riley's head shook slowly, back and forth, long black braids rustling. "You want to worship me from afar, knock yourself out. But don't you go blaming me for you throwing everything away. Man, I don't even know you."

(today's the day the world ends)

He had to get out.

Xander pushed his way past everyone, pushed through people until he was out of the house and staggering toward his car. There was a storm in his head and he felt like he was going to drown. A press of a button and the car unlocked; a yank on the handle and the door opened. He slid into the driver's seat. Getting the key in the ignition took three tries, but hey, the third time was most definitely the charm.

The car roared to life.

Lights on, and then he gunned out of his spot, winging three parked cars and not giving a damn about it. His cell phone was buzzing at him, or maybe beeping, but he didn't care.

He didn't care.

Nothing mattered anymore.

It started raining or maybe he was crying, and that didn't matter, either.

Xander careened down the tree-lined road, and he realized he had nowhere to go.

He couldn't go home, where his parents were furious with him for bailing on Carnegie Mellon.

He couldn't go back to the party, where his heart had been ripped out and trampled.

He couldn't go to his friends. He barked out a laugh. Friends? What friends? Friends like Ted, who betrayed him? Or Suzie? Izzy? Please. They were all with Ted, with Ted and Riley, the Amazingly Perfect Riley Jones.

Riley had taken his love and spat it in his face.

He had no friends.

He had no future.

He had nothing.

He was nothing.

Nothing mattered.

Up ahead, the road gently curved. Beyond the curve was a large tree, big enough to fit a person inside the trunk. It was majestic, a thing of power and beauty, old and wise and able to weather any storm. The headlights hit the tree, streaking the chocolate brown of the trunk, setting it aglow with raw umber, with bronze, with copper.

Xander aimed for the tree and floored the pedal.

He wanted to die.

He wanted to die.

A still, small voice asked him if he wanted to die, and he realized, as the tree rushed up to embrace him, that no, he didn't want to die.

He wanted to live.

He jerked the wheel and hit the brake.

The sound of a screech of tires.

Impact, then echoes of contact, then nothing.

And then, a beep.

And another.

And then Xander was staring at himself, battered and broken in a hospital bed. His body was filthy with plaster and tubes. His mom and dad sat beside him, his mom holding one hand and his dad the other. They were talking to him, begging him to wake up, Son, please wake up.

Open your eyes, Zan.

Next to the bed, a machine beeped with Xander's every heartbeat.

On the bed, another machine allowed Xander to breathe.

He stared at himself as he remembered everything—his plan to follow Riley to college, his reneging on Carnegie Mellon and then not getting accepted to Stanford, finding Ted and Riley at the party together. He remembered all that and more.

In his pocket, his lucky penny burned.

"So here we are," said a cheerful voice.

He looked to his left, to the corner of the room, and there was Death, smiling and leaning against the wall.

"So here we are," Xander said dully, turning back to the bed, to his parents begging him to please wake up, please, please, open his eyes.

"They've all come to see you," said Death. "Your parents, of course, but they never left. Isabella. Suzanne. Edward. Others from school. They've come to pay their respects and share their wishes. Some have said goodbye. Others keep hoping you'll get better. Suzanne's been here every day, yelling at you to wake up already."

"I don't understand," Xander said. "I was with Riley. We were together. Weren't we?"

"In the world you created, absolutely."

Xander's mouth opened, closed, opened again, but no sound came out.

"It's one of the things I like best about you people," said

Death. "Your uncanny ability to create. Goes hand in hand with your innate ability to lie to yourselves, and to believe those lies."

"What . . ." Xander's voice cracked. He licked his lips and tried again. "What are you saying?"

"It was quite the crash," said Death. "Broken bones. Massive brain trauma. You were in surgery for hours. You've been comatose for weeks."

A lump formed in Xander's throat, and he swallowed thickly.

"The doctors have told your parents that tests indicate you're brain-dead. The staff have been speaking to them about your quality of life. Your parents have been praying for a miracle. And you? You created a world within your mind. That was your reality, Xander—at least, for a little while." Death smiled. "You were both the hero and the author of your own story."

"So me and Riley . . ."

"Never dated," Death said gently. "You crushed on Riley for years, but nothing ever came of it. You thought you were in love, so you applied to Stanford. And you know how that turned out."

Xander blurted, "But what about you? Your lost soulmate? Your being suicidal?" Now he was shouting: "What about the Horsemen? The end of everything? What was all that?"

"That was you, Xander. Your world. Your rules. Your story."

"Oh God." Xander hung his head. "None of it happened."

"It happened, Xander," Death said. "Whether in that world or this one, it happened. And one thing is true in both worlds: It really is the end of everything."

Xander whispered, "Today's the day the world ends."

"For you, yes. The doctors have convinced your parents that there's nothing they can do, that all that's left for you is this bed and those machines. Today's the day your parents are going to take you off life support."

By the bed, his father begged Xander to breathe.

"You have to decide," Death said, "right now, whether you want to live."

"I wanted to die. I was going to die."

"You were on your way to wrapping your car around a tree," Death agreed. "But at the last second, you cut the wheel and hit the brake. Something made you want to live. What was it?"

Xander said, "I don't have Riley."

"You never did."

"I don't have college."

"For now? Certainly. But that doesn't have to be for always."

"My best friend betrayed me."

"Only if that's how you choose to see it." Death chuckled. "There are always other sides to every story, even the ones you think you're writing. You just have to be willing to listen."

Xander looked down at his feet. "Even if I die," he said quietly, "Mom and Dad still have Lex. It's not like they can't forget me and move on."

"Xander," Death said patiently, "what did your parents call you when you were a baby? What was your nickname until third grade?"

He remembered. "Oh, no."

"Yes, Xander. You were Lex until third grade, and ever since then you've been Xander."

He whispered, "No."

"You're about to die, Alexander Atwood."

He begged, "Please, no."

"I'm afraid so. You don't have to. There's still a chance. But you have to meet me halfway. You have to open your eyes, Xander. You have to breathe."

He stammered, "I don't know what's going to happen to me."

A soft laugh. "No one does, Xander. That's part of what makes life so interesting. It is what it is."

Xander closed his eyes. "How can life be interesting if there's nothing left to hope for?"

"The thing about hope," said Death, "is that it changes over time."

Xander remembered kissing Riley. He remembered holding Lex. He remembered getting accepted to Stanford. He remembered all of that, and more.

He remembered that was all a lie.

He could take the lie with him to the grave.

Or he could live, and find out whether, after all this time, he could find a different hope.

The coin weighed heavily in his pocket.

"It's time, Alexander Atwood," Death said gently. "What do you want to do?"

He took a breath and opened his eyes. He looked at his body, at his parents, and he turned to face Death, his death.

And then he gave his answer.

THE ATWOODS

Xander's mom and dad held hands as they watched their son lying on what would surely be his deathbed. Hours of tears had left delicate patterns on their cheeks, painting their sorrow on their skin. But now there were no more tears. Eyes burning, mouths grim, they sat in their hospital chairs and stared at their son. Even their prayers were used up, finished.

All that was left was saying goodbye.

And then Alexander Atwood opened his eyes.

THE END

When I wrote *Hunger,* the character Death just happened. I hadn't planned on making him any certain way; he pulled an Athena and sprang fully formed out of my head. I hadn't even been into Nirvana at the time, and yet he was the spitting image of Kurt Cobain, down to playing the guitar and singing. Death: wise-cracking and all-knowing, patient with just a hint of scary. I liked him.

As the Riders of the Apocalypse series progressed, Death revealed himself more and more. In *Rage,* there was a touch of intimacy; in *Loss,* there were flashes of Death as something else —something old and powerful and so far removed from humanity that we can't begin to comprehend what he really is. Something *other.*

And then I really, *really* liked him.

When it was time for me to write Death's book, his origin didn't pull an Athena. Instead, there was music. Sure, there was Nirvana—specifically, Nirvana's cover of the Meat Puppets' song "Oh Me." And there were other songs from other groups that all go on the *Breath* soundtrack, including Breaking Benjamin's "I Will Not Bow" and Linkin Park's "In the End." But there was one song in particular that hit me right between the eyes: "Snuff" by Slipknot, on the album *All Hope Is Gone.* I heard this song, and suddenly Death's origin began to unfold.

At its center were love and betrayal—and how slim the line is between hope and hopelessness. When Death gives up on life, what hope is there for the world?

The answer to that is *Breath*.

Just as this is Death's story, it's also Xander Atwood's. He's a boy with a secret, a boy with a connection to Death—a boy who can save the world. Because at the end of the day, when it's *our* world that's crumbling, it's up to us to save it.

So *Breath* is about Death, yes, but it's also about life, and living, and the choices we make. It's about the shift from being powerless to being empowered.

It's about hope.

If you're wondering about the last scene with the Four Horsemen together, here's the answer: Spalding Gray. It came to me in a dream. Not quite the same thing as pulling an Athena, but it'll do.

Safe to say that we've all been hurt before, some of us more than others. Sometimes, something happens and we get so hurt that all we can feel is that pain. It's like we've become an open wound that will never heal.

This has happened to me before, a few times. And my God, it was bad. I felt like the ground had been ripped up from beneath me, and then I was in a state of free fall. But the bottomless pit wasn't bottomless after all—I hit, and hit hard. And then I was so far down that there seemed no way out of the hole. I walked around in a daze, disconnected from everything. How could I focus on living when I felt like I was dying?

Depression sucks. There's no candy-coating it. There's no bright side. Depression sucks, period.

I got out of that hole, thanks to a small group of people whom I trust completely. That was hard, too, because when the ground had been ripped up beneath me, my trust had been shattered. But the people who love me were there for me, unquestioningly, unflinchingly. And they not only helped me out of that hole, they filled it. None of that would have happened if I didn't trust them and hadn't told them how I was feeling. I talked to them, and they listened. And they helped me.

If you're hurting, don't keep it inside. Talk about it. You can always contact the terrific people at To Write Love On Her Arms. TWLOHA is a nonprofit organization dedicated to presenting hope and finding help for people struggling with depression, self-injury, addiction, and suicide. TWLOHA also invests directly in treatment and recovery. For more information about the organization, please visit the TWLOHA website: **www.twloha.com.**

Just like with *Rage,* a portion of *Breath* proceeds will go to TWLOHA. If you bought this book, thank you for helping to make a difference.